BEAUTIFUL, NAKED & DEAD

& DEAD

A Moses McGuire Novel

By Josh Stallings

D1082385

Copyright © 2010 Josh Stallings

All rights reserved under International and Pan-American Copyright Conventions.

Published in the United States by Heist Publishing

WWW.JOSHSTALLINGS.NET

DEDICATION

For Erika. Without her, none of this would make much sense.

ACKNOWLEDGMENTS

People I owe a debt of gratitude to… The women of Cheetahs, Star Strip Too and Fantasy Island for sharing their stories and more than one good laugh with me. Erika, Jared and Dylan for my life. Larkin Stallings for his sturdy support. My sisters Lisa and Shaun for always picking up the phone. My mother and father for breath. Charlie Huston for his wise editorial insight. And especially Tad Williams and Deborah Beale, who generously shared knowledge and time, but mostly for their endless friendship.

CHAPTER 1

There is nothing quite like the cold taste of gun oil on a stainless steel barrel to bring your life into focus.

I was six years old the first time I honestly considered suicide, not as some cry for help, touchy huggy bullshit. No, for me death was a gift, an escape. Like those vests divers wear that fill with air from a CO2 cartridge and pull them to the surface. At night while the Monster roared through the thin walls of our bungalow, I would pull that thought up and let it comfort me like a warm blanket.

As an adult I have found that a barrel in your mouth forces you to pause, take a moment, ask that all important question. How did my life get this fucked? If I don't need anyone, why am I so lonely? At least I like to think it was that deep, fact was I had a bone numbing hangover, a throbbing head and a fur covered tongue. The gun was on my dresser and if I had any aspirin they were all the way in the bathroom.

Thumbing back the hammer of my snub nose Smith & Wesson .38, it clicked into place. Three pounds of pressure on the trigger would drop the hammer onto the primer, igniting the 4.5 grains of smokeless gunpowder. The resulting explosion would drive 158 grains of lead at 1085 feet per second out of the barrel, plowing up through my pallet, through my brain and out the back of my skull. Sure, it seems like a lot of complex engineering just to end one life, but it was the simplest thing I could come up with at the time. Idiot. All I had to do was hang around long enough and people would line up to do the job for me.

Outside, the warm southern California sun was baking the sidewalk, kids laughed and shrieked as they ran through a sprinkler. Down the street a Mexican radio station was playing some brass-driven ranchero music. Happy, happy LA.

Running my tongue along the gun barrel I could feel the ridges of the front sight.

Was this the day I had the nerve to pull the trigger?

Blame it on the fifteen large I owed Vinnie Bag Of Doughnuts on a string of nags that came in third place.

How about that bloodless whore Jen. Blame her. I owed the heartless bitch five grand in back alimony. An old man in the joint once told me, "You meet a pretty girl, you just want to eat her up, you marry her and son you'll wish you had." To prove him right, Jen had to sic the D.A. on my deadbeat ass so what little green I made was attached. The cherry on top of this little shit cake is my dealer cut me off for passing a bad check for a jar of whites. Hell, what kind of dealer takes checks anyway?

Was it debt that had me sucking on my .38?

I doubt it. I was born broke and would go to my grave broke, only a moron would expect the years in between to be any different. Fact was, my life sucked the big salami. I was just bone tired of trying to pretend I cared what happened to me.

Gripping the trigger, I started to squeeze. Three pounds of pressure and adios mí vida loca...

At two plus pounds, the phone rang. Odds were it was just more bad news. But what the fuck, I could always kill myself later. Or have a beer, or go bowling or what ever it is people do when they are not killing themselves.

"Speak." I said into the receiver.

"Mo?... Are you busy?" It was Kelly, the day waitress at Club Xtasy, a titty bar I bounce at whenever my cash runs low, which has been full time for the last two years. She was also maybe my only real friend.

"Not with anything that can't wait."

"You know you said if I needed help, well..."

"Baby doll, what's up?"

"It's complicated. You're the only one in the whole wide world I trust, you know that, right, Mo?" Kelly was a sweet breath of fresh air in a world that stank of stale smoke and yesterday's beer. She had the looks to be a stripper but not the strength of character, so they let her keep her clothes on and serve slop to the swine we call customers. Even over the phone I could see her winding her brown curly hair around her finger, it was a thing she did when she was searching for the right words. "They want... She um... My sister... well...I'm not who you think I am ok Mo..." Panic made her normal scatter of speech into a flow of meaningless noise.

"Who's the 'they', Kell?"

"They, them - you know... It's complicated. Don't hate me Mo, please. It's just... I... this... Things you know? Things go wrong and we can't always fix it. But I didn't mean to hurt you. It's just she... "

"Slow the train down girl, you left me at the last station."

"Ok, it's, well they, people do things, stuff happens and then, you know, not what you plan but there it is and I need your help or it's all..." her thoughts were a runaway truck, her brakes had failed and she was in free fall.

"Where are you Kell? Are you at home?" I asked.

"I'm at the club...Mo... It's Monday... But they um...You can't hide from them...Why bother right?"

"Pour yourself a drink, I'll be there in fifteen minutes." I hung up the phone. Sitting up too quickly, the room tilted and sent my stomach lurching. Gripping the watery remains of last night's nightcap I gulped it down to quiet my nerves. Suicide would have to wait at least until Kelly could tell me what the hell was going on. Something about her brought out the big brother in me. Maybe it was her Indiana farm girl innocence, or what passed for innocence in my jaded world. This is something the straight world would never understand, we all live with our own set of scales. This girl Piper, she's twenty-nine and that makes her old, past retirement in stripper years. And Kelly didn't take off her top for bucks or give men hand jobs in the back room and that made her innocent. It's all relative. She was the only girl in my life with whom I didn't trade sex for favors. With the other girls it was always give and take. The lap dance for the ride home on my Norton. Convincing a boyfriend to move on for a hand job. Forty-three, rode hard and put up wet too many nights, my life had been many things but never easy and it showed. I had scars from my missing great toe, to the fifteen stitches in the back of my skull. The flesh real estate in between wasn't much better. I knew the only way a pretty girl would want me was in trade. I didn't mind. It was just the way it was. But Kelly was different. She never offered sex and if she had I wouldn't have accepted. When I was with her I felt almost normal, like I had a shot at becoming a good man. A man has to have one pure relationship in his life, and for me she was it. So when she reached out to me, I really didn't have any choice at all.

I set the shower to scald, hoping to burn the stink from my body and cobwebs from my brain. Who the fuck was I fooling, Moses the great white knight, savior of the naked working girls. I could barely keep my body vertical. I let the water run cold before I stepped out.

Searching the pile, I found a less than disgusting pair of jeans and tee-shirt. Laundry was one more thing on my to-do list, right after "find a reason to live" and "go grocery shopping." Slipping the revolver into my coat pocket, I headed out the door.

It only took three stomps to get the Norton to kick over.

It was a black '76 Commando, from the gold lettering on the gas tank to the flawless chrome, it was the only thing I owned that wasn't fucked up. The reason Jen hadn't taken it in the divorce was I think she hoped I'd kill myself on it before the life insurance ran out. Pulling out onto Avenue 52, I turned at York by the panadería, the sweet smell of new bread wafting over me, reminding me I hadn't eaten a good meal in the last day and a half. One thing about riding a bike, you get to know a town by its smells. Highland Park was fresh bread, sizzling meat and chilies from the taco trucks, it smelled warm and hot and sweet all at the same time. It was one of those transitional areas in Los Angeles. Transitional, sales speak for we got gangs but they're pussies. We got biker bars and artists' lofts. It's one recession away from the ghetto and one Starbucks away from good times. Eighty percent of the residents are dark skinned and most of the signs in the shop windows are in Spanish. Whichever enlightened citizens passed the proposition making English the official language of California forgot to tell Highland Park. Hell, bigots and political whores can pass any law they want. Down here we speak how we want, using the words we have to communicate what needs to be said, even the cops speak Spanish in East LA.

Club Xtasy was a smallish single-story, flat roofed building in the shadow of Interstate 5. It stood a block away from the cement banks of the LA River and next door to a chroming shop. Directly across the street was a ancient print shop full of giant machines that stamped out flyers for illegals to place on car windshields. This was the perfect titty-bar neighborhood, light industrial, old, run down but not a ghetto. On the border between Silver Lake and Atwater, which meant both communities could frequent it, but neither had to claim it. To class the joint up, Uncle Manny, the owner had the bright idea of putting plaster replicas of Greek sculptures along the top of the building, Venus de Milo and her scantily clad sisters, all missing limbs. Statues of damaged girls outside, advertising damaged girls inside. The less than classy huge pink plastic letters on the side of the building screamed out "GIRLS GIRLS GIRLS" and "LIVE NUDE", which begs the question, who the hell would pay to see a dead nude? Then again this was LA, they'd probably line up around the block just so they could say they'd seen it. Two planters in front of the door held dying palm trees. Not that the guys who come down here ever noticed. The working stiffs thought it looked good and the cats from the nice side of town were too busy trying not to be seen sneaking from their Lexus' into the club, to ever notice the facade.

Moving through the turnstile into the dark club I was washed in the thumping bass of Eminem's "Cleaning Out My Closet", "...I'm sorry momma, I never meant to hurt you..." The blonde monster sang. I slipped off my shades, waiting for my eyes to adjust to the dim shadows, outside it was mid day, but once you passed through that thinning velvet curtain it was permanent midnight. A short bar ran along the wall next to the entrance, it had room for three bar stools and a waitress station. The back bar was limited, nothing fancy, it was mostly a beer and whiskey crowd. Martini rat-pack madness had skipped the strip scene. Our boys wanted to get drunk, see some tits and ass, pay a filly to grind on their lap and blur on home like it was all real.

"Where's Kelly?" I asked Turaj. He was at his station behind the bar, in his collar-less black silk shirt and slicked back hair he looked every bit the Mack Daddy pimp he thought he was. His Uncle Manny owned the joint, but when Manny was AWOL, gardening or watching his grand kids, Turaj was the big swinging dick. He wasn't a bad kid at heart, he was just one of those pricks who acted like he thought a tough boss should act. He was always a little squirrelly with me because unlike the girls, I knew I worked for Uncle Manny and no one else. He tried to yank my chain once and almost lost an arm in the process, since then he plays nice.

"Fucking cunt walked out in the middle of her shift," he said in a voice that crossed boredom and disdain perfectly.

"What did you just say?" I tensed, ready to jump over the bar.

"Fucking cunt walked…"

"Look around here, don't look at me asshole, look around here." I swept the room with my hand. "You see any cunts in here?"

"Fuck you Moses, what the hell? You going all feminist on me?" He puffed up trying to hold my eyes, but couldn't. "It's just talk Moses, you know talk? Your girl, she bailed and left me without a waitress. It's bad enough she doesn't take her clothes off, but now she won't even serve drinks? If we get a rush I'm screwed."

I'm not sure what I expected, I told her fifteen minutes over an hour ago. I could go blasting out after her, chase her down and let her tell me all about her drama. Or I could have a cold one and try and slow the drum squad in my skull.

"Give me a draft," I told Turaj, he seemed relieved to

see I wasn't going to give him any more stress. Taking a sweet deep swallow, I turned my back on him and scanned the room. On the center stage in the middle of the room China was wiggling her way out of a leather mini-skirt. She was a hard-bodied Asian girl with the best tits money could buy, not those gaudy old school balloons, her store-boughts were round and swooping like soft flesh ski slopes up to her perky nipples. The surgeon screwed up when he moved her nipples, so now she had no sensation, but damn they looked good. A ranked teen tennis pro at one time, her father put a racket in her hand as a child and pushed all the way. China hit the age of consent and decided to show her old man a thing or two. Eighteen months ago she had been a young woman on fire to prove something to the world. Her parents sealed her off like a room they would never enter again. Now she was just another girl working for tips, trying to get through with a minimum of pain. Stripped down to a G-string and prancing around the stage, you might even think she was enjoying herself if you didn't make the mistake of looking too close. Odd thing about LA you can show guys a topless girl and sell him all the booze he can drink, but if that same girl slips off her G-string, you can't sell booze. I guess there is some fear that if a drunk man sees naked poontang he will go wild and take out a city block trying to get at it.

China had her story, every other girl had one just as twisted. The deal was, if the customer bothered to ask, they were all college gals working their way to a degree in child development or nursing or some other non-threatening all-giving career. I knew this one Lithuanian broad, got a square to front her six grand for tuition. She split for Vegas the next day. Hey man, if you believed a single word spoken on this side of the curtain, you got what you deserved. We were in the business of selling fantasies, if booze and naked bodies blurred that simple truth, screw you. The world is made up of hookers, John's, pimps and bouncers. You pick your role and play it best you can even if the deck is stacked against you.

Tits, yabows, massive ta-tas, the guns of Navarone, chee-chees, tetas, mountains, sweater meat, orbs, melons, boobs, knockers, mammary glands, fleshy fun bags, cleavage valley. Oh that I go through the valley of the tits I shall fear no evil for I'm a man. A couple pounds of flesh and men fall apart. Big ones little ones it don't matter, tits, "size just doesn't matter it's all about the shape." "More than a handful's a waste", hell I like two handfuls. Maybe we all want to get back to our mother, suckle at the breast of our childhood. If that bitch crawled out of the grave, came to me and opened her shirt, I'd close my eyes, turn and walk away. There never was any succor there, never was any peace at those tits. She taught me a valuable lesson when I was little. If things are bad now, they can always get worse. Things never change for the better. I hear some mommas say to their babies, "Don't worry baby it'll be alright". That wasn't mine. Momma you said, "If it's going bad, it's probably something you did. Something you did against God and Christ." Religion was a hammer used to make me feel shitty. Tits? No tits in the bible, no sir. So who the fuck wants to read that book.

I was jarred from my gentle childhood reminiscence by a Mutt and Jeff pair of pimped up Armenian thugs stepping out of the private lap dance room. The little one looked around the club with the cold smile of ownership. It was an arrogance I was used to in Glendale, hell they owned that town, they puffed up and you got out of their way or got run over. But these punks were two miles across the border that we all knew Armenians didn't cross, at least not strutting their junk. My boss was from Iran and didn't truck with the Armenian gangsters. They had their own gentleman's club down by the old Southern Pacific tracks in Glendale, it was my job to gently point them in that direction, draw a map on their face if that's what it took.

The punks stopped in front of the stage and leered up at China as she slid her ass up along the pole. The skinny little rat-faced one beckoned with a crooked finger for China to come over to the rail. She looked off balance as she danced up to him. She leaned down to hear what he was whispering. His hand shot out and slid up her leg, two fingers stroked her G-string. Shock flitted across her face. I started to push off from the bar but Turaj caught my arm.

"Let it be, they're good guys," he said, not meeting my eyes. The skinny punk stepped back from the stage sniffing his fingers and laughing to his huge partner who only returned a stone stare. Whoever had worked them in the lap room hadn't come out yet. The girls always beat the men out of there, if the guy still had some cash they might come out on his arm, if not they ran for the dressing room to smoke or drink or do whatever it took to wash away the feeling. I moved quickly but without hurry toward the lap room. The bouncer's strut is a trick of moving rapidly without drawing attention, from the belt up you have to look like there isn't any place you need to be, while you move your legs fast.

The Lap Dance salon is a small back room lined with mirrors, floor to ceiling. It had six raised booths with chairs in them where men sit and get friction dances. Piper was sitting in one of the chairs, reflected on three sides by the mirrors. Her flame-red hair flowed down her back like a burning waterfall. She had on a tube top that was being stretched beyond the suggested limits of its elasticity, her muscular shoulders gleaming in the dim light and her long powerful legs spilling out of her silk tap pants. She'd been in the game long enough not to cry, but I could see the flicker of pain and fear behind her eyes.

"What'd they do to my lil' girl?" I said. She looked up at me, hesitating. "If you don't tell me, I can't fix it."

"God damn son of a bitch...the little pencil dick wants a grand a week or..." She didn't need to finish it. Whatever they said they were going to do to her was ugly and painful. Had to be to scare a pro like Piper.

"How much did you give 'em?"

"Two hundred hard-earned dollars... Bastard didn't even pay for his lap dance... Will you do me one lil' old favor?"

"What's that, baby doll?"

"Cripple those sons of bitches," she said, staring past me into space. Like a benediction, sealing the promise, I kissed her forehead and turned on my heels.

Sunlight exploded pinning my pupils as I stepped out of the dark club and onto the sidewalk, I fumbled my shades on to protect me from the day. The two Armenian thugs were moving towards a ten-year-old BMW 740i. A skinny little thing in a leather trench coat and his muscle, a big boy, six foot and pushing 250 hard. Talk was out of the question, even if I wanted to, which I didn't. Odds were even that the big boy could kick my ass if I gave them any slack. I ran full out, before they even knew I was coming I was in midair. I tackled the big boy from behind, catching his hair in my fist I let the momentum of my body weight drive his face down onto the hood of the Beemer. I heard a crunch that I knew was his nose breaking, and he let out a howl. Pulling his head up I smashed it down again, I could feel the muscles in his back loosen, he was going down. A sweep to the back of his knee sent him sprawling on the sidewalk where he lay holding his face, blood flowing through his fingers.

From the corner of my eye, I saw skinny boy reaching into his jacket. In the two steps it took me to reach him, he had his gun out. It was an ugly Glock 9mm. He swung it up, aiming inches from my face.

I froze, my expression going neutral.

He stood in the street between the hood of the Beemer and the trunk of a rusted-out Chevy. "I'm gonna bust a cap in yo ass muthafucka," he spat out, struggling to sound as Black as possible.

"Do it, please. Come on, pull the trigger. Right here between the eyes." I pointed at my forehead.

"What? You whacked out?" he said, unsure of his position. It's hard to threaten a guy who doesn't give a damn.

"Come on, don't be a squid, pull the trigger. Pull it!" His eyes flitted off me and to his pal. That instant was all I needed. In one movement I lunged forward shoving his gun up, and him out into an oncoming Monte Carlo. The bass thud of his body against metal was mixed with the treble crack of a bone breaking. He bounced off the grill of the speeding car. For a brief moment he took flight, twisting like a broke winged bird up into the air before tumbling down screaming like a little girl. Thank god it was LA so the car just kept going. Grabbing hold of the scruff of his trench coat I dragged his skinny ass up onto the sidewalk, scooping up the Glock on my way. There are so many more guns than brains in this town. His left leg was twisted in a way nature never intended, and he was shrieking in pain. Looking down at this wailing little puke, all I wanted to do was pound his head into the cement, anything to get him to shut the fuck up.

Luckily the big boy got my attention before I could act on my impulse to stomp. Coming around, he stood up looking at me, his face smeared red with blood. His nose was mashed flat against his face. His eyes were raging as though he was about to charge, then he saw the Glock in my hand. He relaxed, shrugging his shoulders and gave me a look that said it was my move, he'd live or die with whatever I chose. You had to respect him, he hadn't been dealt the hand he wanted, but he was playing what he had like a man.

"Get this piece of shit off my sidewalk," I said in as neutral a tone as I could muster. My pulse was pounding, my adrenaline flying high. But this was no time for drama. Things can go ugly in the blink of an eye, and then these boys were looking at the long dirt nap and it's a steel cage for the rest of my life. The big boy looked down at his squealing buddy, a little embarrassment showing in his eyes. Glancing up at me, he hardened.

"You're still trying to decide if you can take me, gun and all." I said flat, "I know I would be. Fuck it kid, take a pass on this one. It ain't pretty any way you play it." I was hoping like hell he didn't attack. If the 9mm didn't stop him I wasn't sure he wouldn't rip my head off. No fear showed in his eyes. He just kept staring at me. Wherever he'd come up it was a hell of a lot rougher than the streets of Glendale. "Whatever you're going to do, let's get to it before the blues roll up and I've got to explain the gun, the blood, the bodies and this day goes from shit to diarrhea."

The big boy thought about it for a moment, turning the options over in his head, I could see the gears click away as his eyes bore into mine, searching for my weakness. He was a street fighter, and not one who was used to losing. "It's over," I said lowing the gun, giving him space to back down into. His shoulders relaxed, hiking up into another indifferent shrug. He moved past me, closer than comfortable, close enough to let me know he held no fear of an old bastard like me. Skinny boy let out a high-pitched squeal when dumped into the back seat of the Beemer. Leaning in, I slipped my hand into his pocket and pulled out his wallet. Taking his driver's license and a wad of bills, mostly hundreds, I tossed the wallet onto the front seat. I leaned my face close to him, tapping my finger on his forehead forcing him to focus on my eyes, with my other hand I covered his mouth silencing his whimpers. I spoke in almost a whisper. "You ever even think about my girls again, even a flitting fucking thought and I will find you." I dropped the clip out of the Glock and kicked it into the storm drain. Ejecting the chambered round, I tossed the nasty plastic gun to the big boy and watched them drive away, wondering what the hell was wrong with the youth of today. Hell, when I was their age, I never would have let some old fuck get the drop on me.

When I reentered the club Piper was on stage dancing to Billy Holiday's "God Bless The Child." Spinning around the pole, running her hands up over her fine natural double D's, fingers dancing circles around her nipples, all the standard moves, moves she could do in her sleep, mechanical moves designed to draw your eye to her body and fill your reptile brain with the need to mate or at least throw dollar bills. The men watching didn't notice the fear in her eyes. Ok, maybe they didn't even notice she had eyes. She was parts, real live moving parts.

The fight had cleared my head, and pulled my spirit up enough for me to remember Kelly and her call and her sweet face. I should have walked out then, but then I wouldn't have been me. Stepping up to the stage I tossed two Benjamins at Piper's feet. Looking down she smiled, her eyes going soft. Even the lonely men at the rail were impressed by the falling hundreds. She danced the rest of the song for me alone. Eyes on my face, it was a dance honoring her valorous hero. The mind may know it's all a sham, but blood wants what blood wants. Watching her work her magic on the stage I knew where we would end up. My blood lust had turned to lust lust that quickly. Tits.

Stepping off the stage, she took my hand and started to lead me to the lap room. "I can't, baby doll, I have to find Kelly," I said half-heartedly.

"Mo, if you were ten years younger," Piper purred, "You'd still be ten years too old for that girl child. Now drop the torch Cowboy, that one's never going to give it up."

"It ain't about that, Piper."

"Tell yourself any little lie you need to, but it's always about *that*. You just want her 'cause she's not up there offering it. You think she's your ticket to Straightsville. Now forget Miss Pure White and come show Momma what you got."

"I think she's in trouble."

"We all were in trouble from those punks, but you handled that," she said, keeping her grip tight.

"Maybe later, she…"

"You plan on banging her?"

"No."

"Then she'll wait. Lordy, lordy, lordy, part of you wants to stay. " Her eyes flicked down to my crotch. "Is that for lil' ol' me?"

I gave up my weak attempt to fight it and let her lead me into the shadows. I lied to myself, saying Piper was right, Kelly must have been afraid of the Armenians. Truth was, my erection was doing all the thinking at that moment. My blood was up and screaming for release. Watching Piper's ass sway before me I couldn't see a damn thing wrong with this deal.

I told myself one more little lie and slid into the

moment, pretending this time it would be different and I wouldn't end up feeling more empty than when I started. Sitting on a metal chair surrounded by mirrors she slid down onto my lap while somewhere in the distance Nicki Minaj was singing about being the best. Rubbing her fine ass on my crotch she moaned in fake but convincing passion. Her hair against my face, her scent filling my nose, rose water hovering over hair spray and buried down below, just the hint of sweat. To the pulsing beat Piper swayed her full, soft, natural breasts across my face, tracing her cleavage across the hair on my chin. All the while her leg expertly stroked my erection through my jeans. Caressing her hands over my shoulders she felt my breathing slow.

"My big strong hero... give Momma a little cream for her coffee." Pulling her leg from between mine she smiled down at me, turning slowly around she bent over giving me a moment to look at her fine firm backside without her watching me. Sliding gracefully back, she sat onto my lap, fitting herself down around the bulge in my pants. Rocking her hips to the pulse of the music and the acceleration of my breaths, she ground her ass against my cock until I finally closed my eyes... let go... and came. Climbing off me, she smiled and kissed me on the cheek.

"Thank you," I said, "Consider your tab squared."

"What?" Her smile faded.

"I took care of the punks, you took care of me. We're even."

"You're such a jerk."

"Me? What did I do?"

"Forget it." She walked out, plastering her sultry *there's nothing I'd rather do than fuck you* smile on as she cleared the doorway. I watched her ass twitch away into the shadows of the bar and wondered if I would ever give up trying to understand women.

Staring into the mirror I had to ask myself who that man was. The scruffy red beard, four gold earrings in one ear, a Celtic knot tattoo on his neck, placed there to commemorate the love for a girl he no longer knew. The scar above the left eye from a broken beer bottle. And cold blue eyes, eyes that had seen too much for one life. The Viking heritage showed in the man's body, he was built for wielding a battle-axe and pulling an oar. I wondered if that man in the mirror came into the club, would we be friends? Probably not, he didn't look like he had many friends. I'd probably throw his trouble-making ass out on the street.

After the rush of the battle and the bad sex settled, after staring at my face in the mirror for too long… Kelly's face came into my mind. Her call was the reason I stepped into this mess in the first place. I came in looking for Kelly and wound up getting tossed a thank you lap dance from Piper. Life does have its ups and downs.

With a guilty smirk, I stepped into the men's room to dab the stain off my jeans. I wasn't guilty about the lap ride, hell we were both consenting adults and I figure as long as the donkey didn't die, what adults do behind closed doors is their own damn business. I did feel bad about leaving Kelly hanging while I got my nut off though. It was no way to treat a friend. Men can be jerks sometimes, just a fact. Any possible warm afterglow of the ejaculation was gone before I left the john.

Dropping some change into the pay phone, I dialed Kelly's number. I was rewarded for my effort with a busy signal. I dialed again but got the same irritating blatting tone. Why would the Armenians have threatened a waitress? She didn't make the kind of cash the dancers did. When she called, Kelly had said she wasn't who I thought she was. What did that have to do with the Armenian shakedown? Somewhere between the pay phone and the bar I decided I was going to have to go see Kelly, if only to stop my brain from thinking about it.

Behind the bar Turaj's eyes were in full flight, lighting on anything in the room but me. I slapped my hands firmly down on the bar top. Turaj gave a little jump then turned a sheepish grin on me.

"You are one slick mother fucker, right?" I purred.

"What? Moses my man, what are you thinking?"

"That you are one slick mother fucker. How much were those Armenian pricks planning to pay you a week, for the right to scalp our girls?" He looked mock stunned.

"I didn't, they, I never saw-"

"That's it, just keep digging that grave deeper and deeper."

"Trust me, I don't know those punks. What kinda man do you think I am?" A line of sweat was collecting on his weak brow.

"The spineless kind. The kind that gets his rocks off holding power over these girls because they'd never give it to him willingly. That answer your question?"

"Screw you," he said with no conviction.

"Hand me the phone, I need to talk to your uncle." At this his mask of cool started to twitch.

"Who's he going to believe, huh? I'm his blood."

"Hand me the phone, we'll find out." What I really wanted to do was jump over the bar and turn him into a stain on the carpet. I guess he saw it in my eyes because he fell apart, his upper lip started to tremble, he looked down at his hands as though they held some mystic secret.

"Here's how it works, those fucks or any puke like them comes in here after our girls, you're going to call me. And if you don't, what do you think will happen?"

"You'll tell Uncle Manny."

"Beep, wrong answer. Forget about Manny, I'll be coming for you. And I won't be happy… are we clear?" He nodded ever so slightly, fighting to hold his face from completely falling apart. "All right bitch, I need Kelly's address."

"No, no. If she wants to fuck you, she'll give you her address, not me. You know the rules."

"I wrote the rules. Now get me Kelly's address before I remember how pissed off I am at you."

"Fine, but you don't tell her I gave it to you." He scurried off across the club toward the office, glad for the excuse to get away from me. His head was down, and his shoulders sagged. Beating down a whipped dog gave me no pleasure, but screw him, he made his own lumpy bed when he climbed in with wanna be gangsters.

"Did I ever tell you you're my hero?" China asked, sidling up next to me.

"Just doing my job, like everyone else here."

"What a man, what a man, what a mighty fine man." She sang. Winding her small pale finger into a buttonhole on my shirt she pulled me close to her. The word had spread quickly that the Armenian tariff had been lifted. Looking around at the other smiling girls I knew I'd be offered enough free lap rides to keep me happy for days... If only that was what would make me happy. Maybe if I knew what happiness looked like I might know how to go after it. But, forty-three years on this miserable planet only taught me how to survive, not thrive. Every day I felt like just one more soldier trying to make it back to the world in one piece. If I was smart I would stay in the trenches, keep my head low and never play the hero. If I was smart.

.

CHAPTER 2

Kelly lived in a small 1950's apartment complex clinging to the sheer green hillside above the reservoir in the Swish Alps. Silverlake, a trendy, oh-so-hip, gay community nestled in the steep hills between the gritty streets of Hollywood and the harsh reality of East LA. From her porch you could look down the sudden incline, past the Spanish tile rooftops to the shimmering blue water of the reservoir, water surrounded by chain-link and razor wire. Here in LA water was better protected than our children, I guess to some degree it was simple economics, one was more valuable than the other. Water turned this desert into a city, what had children ever given us?

Walking past Kelly's little red Miata, I climbed the stairs. The curtains of one of the ground floor apartments parted and a pair of rummy eyes surrounded by white hair watched me pass. If the old woman didn't like what she saw, she didn't say so. I knocked on Kelly's door but she didn't answer. A string of miniature Japanese lanterns hung above her door, and a hand-painted Mexican tin heart was tacked below the peephole. I knocked several more times, but the apartment was silent.

Standing there on that peaceful afternoon, sunlight dappling down through a eucalyptus tree I started to feel a bit silly. A knight in rusted armor charging off to rescue a damsel who probably took her new puppy down to the dog park for a stroll. While sharing Chinese food in the dressing room she had told me about the puppy Angel, and how much she loved watching it play with the other dogs. Some breeder gave her a purebred Bullmastiff pup in the hopes it would buy his way into her shorts. She blew the guy off but kept the pup. She said the dog world was simple and pure, love without deceit. She didn't have to say it, I knew she meant it was the opposite of everything around us. Strip joints act like they're honest. Straight transactions, sex for cash. Bullshit. It's all smoke and mirrors and denial and deceit. Every night the deal goes down all across America, and no one goes home with what they bargained for. Not the girls or the marks or dumb bouncers who think that just because they're smart enough to see the crooked deal they're immune to it.

Riding down the hill towards the dog park, I decided to give Kelly a verbal ass paddling. Chicks love drama more than they love new lace panties, but she had to know that when she reached out to me I took it seriously. Cruising past the large fenced park there were lots of happy pooches but no Kelly. She might have taken the dog down for a cup of coffee. Or she was asleep in her apartment with her earplugs in. Whatever, I was sure she'd call me sometime that night, all apologetic and chump that I am, I'd say it was no big.

24

Back in my bungalow I poured myself a tall McCallans. The scotch cost forty-five bucks a bottle, but a man has to have some extravagances. Sitting in my lazy-boy I cranked up U2. Bono was singing about a girl packing for a trip to a place none of us had ever been before. I couldn't get Kelly out of my head, as if the song was about her. I saw her standing in an empty airport late at night, a cheap suitcase in her hand. Maybe it wasn't her I was worried about, maybe it was me. Was Piper right? Did I think Kelly was my ticket to a normal life?

No, it was more, she stood for hope, hope that the whole planet wasn't full of cheap scams and low-class trades. She was real in a life full of fake. Fake tits, fake passion, fake vows given to fake friends. Everyone looked out for Number One and everything was for sale if you just knew the price. But not Kelly. She was the only person I counted as a true friend, and I had never seen the inside of her apartment. What did that say about my life? We spent so much time in the dressing room chatting, goofing off, sharing take-out, that rumors spread that we were lovers. Most of the dancers had no reference point for a man and woman being friends. Fuck them if they didn't get it. Hell I didn't get it, what did she see in me that was worth her time? Finishing my drink I dialed her number, more busy signal. Not good. Climbing onto my bike I headed the Norton back to Silverlake.

Night fell soft and gentle as I moved up the apartment building stairs. I was moving quietly but not enough to avoid the watchful eyes of the white haired sentry, when she saw me looking at her she stepped quickly back behind the protection of her curtains.

There were no lights on in Kelly's apartment. After knocking I pulled out a thin piece of stainless steel. It was the size of a credit card. As long as the dead bolt wasn't set, it would open any door. Slipping the card into the doorjamb, I felt it click, and the door opened. Stepping into her apartment uninvited, I knew it was a betrayal. But, if nothing was wrong, she'd never have to know I'd been there. Sweeping the living room with my Maglite I could see it was a nice, friendly room as inviting as her smile. She had an overstuffed sofa with an old-fashioned floral print slipcover. A framed print of water-lilies hung over the sofa, it was a Monet; I could tell because it said so under it. A scarred coffee table held a small ghetto blaster and a stack of cd's. What was missing was any of the normal flotsam and jetsam one collects in life. No books or knick-knacks, no memorabilia, nothing to personalize this apartment to Kelly. The kitchen was tidy, a few dishes in the sink but other than that everything was in its place. In a dish-drainer were four plates, in the cupboard, four water glasses stood next to four coffee mugs, all matching and relatively new. It made me embarrassed to think of the Salvation Army rejects that filled my shelves.

Opening the bedroom door I moved the light across the tan carpet and up onto the bed and across her pale feet. She was lying sprawled naked on a daisy print comforter, she looked peaceful as if she'd fallen asleep with her head resting on a rust red stain. The world skipped a beat slipping sync for a moment. She was Sleeping Beauty, this was a cartoon; any moment seven dwarves would burst through the door. I felt myself drifting in and out of my body for a moment as I looked down at her, no way this was real. I pulled the light off her face hoping that when I looked back she would be fine, but I found myself staring at the wall, it was splattered with blood, hair, bone chips and gray matter. Facts. Hard cold facts. From splatter to victim. No entry wound on her face. I could see it go down. They had forced her to suck on the barrel before they pulled the trigger. Entry wound back of her throat, exit wound back of her skull. I traveled down her body. Her left nipple was hanging on by a ragged piece of skin. They used pliers on her. Random small brown circles on both breasts, her belly… they burned her with a thin cigar too large to be a cigarette too small to be a robusto. A browning red stain smeared from her pubic hair down to her thigh. Jesus Christ they… back to her face. Her lifeless green eyes stared up at me. My knees went weak, I slipped to the floor, tears rolling out of my eyes. I hadn't cried in years. I felt the weight of it all pressing down on me. In this whole shitty world couldn't they leave this one perfect flower alone?

I don't know how long I sat there, but slowly out of the darkness a sound found its way to me. It was a soft whimper coming from behind the bathroom door. Crawling to my feet I opened the door. A four-month old strawberry blonde puppy bounced out. She had huge paws and a wrinkled loose skinned sloppy face. Her wild wagging tail swung her butt around as she showed me her joy at being set free. Suddenly, the pup stopped dead still and stared at the bed. Tail and head down she edged towards her dead mistress. She sniffed the hand that hung off the bed. Gently the pup licked Kelly's limp hand.

Leaning over, I kissed Kelly's cold lips. The last thing on her mouth should be a kiss, not a gun. Looking down at Kelly I wiped the tears off my face and felt myself go cold. Tears never helped anyone, tears were a luxury for folks living in safe little houses watching flicks about kids with cancer. Out here in the real world, they didn't do shit. Taking a dish towel from the kitchen I methodically moved through the apartment wiping my prints clean from every place I had touched. Using the towel to open the front door I was almost out when I felt eyes on me, the damn pup. Looking out from the bedroom with those big lost eyes. "What the hell do you want me to do with you, huh?" I said. The pup looked at me with a depth of sadness I had never seen in a dog so young. "Fine, come on then, but I swear to God the first time you piss in my house I'll sell you to the taco truck." She didn't resist as I picked her up, she crawled up to look over my shoulder, watching her dead mistress all the way out of the apartment. The damn beast weighed at least forty pounds and was well on her way towards monsterhood. But one look in those sad eyes told me her heart was even bigger than her massive paws.

I called the cops from a pay phone outside a liquor store. When they asked for my name I said it was Tom Waits, and that I lived at the corner of Heart Attack and Vine.

Climbing onto my Norton I nestled the pup under my leather jacket and rode towards home. A heart-shaped tag on her collar read Angel, no phone number no address. No evidence to lead anyone back to her mistress. John Q Straight put his name on everything he owns, but fringe dwellers know better. Kelly knew it. Information is power so don't give any out for free. I didn't save Kelly, I guess caring for her dog was the best I could do... I knew it wouldn't be enough. Wind whipped at my face and Angel snuggled down against my chest. I had seen death before. As a soldier in that mess they called a war, I had even caused it. Somehow this was different. She mattered more than all the rest, maybe because she wouldn't matter to anyone else, not the cops, I knew how hard they would try for a dead cocktail waitress from a strip joint. Not the straight world, to them the women of my world were as expendable as last night's condom. But she mattered...If only to me and the goddamn dog.

Pounding down Highway 2 where it rose up over the 5, the Girls Girls Girls sign of Club Xtasy winked up at me from forty feet below. At seventy MPH, it would only take a flick of the handle bars to send me slamming into the low freeway wall. One quick crunch of metal and I'd be soaring out over the LA river headed for the great beyond where crap like this was all a dull memory. My knuckles went white on the hand grips. The will to survive battling it out with desire for oblivion. The pup trembled under my leather coat, it was as if she could sense how close we were to ending it all. Taking her with me wasn't part of a deal I was willing to make. Carry your own water, leave the innocent be and if you have to step off the board do it alone. No passengers for that ride. We come in alone, we go out alone, end of story. Breathing out a breath I didn't even know I was holding I loosened my grip. The green of Forest Lawn on my right, the brown green of Mount Washington on my left, and ahead in the distance the steep peaks of Angeles Crest. Just when you're ready to burn it to the ground and walk away, this aging bitch we call a city can still catch you off guard with her beauty. Sure, she's only a tarted up old whore, but when the light is right and you squint just a little, she looks young and fresh and almost hopeful.

I pulled down an old sleeping bag and made a nest for Angel on the floor. After three or four therapeutic scotches,

I curled up in bed and hoped for the noise in my head to stop. There was a thump on the foot of the bed as Angel pulled herself up. She curled up very small and didn't look at me, like maybe I wouldn't notice her if our eyes didn't meet. I closed my eyes until they were only open a slit and watched her as she ever so slowly crawled forward, finally resting her head on the pillow next to mine. Only then did she fall asleep. I wasn't so lucky. I lay for a long time in the dark haunted by my fallen friend's face. Haunted by what I knew of her last hours, by what I should have done...She reached out to me and I had failed her. I blew her off to play the hero for Piper and collect a lap dance. While I was squirting in my jeans, some freak was raping her. She was dying while I sat at the bar fucking with Turaj. If only I had gone straight to her place... If only... if... When at last I fell asleep it was listening to the rhythmic breathing of the pup.

In the dream rivers of blood flow down off the granite mountains into a boiling red ocean. I can taste sweet, iron and salt in my mouth. A young Lebanese woman lays in the white sand, the pulpy surf pounding her dead bullet riddled body. Beyond the breakers, where the sea grows calm, Kelly floats on her back. She cranes her neck to look back at me.

"Come on in, the water's fine," she whispers, a slight smile curling up her lips. That mischievous twinkle in her eyes invites me to chuck it all and join her.

"I fucked up, Kell."

"You just did what you always do." We spoke without moving our lips.

"You paid the price."

"Women always pay the price. Now come out here and join me." I wanted to obey her. I really did. But as I watched, she slowly sank below the surface and was gone without even a ripple.

When I woke my first thought was of suicide. Again. Who would care or even notice? Closing my eyes I wondered if I even had enough drive to get up and look for my pistol. Something wet and rough dragged across my cheek. A big sloppy puppy face looked down at me with anticipation.

"What the fuck do you want?" I asked, Angel stared at me, her tail starting to wag.

"What?" Nothing, just big empty eyes. "Thanks a lot Kelly, what the fuck am I going to do with a dog?" I asked the ceiling.

Pulling myself out of bed, I fried up some eggs, smoked ham, six cloves of garlic, a yellow onion and strips of stale tortillas into a hash. I split the steaming tasty mush with Angel. She wolfed the grub down in three big gulps filling her face wrinkles with egg. Grabbing a dish rag I scrubbed her face clean, "I don't know what you are, but you sure ain't no lady."

I rode out with her smiling face peeking out of my jacket, ears flapping in the wind. It was ungodly early,

31

another strong point against me as pet owner. The only time I got up before noon was when I was in the Marines or the joint, and both places it sure as hell wasn't willingly. But I had a plan, a way to duck my new best friend, so we hit the dog park. To enter we had to clear a small chain-link sally port. I closed the first gate behind me before opening the gate into the park. Chino Prison had one just like it, only this one had no razor wire or guards with high powered rifles sighted down on me. Across the dying lawn, a group of dog owners sat and stood around a cement picnic table drinking from travel mugs and laughing at some joke I couldn't hear. They were all young, good-looking squares. Some had tats and piercings, the kind they got to impress the world with how edgy they were. All looked up when I cleared the second gate, smiles faded as if I had farted in church. A cute little blonde gal with spiked hair and army boots looked down, afraid that meeting my eyes might be an invitation for trouble. I was used to this reaction from the straight world. Their style came from ghettos and jails, but God forbid they actually had to meet one of us face to face. Maybe it was fear, maybe I called their street cred into question, or maybe I was an ugly motherfucker who nobody wants around unless they need him. Fuck them and the bitch they rode in on.

I set Angel down, and she immediately ran past a pile of dogs fighting over a stick and over to a huge Rottweiler. Leaping up, she latched her needle teeth onto his upper lip. The big dog tried to shake her off, but she would tumble in the mud, get up and charge again. She made up for her lack of poundage with pure guts and tenacity.

"Bruiser!" A large lady in a faded denim jumpsuit called out to the Rottweiler. "Play nice, or when she gets her size, you'll wish you had."

I turned and started to walk away. Angel was cute enough, one of these dog lovers would take her in and I could get on with whatever the fuck I was going to do.

"Are you friends with Kelly?" The big woman called out to me, "Well, I mean you must be, you're walking her dog."

"You know Kelly?" I asked, startled to hear her name spoken here.

"Yeah, I know that beautiful girl." She was smiling openly as she came over to me. "Angel loves my Bruiser. She attacks him like this every morning. Luckily he's so not alpha." She talked to me in a comfortable way I wasn't used to. Like Angel was my ticket into her secret society. "Every morning for the last month Kelly's brought Angel down to play with my Bruiser. Sometimes we go get a cup of coffee at an outdoor café down the street. Tell you the truth when I first met Kelly I was hot for her. She told me she didn't swing that way but I though I might convert her. Men can be such pricks... I mean not you, well maybe you I mean the jury is still out on that one, but you know what I mean." She was speaking a mile a minute, like a speed freak on the end of an all night jag. But, it turned out Helen was a TV crime writer who drank too much coffee and spent way too much time alone, just her, her keyboard and Bruiser. After it was clear she wasn't getting into Kelly's shorts, they had struck up a true friendship. Kell was like that, easy to like, and I don't ever remember her judging anyone. Once I asked her what she thought about the men who came into the club, the men who got lap dances. She said, "Like my grandma used to say, just people doing people things."

"Look, I don't know you from nobody, but do you think you could take Angel. I'm just not up to being, whatever."

"Where's Kelly?" Helen's face dropped, she braced herself for bad news, as if she knew it was coming.

"I don't know, she's gone, ok. Can you take the dog or not?"

"Where is Kelly?"

"Fuck, I'll keep the damn mutt." Picking up Angel I walked out of the dog park. I could feel Helen's eyes following me all the way to the street.

After depositing Angel back at my crib I went into Club Xtasy. Parking my bike I noticed the unmarked LAPD car out in front of the bar. I thought about rolling on, but they would want to talk to me sooner or later so it might as well be now. I slipped my .38 into a specially built hidey-hole under the seat of the Norton, the last thing I needed was to have them find an unregistered piece on a registered felon.

Inside the club, Piper came rushing over to me, "It's Kelly, Mo. Did you hear?" Before I could answer her, a thick-necked, short-haired, butch detective moved in on me. She had on jeans, running shoes and a nylon windbreaker. She was six feet if she was an inch. Big but not soft, she looked as though she lifted weights and hated men, me most of all.

"You Moses McGuire?" she asked, daring me to deny it.

"Yes." I said in a dead tone. I'd spent enough time with cops to know smiling and saluting them only bought you contempt. The moment she saw me she knew we stood on opposite sides of that thin blue line that most straights don't even know exists. She could smell the time I'd done.

"Would you mind coming with me?" She asked, but it wasn't a question so I followed her into the back office. Turaj was there, looking less bold than usual. An older White detective was sitting behind the desk; he had a crew cut, graying hair and sad tired eyes. "Take a seat," the female detective told me. So I sat facing the White detective, with his partner towering behind me.

"Moses McGuire?" The older detective asked. I nodded yes and he continued in a calm, even voice, "I'm detective Lowrie, that's Sanchez, would you mind telling us where you were yesterday afternoon?"

"If you tell me what's going on," I said. Sanchez smacked the back of my head, not as hard as she wanted, but hard enough to get my attention.

"We ask, you answer. Is that simple enough for you?" Sanchez said, resting her hand on my shoulder. I looked at her hand then coldly up into her eyes.

"Unless your next move is to bust my ass, you better take your hand off me."

"Or what? I'm not one of your bikini bimbos. I'm not your punch of the week. I'm Detective First-Class Sanchez. You want a dance, then we'll step out back. No? Afraid a girl might kick your ass?"

"Mary Cruz. I'm sure Mr. McGuire wants to help us out." Lowrie's eyes flicked to her hand on my shoulder.

"I'm sure he does, Stan," she said, clamping her vice grip before removing her hand in a show of mock politeness. Rodney King, the LA uprising, the descent decree and two new Chiefs might have made the LAPD more citizen-sensitive but it hadn't changed their hearts. Sanchez was a bully who would love nothing better than to play racquetball with my head while her partner held a gun on me. Lowrie looked up at her, shaking his head slowly.

"My partner doesn't like you. I keep telling her to switch to decaf, but she doesn't listen," Lowrie said in friendly tone.

"You the good cop?"

"No, I'm just a tired civil servant who's been up all night staring at a girl's brains on a wall and I would like some straight answers."

"Ok, I was here 'til after four, then I went for a ride, ate a Tommy's burger around ten then hit the rack," I said, trying to keep my voice even and calm. Lowrie let out a long sigh. Rubbing his temples he stared at me with his tired eyes.

"We know you went to see Kelly Lovelace after you left the club," he said. My eyes flicked over to Turaj who looked down, the spineless prick had sold me out.

"What happened to Kelly?" My question was answered with another smack to the head, this one harder.

"Not real good at following directions are you?" Sanchez said. "We got you. Your life is a turd circling the toilet bowl right now and you don't even know it."

"What happened to Kelly?" I said, looking Sanchez square in the eyes.

"Here's a hint, I'm a homicide detective. Help any smart guy?" she said. I looked from her to Lowrie, who simply nodded.

"Should I lawyer up?" I asked him.

"Only if you want to go down to the cop shop, make me fill out a bunch of unnecessary paperwork." Lowrie said. I liked him. He was just another guy doing a job.

"Ok, straight deal," I leaned in close to Lowrie, making it clear I was talking to him, not Sanchez. "Kelly called me yesterday from the club. She sounded scared so I told her I'd come get her. When I got here, she was gone. So I went by her crib, but she wasn't there either. Truth is, I figured it was just stripper drama."

"What was your relationship to Miss Lovelace?"

"We were friends. Just friends."

"That's not what we heard." Lowrie said with no judgment.

"Yeah, but it's the truth."

"Did you wish it was more?" Again no judgment.

"No, in this business chicks are easy, but friends are few and far between... I've dealt straight, now will you tell me straight, do you have any idea who did this, or am I the best you got?"

"You're it, sweetheart," Sanchez interjected with a

smile. "Can you hear those bars closing around you?"

"I've been inside, it ain't no big." I said, keeping my eyes on Lowrie. "What scares me, is that the asshole who did her is walking around free, and you've got nothing to stop him." And that was it, my interrogation was over. They wrote down my address and phone number and told me not to leave town. Lowrie gave me his card and asked me to call if I thought of anything else. As I was walking out, Sanchez stepped in front of me, she just had to get one more shot in.

"Pack your bags, and get ready for the cell. I know you did it, can't prove it, yet. But you did it," she hissed. I didn't have any snappy comebacks, and I was all out of tough bravado, so I just moved past her and walked out.

The girls were sitting around the club, some on the leopard print couches, some on bar stools, they all looked stunned. Their sadness surprised me. It wasn't like this was the first time someone they knew had died ugly. Maybe they knew Kelly was different, or maybe it never got any easier no matter how many soldiers you lost. Piper came up to me. Wiping away a tear, she hugged me. "Sorry big man, I know..." Her words drifted off.

"It's all going to be alright, baby girl." I said, patting her back. But that was a lie, a whore's promise. Nothing would be ok, not for me, not for Piper, not for any of us.

CHAPTER 3

When the cops finally left we opened the club. I went through the motions of working my shift. Luckily Tuesdays are dead nights in the flesh game. When I got home I was greeted by the odd feeling that it had snowed in my living room. A thin dusting of white feathers covered every surface. In the center of it all Angel was sleeping, curled in what was left of my down comforter. I didn't know if I should laugh, cry or boot the pup across the room. I settled on cleaning up the feathers and being thankful she hadn't crapped on my floor, me being stupid enough to leave her alone for eight hours. From a taco truck I bought a box of carne asada tacos. The spicy meat didn't seem to dull Angel's appetite any. Maybe she could stay. Maybe.

The dog farts started around four in the morning, eye watering silent stink bombs. How such a small creature could contain so much foul odor was beyond me. I moved to the living room and left her to sleep happily in the stench. I was miles from sleep long before she smoked me out.

Dry blistering air rattled the leaves on the magnolia tree outside my window. Earthquake weather. Suddenly all the night's chill was gone. The crickets went silent, their sound replaced by the slapping of tree branches and the rush of air. I knew there would be no more sleep tonight. It's earthquake weather in the city of angels and no one is at peace.

Three fingers of single malt did little to quiet the choir of condemning voices in my head. My ex-wife had called me a hopeless drunk. But that was bullshit, a little whiskey was all I had some days to keep from dropping into a dark hole I might never climb out of.

I put The Pogues into the stereo. Shane McGowan was rumbling drunkenly about a dirty old town and the axe he was going to make to chop it down. I raised my glass to the speaker, I knew just how he felt.

The winds brought no trembling earth this time, Angelenos had been spared for one more day. By six most of the toxic gasses had escaped the bedroom. I crawled back in next to my pup and drifted off stroking her soft coat. Wednesday started about as bad as possible.

"Hands on the wall, assume the position." Sanchez wasn't taking any chances. The detectives had woken me by pounding on the door. She had her gun out and me against the wall before I could say word one. A high-pitched growl came from the bedroom as the puppy charged out. She stopped a few feet from the detective, her hackles up. She looked ready to attack regardless of their gross weight advantage or the gun I was sure Sanchez wouldn't mind discharging. "Angel!" I snapped, and to my surprise she backed down. Sitting on her rump, she watched us warily but the growling stopped.

"Cute dog," Sanchez spat.

"Real cute," her older partner said.

"Strange, we found a dog bowl and puppy chow at Kelly's apartment, no dog. And here this skell who never went into her place has a new dog."

"She makes a good point," Lowrie said to me.

"Owning a dog illegal now?" I said and wished I hadn't.

"No, but rape murder is." Sanchez wrenched my arm down and slapped the cuffs on.

At Parker Center they hooked me to a bench next to a Black banger with a swollen eye and crusted blood rimming his left ear. On the ride down they hadn't told me I was under arrest. They had given me the big silent treatment, hoping to rattle my cage, it was working. For all my tough bullshit, I didn't think I had another jolt in me.

My pulse was starting to climb when a young uniform took me into a long shallow room and had me line up with six other men, all roughly my size. Facing the mirror I racked my mind, who was was their witness. The old curtain watcher from Kelly's apartment? Had to be. If she I.D.'d me I was fucked, add that to the fucking mutt and they might have enough to nail me. And that would be it. Judge and jury would take one look at me and my rap sheet and I would take a lifelong fall.

After the line up, I was placed in an interview room with muddy smudged walls that possibly had been white once.

"This could go a lot easier if you'd confess," Lowrie was sitting across the steel table from me. Sanchez had been left out of the interrogation. My bet was she would bust in if Lowrie's nice guy act failed.

"I want a lawyer." I stared coldly at the old cop.

"No, you don't. Get the lawyers involved and we lose any wiggle room. Why don't we get our story straight before we go there."

"I got my story straight."

"Only problem son, it's bullshit. We have you at the scene, we know from your record that you have violent tendencies. That's two out of the big three, all we need is motive. What happened, if let's say she was stringing you on, showing you a little piece then slapping your hand for touching. I think you may have a shot at a crime of passion defense. Is that what happened?"

"I didn't kill Kelly. She was my friend."

"You're a broken record Moses. You were there, and you lied about it. It doesn't look good." He looked at me with as much fatherly concern as he could muster. I gave him stone in return.

"I want a lawyer."

Lowrie twiddled a pen in his fingers for a moment, then picked a file off the table and walked out. After a while the young uniform came and led me out.

"You are one lucky piece of puke," Sanchez said as she unlocked my cuffs. The banger kid was still on the bench, only now he was passed out. It had taken an hour after the interview for them to get me. "This is far from over, you did that girl and I'll prove it, end of story."

All I could figure was that the old lady must have been either too old or too blind to make a positive I.D. Rubbing the blood back into my wrists I started to walk out. I was almost to the street when Lowrie caught up to me.

"Hold up McGuire."

"What you want to do a quick cavity search, make my morning complete?"

"No. Believe it or not, I'm not half the hard ass you think I am. My partner hates you though, that's a fact."

"This leading someplace, I got shit to do."

"I know you were in her apartment."

"Then prove it." Turning I gave him my back and walked out to find a cab.

After a quick stop at Petco for chew toys, a dog door and what I hoped would be flatulence-free puppy chow, I went home and puppy proofed the house. Angel took the large stuffed green arachnid in her jaw and shook it to death, looking up at me for praise.

"Oh yeah, girl, you're a stone cold killer," I told the pup, sending her tail into a wild flurry of wags. I was bolting the flap over the hole I'd cut into the back door when it occurred to me that this was the first home improvement I'd made to the place. In the years that I had lived there I hadn't even driven a nail in to hang a single picture. Kelly had only been in LA for six months and yet she had decorated her door, hung art, made her house a home. Where had she come from? She grew up in a small town in the Midwest, was the only detail she had offered. Thinking I had plenty of time I hadn't pushed her for more.

After finishing the dog door, I poured a short drink, yes it was early but fuck it, it had already been a long day. Lack of movement was making me crazy.

The pain of the ink filled needle felt honest and real. For a moment, it pierced the dull numbness that had settled over me. I was in Cardo's kitchen in his small Hollywood apartment. He was a soft faced ex-banger who I'd helped out with some AB boys when they jumped in his shit down in county lock-up. After his last jolt he had left the life, moved from Pico Rivera to Hollywood, crawled out of the closet and reinvented his brown ass. Now he made the bills painting storefront windows and when he was lucky he was hired for a mural or sold a painting from one of the small galleries that carried his art. His soft electric colored view of the world hung on his walls. All dreamy paintings of women, most of whom I knew. He'd come down to Xtasy to sketch the girls. At first he pissed them off by not buying laps. But, when they saw themselves in his work, how beautifully perfect he saw them, they learned to forgive his lack of cash.

"She was a rose in a garden of thorns, Loco," he said wiping away the blood and ink off my shoulder, so he could see the art he was drilling into my flesh. "Sweet and gentle in a world grown hard."

"She was something all right."

"Women are like gem stones, no? They sparkle to get your attention but if you look in a loop, see close up, every one is different and totally unique. It's the flaws and inclusions that make them special." With a homemade tattoo gun he was drawing Kelly's face freehand. Doing it all from memory and capturing her just right. I got my first tat in the joint. In a cage, they take all that is yours, all that is personal. The first ink was there to remind myself I was still alive, still had some control over my body. This was how we marked our time, writing our history in ink and blood.

"Explain something to me," I started, looking with awe at how perfectly he was capturing all that was beautiful in Kelly.

"If I love women so, why am I gay?" he said, guessing the question.

"Something like that."

"You breeders get it all wrong. I love roses, no? But I don't want to fuck them. You can't imagine love without penetration. I can't imagine life without beauty. The form it takes is so much less interesting than the beauty itself," he said, reminding me once again why I hung with him. Like him or don't what you heard was who he was. He finished the work giving me his usual admonition, not to get in any fights or fall off my bike until the skin had healed. I'm not sure what he cared about more, me or the canvas he painted on.

The next week passed slowly. Every morning I took Angel to the dog park for her daily romp. The fear in the locals' eyes faded bit by bit every day, but it was never replaced with warmth. If our eyes met they still looked down or away. At some level I would always be the boogie man under their beds. Helen, Bruiser's owner, and I would chat about the weather and life and dogs. Some mornings we went down the street for coffee. She was a link to Kelly, she kept her alive for me. I shared her deep grief but I was done crying. I stuffed that pain down deep inside and let it work on my ulcer.

I called Lowrie to see if he had made any progress in finding Kelly's killer. He told me I was still the best suspect they had. The next day I called him again and this time I took a shot and told him the truth. I told him I had been in Kelly's apartment, what I had seen and again restated that I hadn't, couldn't have killed her. By my fourth phone call we slowly began to build trust, if not friendship. My initial feelings proved right. He was a straight shooter. He told me they hadn't been able to locate any next of kin. The name she'd been living under didn't show up on any record search, the social security number she'd given to the club was bogus. It was strange he said, he had been through her apartment three times and hadn't found as much as an address book or a letter from home. I told him I thought she was from Indiana, but it didn't help much.

"They're going to cremate her on Friday," he told me. "You're the closest thing to family we can find... If you want to claim the ashes, I'll back you up."

"What do you want as payback, I don't snitch. You

46

have to know that straight up."

"Son, you don't have anything I want... You're alright Moses, I just don't think you know it yet."

"How many days 'til they put you on another case, and she becomes a dead file?" I asked.

"Two days ago. But that hasn't stopped me. You may not believe me, but I'll keep looking," he said, and I did believe him, but also knew how little he had to go on. After I hung up, I filled a tumbler with ice and poured in my Scottish Prozac. I had no idea what Kelly would want me to do with her ashes. It wasn't the kind of subject that came up much in strip club dressing rooms.

"You committing suicide on the installment plan?" Piper asked. I was sitting at the bar knocking back my third scotch of the shift.

"Just trying to slide through the night," I told her, motioning for Turaj to fill it up again. It took the drinks to quiet my head down enough to go to work wrangling the straights, it dulled my building rage to the point where I might not tear any heads off. Truth was I did very little bouncing, I was just the big scary guy there for show. My experience has been that naked ladies turn most men into drooling pussycats. I watched a tattooed Mexican kid get a lap dance, Ginger told him to keep his hands at his sides and he obeyed like a kid in school.

"So what are you going to do with her ashes?" Piper

asked, leaning against the bar.

"I don't know, I really don't," I told her.

"If it was me, I'd want to have my ashes spread into the waves, up by Malibu. Up where the livin' is easy and the greenbacks grow tall. Get stuck on some matron's feet and stain her white shag."

"I don't really think Kelly was a Malibu kinda girl," I told her.

"No she wasn't, not enough irony in her... You'll know what to do when the time is right. You always do," she said resting her hand on my shoulder.

"You have a lot of faith in this old man."

"Yes I do... And you're not that old," she said with a wink. Looking past her I saw Sasha, that chestnut haired little Czech vixen, fixing to haul off and hit a dread locked customer. I caught her cocked arm just before she swung. She spun on me, eyes flaring.

"Jesus Christ Mo, this cheap bastard says he give me one hundred. Like I don't know what a twenty looks like. Am I blind? Am I stupid? "

"No baby girl, but you look pissed off."

"Pissed off?" She let out a long stream of unintelligible Russian curses, her face growing redder as the volume climbed. It would have been funny if it wasn't my job to keep the room chilled and blood off the carpet.

"Breathe baby girl, breathe. Go in back, do some of that yoga crap you're always spouting about and let Moses handle this."

"He's trying to steal from me!" I put a firm hand on her head, pulling her towards me. I smiled, to anyone else it looked like I was kissing her ear.

"Keep this shit up, and in three seconds you are over my shoulder and out of here." I whispered. "That how you want it?" I kissed her neck and stepped back, continuing to smile at her. Sasha's eyes flared then dropped to a low burn, and like a good little girl she started to walk away. But then Dreadlocks had to open his mouth.

"Mon dat bitch is crazy," he slurred. Out of the corner of my eye, I saw Sasha flying at him. Catching her around the waist I lifted her off the floor and I let her momentum spin us both around. Dreadlocks jumped up, knocking his chair over. Now the whole club was looking at us. Dreadlocks was angry now, his hand reached up into his jacket. I set Sasha down shoving her into Piper's waiting arms.

"Take her in back," I said. Sasha was struggling, but Piper was a gym rat and had no problem marching the smaller girl out of the room. Even the girls on stage had stopped to watch. I could see that Dreadlocks felt his manhood was on the line. His hand was still up under his jacket. I moved in close, speaking softly, forcing him to lean in to hear me. "I don't even want to know what's in your jacket. But the last thing you want to do is pull it out. Trust me on that pal." Blood rushed thumping in my ears. It took real strength to keep myself from clocking the stupid ass muncher.

"Dat bitch stole my money."

"Right now, at this moment, all you are out is maybe some cash. But you push it, and one of two things will happen. Either you'll be fast enough to pull whatever is in your jacket, in which case you might kill me and spend the rest of your days in the pen. Or, and it's a big or so pay attention, you won't be fast enough and then brother, your ass is mine. I will bitch slap you down in front of all these fine ladies. Honest, odds are I bet you kill me. I also bet you're smart enough not to want to spend your life in the can over eighty bucks." I knew I had talked long enough for his pulse to slow and a bit of reason to settle into his booze soaked brain. Slowly his hand dropped out from his jacket.

"You tink I'm ghetto poor?" he said. From his pocket, he took a wad of singles and tossed them at the stage. Lupita looked stunned as the bills fluttered down at her feet. "Mon, I could buy and sell your white trash ass like dat." He snapped his finger in my face. I shot him a quick smile. "You tink dat funny?"

"No, I think it's true."

"Dat's right," he said puffing up his chest. "I don't need this place with all its crazy bitches." He said for the room to hear and walked out. As the door slammed behind him, I nodded up to Lupita. She moved back into action, pressing her breasts together and swaying her full Aztec hips to the beat of the pulsing Cee Lo Green tune. The men all turned back to the stage, as if the moment had never happened. I thanked God for tits and their amazing power to make men forget.

"Always a party." Piper said as we leaned back against the bar.

50

"Got that right." I said downing a quick shot. I almost never drank on the job, but strange times called for strange ways. Turaj raised an eyebrow as I reached over the bar filling my shot glass again, but I withered him with a cold glare. We hadn't spoken two words since he sold me out to the cops. I found I could almost stomach the son of a bitch when I didn't have to talk to him.

"Do you know what we should do?" Piper asked.

"Get drunk, get naked and forget this whole sad mess?"

"Freak. No, about Kelly, we should have a send off for her, here at the club. That's it, that's what we'll do. Sundays are dead anyway, Uncle Manny will close the place if I ask real nice. Toast a glass, kick some ass and say goodbye. You in? Would that make you feel better?"

"Yeah, sure." I lied again. Nothing would make me feel better. But she was right; the moment did deserve to be marked. If a tattoo and a bunch of strippers in black was the best we had to offer, it would have to do. Kell would have gotten a kick out of it, the idea of all her backstabbing co-workers coming together to mourn her.

CHAPTER 4

I woke Friday with a head full of dread. Even Angel and Bruiser's game of battle bots couldn't make me smile. At noon after three beers and a couple of Tommy burgers that against my better intentions I shared with Angel, I rode down to the county morgue to retrieve my friend. It was hard to believe that all that was Kelly fit in a small plain brown cardboard box. Lowrie had been true to his word, they let me take her ashes without question.

Back at the house I poured myself a little more Scottish anti depressant. I set the box on the kitchen table and cranked up U2. Bono was singing again about that girl packing a bag to a place we'd never been, a place that had to be believed to be seen. "Come on Kell, what do you want me to do?" I asked the box, but no answer came. One thing I was sure of, a cardboard box with a county morgue form on the side wasn't going to cut it. From a cupboard over the sink I found an old cookie jar in the shape of Marilyn Monroe, one of the club girls had given it to me for Christmas a few years back. It had a screw top and sealed with a fat red rubber gasket, meant to keep cookies fresh, it would serve to keep Kelly's ashes safe until I could sort out what to do with them. It seemed like a fitting container, Norma Jean and Kelly Lovelace had both been small-town girls caught up in a life they didn't understand. Both had been ogled by men. Men too blinded by their beauty to see that the real magic was inside. And in the end, they both died alone. I cleaned the cookie jar out and poured Kelly into it. Then I took Angel down to the panadería and bought some pan dulce from an ancient Mexican woman. Her granddaughter wanted to play with Angel, so I let her off her leash. Giggling and yapping they ran around the bakery. The old lady and I smiled at each other. We didn't speak the same language, but we both understood that watching a little girl play with a puppy made a hard life better, if only for the moment.

Piper was the oldest woman in the club, the girls who didn't look up to her at least respected her. So when she told them to show up for Kelly's memorial, they did. All dressed in black, most of them tarted up in evening wear, with long slits up the legs and plunging necklines. Uncle Manny and Turaj both showed up in dark suits. I was touched, even Billy the D.J. put on a black tee-shirt. Manny brought a beautiful flower arrangement, we placed it on the center stage next to my Marilyn cookie jar. Billy lit it with a single spotlight, and he played a mix of Kelly's favorite songs. Upbeat happy music, Beach House, Florence & the Machine, and U2, the band Kelly and I had shared a love of. Uncle Manny brought out a magnum of good champagne. He poured a glass for each of the girls, then stepped up to the stage. He was a short, round, balding man of sixty, his skin olive tan from working in his garden. Raising his glass he spoke in his high squeaky voice, a voice that never matched the gravity of his body, "Kelly was a good girl, always on time, never gave me any grief." That was it. That was his eulogy. A couple of the girls got up to speak, Sasha liked the fact Kelly had never stolen any of her cigarettes, unlike others she wouldn't mention.

"I remember I came in one night, I had had a fight with my girlfriend and I was a wreck, and I had forgotten my make-up at home," China said. "And Kelly handed me her purse and told me to take what I needed... she was always so giving."

"She watched Jessie for me one day, when my mom was in the hospital," Lupita said, her dark eyes hid any emotion behind their pot-fueled glaze.

"I'm afraid to even go home alone anymore," Madison said through her tears. "This could have been me. There is still so much I want to do with my life, I still haven't gotten my headshots done. I want to get an agent, and this happens. It could have been me." A number of them mumbled agreement to this last statement.

No one said anything personal about Kelly. No one really knew her that well. She had been a visitor in their life not a resident. I knew I should speak up but I had no words so I poured a tall glass of Jack, said a silent prayer and proceeded to get drunk. Turaj came up to me at the bar and started to speak, but before the words could come out I shut him down. "Don't do it Turaj. Walk away." He must have seen the danger in my eyes, looking down he moved to the other side of the club.

"Do you have a problem with my nephew?" Manny asked, stepping in beside me and pouring himself a short shot of Jack.

"He's a weasel Manny, and if he wasn't your kin I probably would have busted his ass a long time ago."

"His father, my brother gave his life so that I could make it out of Iran, did you know that?" Manny said looking out at the room.

"No I didn't."

"Family, honor, very important Moses. When we grew up we were very poor, had nothing. Grew up fighting in the streets my brother and I. Whatever we had we got and held onto by knife or by gun. In the last days of the revolution it was a running gun battle for the border. Get out with what you had. At a roadblock my brother drew fire allowing me to get our families across. He died in those sands so I could be here today. Did you know I have a son who is a doctor and a daughter who writes for the New Yorker, she says I am an exploiter of women. And Turaj, he dreams of one day following in my footsteps. I know he steals a little here a little there, but he only steals from what will one day be his, so what is the crime?"

"What do you want from me, Manny?"

"I want you to give him the respect you give me."

"Tall order," I said, letting the amber booze flow down my throat.

"I wish he was tough like you, most Americans are soft. It is my fault, I wanted to protect my children from the hardness I grew up with. But you must respect him. Ok?"

"I'll try, for you Manny."

"Good. Now I have to go home. Junie is waiting up, and after thirty years I know better than to keep her waiting long." With a laugh Manny walked out of the back of the club. He was living proof that the American dream was alive and well. Turaj danced in jerky motions with Taylor, who had given up her grief and was now seeing if seducing the manager could get her better shifts.

It didn't take long before the wheels came off the affair. It turned from a memorial to a wake to a party. I sank into one of the leopard print couches and let the room swirl around me like an Impressionist painting. The whiskey washed up and over me, leaving me beached on the couch in its warm glow. The room was all light and color, Florence Welch was singing *Kissed with a Fist*. The girls danced and laughed drunkenly. China pulled the new girl, Roxanne, into an embrace slipping her tongue into her mouth. Roxanne looked surprised at first, but she didn't pull away. If I knew China, they'd be bumping rugs before the end of the night. Somewhere in the haze, a Marilyn Monroe cookie jar sat silently in a spotlight.

"He looks so sad, don't he look sad, Ronnie?" Lupita swayed at the blurred edge of my vision.

"Pitiful baby, just pitiful." Ronnie's ebony form slipped up. Her face soaring high in the distance above me. They were both a step past tipsy, one shot shy of drunk.

"Let mamacita make you feel better." Lupita slid

her soft fingers over my forehead.

Ronnie giggled, filling my vision with the sloping valley of her cleavage. "I hate to see a good man down." Swinging a leg over mine Ronnie sat on my lap, facing me, she started to gently grind to the beat. Lupita crawled onto the cushion beside me rubbing herself against me. Somewhere in my reptile brain the blood started to rush. "Give it up baby, you're in Queen Ronnie's house now." She moved her lips close to mine, our whiskey-laden breath mingling in the tiny space between our lips. Looking deep into my eyes she rubbed her breasts against my chest. I could feel her thighs rub against me, pelvis against mine. Lupita was all over me with hands and body. Like that Hindu goddess with all the arms, I couldn't tell where one woman stopped and the other started, but it all felt soft and good. The music changed and Sinead O'Connor was wailing out *Nothing Compares To You*. Past the blurred girls working to get my attention I saw the stage. In the spotlight I saw Kelly spinning around the pole. She looked down at me; a laugh rippled from her. Suddenly, my erection and desire were gone. I felt shame drift over me. This was my friend's memorial. What was I doing? "Just people, doing people things." I heard Kelly say.

"What's wrong mi amore?" Lupita purred in my ear, her hand fumbling on my limp member.

"It ain't you girl...I just... I don't know. Maybe I'm just getting too old for this..." If they heard me they didn't react. They stepped up the rhythm drunkenly laughing while they stroked me from all sides.

"Off." They both froze at the sound of Piper's voice. She stood planted firmly in the swirling room. "I said off."

"Shit girl we weren't doin' nothin'." Ronnie stood up, swaying on her feet.

"We just want to make him happy," Lupita slurred. "Tell her, Moses." I reached out for words, but only found a thick tongued mumble.

"Scram. Go on, I'm not playing." Piper said shooing them off with a wave of her hand. Sitting down next to me she patted my thigh, looking out at the building debauch.

"You wan' a drink?" I fumbled the words.

"No. I drink for boredom, tragedy I take straight up." Drifting her fingers over my face she spoke quietly, "You're going to be ok, you know that don't you?"

"Sure, I'm going to be fine." Lying was getting to be a habit with me. I lay back into the cushions closing my eyes. I felt the room spin as I fell into warm silky blackness.

CHAPTER 5

Somewhere on the other side of the worst headache known to man I could hear the distant thunder of a leaf blower. I peeked out through puffed eyelids and saw crystals hanging in the window. This was not my home. This was not a home I had ever been in before. My mind felt thick, like I had pickled more than a few brain cells. I was clearly not up to the task of figuring out where I was. Above me, a brass and oak ceiling-fan spun in lazy circles. Piper leaned down into my field of vision. She was wearing an oversized Raiders tee-shirt. "Don't look so nervous, it's me." Apparently we were in her brass bed. This scrap of information cleared nothing up for me.

"How did I get here?" I asked, my voice sounded like a distant growl.

"You said you wouldn't survive unless I let you fuck me... I'm joking, Mo. Relax, your chastity is intact. I drove your useless ass home. Helped you stumble into my bed." I let my neck muscles go, my head sinking backinto the pillow. My temples throbbed and my mouth felt like I had spent the night chewing on an old running shoe.

Piper traced the scabbing tattoo of Kelly on my shoulder. "That's going to be hard for us real girls to compete with."

"Not a lot of real girls lining up to compete with anyone for me. Maybe you hadn't noticed."

"Christ, Moses, there were girls all over you last night, or were you too lost to notice."

"Ohhh... Did I get a dance from Ronnie?" Blurred memories flitted in and out of focus.

"No, she tried but you shocked us all and declined. We may have to change your name to Saint Moses."

"That's good." She was gently stroking my hair while the world slipped away.

When I awoke again, Piper was standing by the side of the bed, she had on a short Catholic schoolgirl's skirt, knee high white socks and saddle shoes. Her cleavage spilled out of a Wonderbra as she leaned over. In her hands, a glass of O.J. and a bottle of aspirin. "Come on big guy, I need to get to the club, and you need to go home and shower 'cause you be stinkin'," she said with a laugh.

"How come you look so good and I feel so bad."

"Maybe it's youth, or maybe I didn't try to drink the bar dry. Now take your aspirin like a good little Moses, and let's roll." I did as I was told, nothing I ever drank tasted as good as that O.J. Sitting up, my brain seemed to slop around in my skull. I was naked, my pants and shirt were folded and sitting by the side of the bed. Piper let out a laugh. "Don't worry, I had my eyes closed when I undressed you." I cocked an eyebrow. "Ok, I might have peeked, but fair is fair, I mean you've see all of me. Now I've seen all of your scar-tracked fine self. Now get dressed, or I'm going to be late," she said tossing my clothes to me. In a show of false modesty she turned her back as I dressed.

At the club, I retrieved my Norton and drove home with Marilyn tucked under my jacket. Back at my crib, Angel had lived up to her name, I had half expected to find the place trashed, but no. She had eviscerated a stuffed bunny but had left my furniture alone. We walked down to a taco stand where I had a bowl of menudo, Mexico's sure fire hangover medicine. Walking home I felt like a new man. And the first thing the new man wanted to do was vomit.

It had been nine days since I found Kelly. Nine days blurred with booze. Nine days of stuffing my feelings down into a tight little lockbox in my stomach. I poured myself a scotch, but when I rose the tumbler to my lips I saw Kelly's face. *"Mo?... I really need your help... They want... She um... My sister... well...you can't hide..."* She whispered to me, her eyes afraid. I set the tumbler down. What kind of a limp dick punk was I? Some bastard had raped and killed my friend because I'd been too fucking busy to check on her. And all I'd done since was to try and drink Scotland dry and hang my head like a broke neck weasel. I hated the face that looked back at me in the mirror, I was sick and tired of being sick and tired.

I was down to only two options, gather my balls up and finally kill myself or find the freaks who had killed Kelly and make them pay. The numbness in my soul shifted, replaced by a building rage. An eye for a fucking eye, a tooth for a tooth.

The rage felt clean and simple, blowing the cobwebs from my mind. Someone must be made to pay the price for the ride Kelly had to take. If the cops couldn't find them, I would.

I had two leads to chase down, one was the Armenians. I still had the skinny one's driver's license, his address was in Glendale. The other was the word "sister". She had never talked about having any family, but it wasn't the kind of word she would use for any of the club girls.

I rode back to Silverlake, maybe Lowrie had missed something. Pulling off the crime scene tape, I let myself in. The bloodstains had all darkened to a deep brown. A line of ants climbed up the wall over her bed. I went through her dresser but found nothing. She had an antique dressing table with a round mirror. In her jewelry box, I found a tarnished little girl's charm bracelet amongst the cheap costume pieces, rhinestones and paste worn to attract diamonds and gold. I picked up the charm bracelet, feeling the little shoe, the Golden Gate Bridge, the Scottie dog. I was sure they all meant something, each had a memory if only Kelly were there to decode them for me.

I let myself in the back door of the club. The cleaning crew was busy vacuuming. Kelly's locker was almost bare, a cute furry sweater she wore when the air-conditioning froze her out and a small makeup bag. Slipped into the lining of the bag was a postcard from the Cock's Roost, one of Nevada's many legal hot pillow joints. The postcard had a cartoon picture of a rooster surrounded by big-titted hens in lingerie. On the back was a Nevada postmark. It was addressed by hand in flowing purple cursive. The note read, "Kelly, all is swell, peachy in fact. I'm making mucho ducats, and if you don't expect much from the guys you don't get disappointed. For the first time in my life I feel that I am in control of my fate. I hope all is well with you... Write me! Cass." It wasn't much but it was all I had. My search turned up nothing else of any use.

Back at the crib I cranked up a little Black Market Clash, I needed the edge. Four calls to different area codes in Nevada finally delivered a number for the Cock's Roost. A woman with a thick sultry voice answered the phone, "Cock's Roost, how can we pleasure you?"

"Yes, I'm looking for Cass?"

After a brief pause she said, "We have no one by that name here, but if you want to stop by I'm sure we can find you a pleasing substitute." I told her I would and jotted down the address, not that I knew what the hell good it would do me.

"An old Jew, a Black guy and a cop come into a bar. 'What'll you boys have?' says the barman. 'Goys?' says the old Jew, 'Goys? I didn't survive two years in the death camp to have to listen to this crap.' And he stomps out." Bob the bookie and I were sitting in his booth at Bordner's, a local low-life watering hole. "Now the black guy looks the bartender up and down real slow. 'You call the Amazon a creek?' he says, 'You call King Kong a monkey?

No? Then don't call a man a boy.' And he walks out. So, the cop, he walks up."

"What color was he?" I asked.

"Who?"

"The cop?"

"It don't matter."

"Well you got a Jew and a Black guy, so what color was the cop?"

"Blue, ok? Blue, like all of them bastards. Now can I go on?"

"Go ahead," who was I to stop him. "I just wondered."

"Ok, ok so the Jew, no the cop, yeah ok, so the cop steps behind the bar and shoots the bartender in the knee and then arrests him for resisting. Moral of the story, don't call a man a boy, unless you're sure he doesn't have a badge." Bob looked at me, waiting for a laugh that wouldn't be coming any time soon.

"You make that up?" I said.

"Sure, this morning while I was in the crapper. Get it?"

"I got it. I think the cop was probably White."

"Who the fuck cares what color the cop was, it's not the point." Bob was a fur covered fireplug of a man. He kept his moon shaped face clean-shaven all the way down his neck but through his open collar a tee-shirt of chest hair showed. We had been friends since we hooked up in Juvie. I was twelve at the time, he was two years older than me, but even then I had size on him. The Mexicans were all crewed up as were the Black kids, that left Bob and me to fend for ourselves. We covered each other's asses in there, but when we got out we drifted back to our separate worlds. He had the good fortune of being born Italian. He had never been made, but that didn't stop him from being a good earner for the LA family. And when he was busted in the eighties he did his jolt like a man and never rolled on anyone. That earned him a new Cadillac and a permanent place on the team.

"Tell me you brought me some cabbage," Bob said. "We're pals and all but cheezus I can't keep covering for you." I slid an envelope across the bar. I had $600 donated by the Armenians, cash I had meant to give to Kelly. Bob flicked the envelope open and closed. That was all it took for him to count it.

"Couple of grand light, aren't you?"

"It's a start. I need you to take me to the Pope." You never knew who was listening so we always call Don Gallico the Pope, his lieutenants we called the cardinals.

"No, you don't," Bob said with as much steel as his pudgy face could muster.

"Yes, I do."

"He doesn't have a real soft spot in his heart for you. Not since you ankled it out on him."

"Old news." I said. Years back the head of the LA family offered me a job in collections as a way to get out from under some cash I owed them. I tried, really, but it just wasn't me. "He said he understood."

"He says all kinds of stuff. You hurt his pride. It was like you were saying you were better than him."

"I'll take my chances. Come on, Bobby, it's a short drive and 'a hello how are you'."

"Forget about it. Ain't going to happen."

"I'll tell him you sent me."

"You wouldn't."

"I need this."

In public we may have called the old man The Pope, but to his face we called him Sir. He'd been the head of the LA family going back to the day. In all those years the man had never seen a single night in the cage. In part this was because he never let the business actually touch his hands, also he insisted that the LA family stay clear of drugs, but the main reason for his lack of jail time was that if anyone even thought about ratting him out, they wound up as so many body parts floating in the LA river. He was old when I was a kid, but walking into the restaurant I wasn't prepared for what fourteen years had wreaked on his body. His once large frame had collapsed in on itself. His skin hung grey and loose like a cheap suit after a two week run. His silver hair had gone to near transparent white and fringed his shiny cue-ball of a skull. Cigars had taken his larynx so that when he spoke he had to press a finger against a small voice prosthesis in his throat.

"How you doing, sir?" I asked, sitting down across from him.

"I speak out of a tube in my throat, I shit in a bag and my dick only gets hard when I pop six Viagra. How the hell you think I'm doing? You come here to bust my chops you little cock sucker?"

"No, sir. I meant no disrespect."

"Hell you didn't. Look at you, you're a walking disrespect. Manny don't pay you enough to buy a suit? Or even a razor?"

"I, um…"

"Johnny," his metallic voice squawked to the waiter. "Get the kid a slice with prosciutto and peppers." Refusing to eat in front of The Pope was a sin, one he never let you commit. "I can't take good food any more. Not that it would matter, I got no more taste buds see? Do yourself a favor kid and die young. This growing old is the craps."

We were sitting in Figueroa's, a small Italian restaurant and bakery in the Los Feliz area. His crew looked more like a V.F.W. meeting than a mob. Fifty would have been a youngster with this group. Not that their age made them any less dangerous. Most of these guys had more bodies to their count than I had bad debts. Bob had gone in first, cleared my way and then faded back onto the street. He had no desire to be around if it went sideways between me and the old man.

"I need to ask you a question," I said, my eyes darting around the room.

"So ask. Don't worry, I have this place swept daily."

"I know Uncle Manny kicks you a piece off the top, not that it's any of my business."

"Did that little towel head send you to me?"

"No, he doesn't even know I'm here. Problem is I may have to jam up two Armenian punks, caught them running a protection racket on my girls."

"Inside the club?"

"Yeah."

"Cock-sucking sons of bitches."

"I don't want to step on any toes. But you know I can't let it pass."

"These Armenian pricks have some balls, huh? If it was ten years ago, I'd just take them off the count and call it a day. New York wants us to make peace. They're trying to strike a deal with the Russians. This is the golden age of mergers, huh kid?"

"I've heard they have a mob set up out of Glendale."

"Fuck that. A few crews at best. But they're growing balls fast. Gas station tax scams, credit cards, cloned cells, some loan sharking. They keep it in their neighborhoods and out of the press. I had a little boundary dispute with them. These Russian bastards don't scare easy I'll tell you that. I put three of their pawns in the grinder before I even had their attention. Now this crap in my territory. If it's sanctioned, bodies got to drop. Let a man shit on your lawn, he'll be screwing your wife by nightfall."

"You're a poet, sir."

"Whatever."

"If these punks are freelancing?" I asked.

"Then you'd be doing me a favor by squashing them."

"Who do I have to ask before I pull the switch?"

"Rafael Hakobian, he's running things since his brother took a federal fall two years ago. I'll have Frankie make a call, an introduction, nothing else. You go in alone, you come out if you're lucky." The waiter placed a slice of pizza in front of me. Say what you will about the Wops, they make a mean piece of pie. "No shit, kid, these fucks are some evil pricks, kill cops, kids, girls, they just don't seem to care. In ninety-four, we had a council meeting after bodies started washing up on Brighton Beach, I said we should take them down, but the New York families wanted to wait and see. Well, we saw. Now, I say go to the mattress and they say we negotiate. When did the world go to the pussies?"

"Maybe they're all just looking out for their piece of the pie." I said, taking another bite of the thick-crusted pizza.

"Yeah, and we're going to lose the whole pizzeria in the deal. You don't come out of this Russian fuck's crib, ain't shit I can do, we're clear on that, right?"

"I'm on my own, Sir, I got it."

"And you still want to go in?"

"No, but I have to. Nobody fucks with my girls, you know that."

"Uncle Manny don't pay you enough to die, so why?" I could tell he really wanted to understand what would make me do it. I thought about it for a moment looking out the dirty window. On the street a Latin immigrant woman pushed a shopping cart with all of her worldly possessions piled high, her face was deeply wrinkled. I wondered if this was the promised land she had hoped it would be. Two Cholos in a candy apple red Impala rolled by like a cool jet of red steam.

"I guess the truth is, there's only so much you can let pass, then you start drawing the line. Don't draw the line somewhere, it all turns to shit. It's like live and let live, but you cross the line and fuck with what's mine and you will go down." He looked at me for a long moment then nodded appreciatively, he motioned for one of his boys and sent him to make the call. While he did, we talked about horses, who we liked, who was overrated. He told me about his son, a big time lawyer, lived up in Santa Barbara. There was no pride when he spoke of him. I think the Pope was aware he was the last of his kind, a dinosaur who could feel the cold breath of the ice age on the back of his neck. The new generation of mobsters had M.B.A.'s and law degrees and when they stole it was all legit. Enron alone made his whole career look like boosting hubcaps. His man came back and whispered in his ear. The Pope nodded briefly then turned back to me, slipping me a piece of paper with an address on it.

"Go with God kid," he said, making the sign of the

cross. "If it turns out freelancers are pissing on my turf, I would consider it a personal favor if you put the hammer down on these stray dogs." The steel returned to his eyes, reminding me that deep down beneath all his age and ailments was a man who could kill you with a claw hammer and not have it ruin his appetite, such as it was.

CHAPTER 6

The address was in the Glendale Hills, expensive sprawling California ranch-style homes littered the steep streets. Most of the houses were designed to cover every inch of available building space, a perfect example of the mansionization craze: take what is already fatally ugly and make it bigger. The thin roads were clogged with gold trimmed BMW's and Mercedes Benz's, it was ghetto rich, all flash, telling the world you had made it up the hill, ornate iron fences, huge brass door knockers. It screamed like a ten-pound gold neck chain "I have cash, look at me." It was all show, no go, just more fools spending every cent they have to prove to the world that they are here, that they are worthy. If they thought all this stuff would protect them from the random spin of the wheel, they had an awakening coming.

Rafael Hakobian's house was on the crest of the hills. In front of a security gate I spoke into a video camera and waited. A deep voice told me to follow the driveway up to the house. What a house it was, a three-storied box that looked more like a motel than a home. It had to be five thousand square feet of ugly gray stucco with balconies jutting out at odd angles, as if added on as an after thought. The windows were all multi-paned and looked expensive but the brushed aluminum they chose for the frames made them look cheap at the same time. The garden was all grass, not a flower in sight, just a huge expanse of rolling green. In the center of the lawn a tall maiden stood on the back of a sea serpent spraying water up into the air, the mammoth fountain looked painfully out of place in front of the modern house. Beyond the house the view was magnificent, all of Glendale spread out below us and past that, the gleaming glass towers of downtown. Two men, only slightly smaller than Mac trucks stood waiting for me. I'm a big man and not too used to being looked straight in the eye. Under their matching black collar-less jackets were large, not so hidden pistols.

"Here to see Mr. Hakobian," I said, their expressions didn't change. I climbed off the Norton and they moved in blocking my path. One of them held a small metal detector, with a flick of his finger, he motioned for me to raise my arms. "Big talkers huh?" I said, the huge man just stared at me with cold dead eyes. So I lifted my arms away from my body and let him give me a quick sweep with the metal detector. The thing went wild when they got to my leg. Both men tensed. "It's bolts in my leg. Motorcycle accident, titanium rod in the femur, two bolts in the knee," I told them, but they didn't relax a bit. "You got a scalpel I'll show you," I said with a grin.

"Drop you pants," one of them said in a thickly accented growl.

"Fuck off." I said, turning back towards my bike. "Tell your boss it was nice not meeting him." Two huge hands clamped down onto my shoulders spinning me around and locking me in place, my face inches from his ugly mug. I rocketed my knee quickly up into his crotch, he gasped a stream of hot garlic breath into my face. I pulled the short barreled heavy frame .357 from under his arm, smashing the pistol into the side of his face. He stumbled back and went down. His twin was reaching under his coat when I pulled the hammer back and drew a bead on his forehead. "You really want die over this shit, Huh? Do it! Keep moving that hand and see if I give a fuck."

"Yuri, kak dela?" A voice came from the front door. I flicked my eyes over long enough to see a large barrel-chested man in a silk shirt.

"Tak sebe," the standing twin said with a small shrug.

"Horosho," the man in the doorway said, "Vlady?" The twin on the ground groaned pulling himself up, a burgundy bruise was blooming on his cheek from his eye to his hairline and he was having an uncomfortable time walking. He looked at his boss and tried to force a smile.

"Mr. McGuire, please either shoot my worthless bykis or come inside for a drink," the man at the door said disappearing into the shadows of the house. Looking from one thug to the other I smiled briefly then opened the cylinder of the .357 and dropped the shells on the ground. Walking toward the house I tossed the revolver over my shoulder in the general direction of the stumbling giant.

The entryway was built to impress, marble tiles and a vaulted ceiling that went up the full three floors, in the center of it hung down a huge crystal chandelier. Tall Chinese vases held dried flowers and gold mirrors flanked the walls in thick ornate frames. The entryway alone was bigger than my entire bungalow. Two slender legs appeared from above, stepping silently down the plush carpet of a wide curving staircase. Bare feet and legs made long by the short purple leather skirt they disappeared into. A tight baby doll tee-shirt with the word "Brat" stretched across her teenaged frame, big-chest, tiny waist, and about a can and a half of hair spray struggling to control her hair. There's something sweet about a teenager wanting so bad to be a woman and having no idea what it entails. Long black wild hair framing a sad face. Fresh makeup covering a bruise on her left cheek. Her feet left small tracks in the freshly vacuumed white carpet. Hitting the marble floor of the entryway she looked up, surprised to find me there watching her. I shot her my best smile, the one I wish said I'm ok I don't eat the young. Looking me over she raised her nose in the air like she smelled a bad fish.

"Who the hell are you?" she asked.

"No one important."

"That's an understatement," she said without a hint of humor.

"Maral!" At the sound of her father's voice her face flashed from arrogance to fear to complacence all in the flick of an eyelid. Without a glance in my direction she walked out of the room.

In a large library, Rafael Hakobian sat in a deep red leather club chair smoking a cigar and looking me over. Behind him the walls were filled with leather bound books I was sure he never read, like everything else in this house it was all for show. "Sit, have a vodka and tell me what you are here for," he said motioning me to the chair across from him. From a crystal decanter he poured a tall shot of clear liquor into a shot glass and passed it to me.

"To your health, Mr. Hakobian," I said and powered down the shot. He smiled and drank his. He poured us each another.

"I would drink to your health, but I despise hypocrites," he said. "And as I may have to kill you, that would be the wrong toast. So we say udachi! Good luck!" Raising his glass we drank again, and again he filled our glasses.

"Kill me huh?"

"Neizvestno, chto teper' budet." He blew out a slow stream of blue cigar smoke.

"What's that mean?"

"There's no knowing what will happen now. You think that decrepit Italian can protect you here?"

"No, said he wouldn't. Said I was on my own. He also said you'd probably kill me for coming."

"This didn't scare you?"

"Not much. It's not like I have some swell life to protect."

"Ha, have you ever been to Russia?"

"No."

"Too bad, you would fit in very well with all the other weak fatalists."

"Fatalist, just another word for nothing left to lose," I said with a smile.

"You think this shit is funny?"

"Yeah, I do. You're all puffed up showing me how tough you are. Why bother, you want to put one in my brain and drop me off the hill, nobody would give a damn, some would celebrate."

"Why do you tell me this?"

"I don't think you have any reason to kill me. That, and I think you know it's going to cost you heavy to do it. I won't go down easy."

'Provda, so why are you here, Mr. McGuire?" he said letting a fresh stream of smoke slip towards the oak-paneled ceiling.

"This," I said, handing him the skinny boy's driver's license. "Two Armenian punks have been poaching on the girls at the strip club where I work." He turned the license over in his hand looking at it carefully.

"And this involves me how? An Armenian farts in an elevator and the feds come looking for me. You think I have time to worry about what every Armenian does in all of California?"

"Yes I do. Personally, I don't think an Armenian steals a glance without you hearing about it."

"Ha, you think I am very powerful, omnipresent almost? And then you blame me for these wild young fools?"

"I don't blame you for anything."

"Then why are you here?"

"Out of respect. I'm going to put them down. I thought if they were with your crew I'd give you fair warning."

"And if I told you not to touch them?"

"I'd leave you my address so you wouldn't have to look too hard for me after I dropped them." I looked straight into his hard eyes. It was clear he had seen a lot of bad shit in his time, but so had I. Slowly a deep laugh rumbled up out of his chest.

"Tough guy, huh? I like you, be a shame to gut you like a fish. Lucky for you, I don't know this boy." Then he raised his glass, "To your health."

The twins tried to burn holes in my back with their eyes as I walked out, but they didn't say a word. Climbing on the Norton I gave them a two-fingered salute and rolled down the hill, heading for the flats of Glendale. The address on the license was one of many graceful apartment buildings built in the twenties, back when craftsmen actually gave a shit about their work. The windows were arched and thick, the lines of the building flowed down to the sidewalk. Even the shit brown the latest owners painted it couldn't disguise its grace. Moving to the second-story landing, I took out my .38 and knocked. After a long moment the door opened a crack, with the chain still on. I put my shoulder to it with all my weight. The chain ripped out of the jamb and the door flew open, knocking the big boy tumbling onto the tan carpet. I stepped quickly in. Slamming the door behind me I swept the room with my .38. On a stained sofa the skinny boy sat with his leg in a cast from hip to toe. He was scrambling to reach his Glock on the coffee table, but when he saw my gun he gave up. The big boy stood up, he had a plaster patch over his nose, if he was in fear of me he sure hadn't told his face the news.

"We haven't done shit!" the skinny boy yapped.

"Is that any way to talk to a guest?" I motioned with my .38 for big boy to sit on the sofa. "You boys really screwed the pooch this time. You know a man they call the Pope of Figueroa?" They both nodded, worry starting to show. "Turns out he didn't take kindly to you running a scam in his neighborhood. I may be able to square it with him, if you're straight with me. Lie to me and you better pack your bags and head to the old country. Did you sweat the girls alone, or did you have help?"

"We're with the Broadway crew, so if those Italian fucks want..." I didn't let him finish. I put my .38 in my pocket and went for the door. I had it open before he stopped me. "Hey, where are you going?"

"I told you what would happen if you lied to me."

"Fuck you and fuck your friends in their fat grease-ball asses, the Italians are over and we're running this town now bro, or didn't you get the E-mail?" the skinny boy said, puffing up.

"Only thing you're running is your mouth. Gonna get you a slow death. See shit for brains, I just came from Pakka supreme Rafael Hakobian's house, he never heard of you. Have a good life kid." The skinny kid's eyes darted wildly around in their sockets searching for the hidden camera and perky host to tell him it was all a big joke.

"Tell him the truth," the big guy said in a deep baritone.

"We're alone," the skinny guy said.

"You sure are," I said. "Now the six-million dollar question, where did you go after I met you at the club?"

"Where the fuck do. . ." the skinny boy started but was shut down by a look from his friend. "We went to Glendale Adventist's emergency room, they were backed up with a drive by, we didn't get out 'til the next morning." I looked at him long and hard. "Call the hospital if you want, they'll tell you."

"I'm going to." I said and walked out. I didn't need to make any more threats, they were scared little rabbits as it was, at least the little squid was. As for big boy, who the hell knew what was going on behind his stone face.

I headed home tired, no closer to an answer then when I started. Back at the crib I fed Angel a half-pound of ground beef. After watching her wolf down her dinner, I lay down on the bed to play with her. I fell into a dreamless sleep for two solid hours. I woke up, showered, drank a cup of strong coffee and rode into work.

It was a typically dead Monday night at the flesh palace, a few stragglers came in for a quick lap dance, then slunk out with a stain showing on their slacks. I asked Piper if she had ever known any girls that worked at the Cock's Roost. I guessed right, it was one of Nevada's infamous legal brothels. She'd known girls who went there, but none had come back to stripping. On the long twisted road of the sex trade, the direction was one way. Most started out bikini dancing, then moved to stripping, some went into porno, and others to prostitution. At every stop they drew lines in the sand, demarcation lines they would not cross, until time and cash blurred the lines and they had to draw new ones.

"You're a good boy, Moses, why you want to go chasing dragons?" Uncle Manny asked when I told him I needed to take some time off to look for Kelly's killer. We were sitting in his office, his desk strewn with the week's books.

"You can have Doc take the extra shifts," I said. "He can use it, I hear his old lady's going to give him another rug-rat." Doc was a huge, bighearted man, with skin as dark as night and a smile that could lighten the darkest room.

"He is a good man, but you I trust. You understand?"

"She was one of ours, Manny, we owe it to her."

"Very noble."

"No, it's just something I have to do."

"Still, it is noble," he said, thinking for a moment. Then from the open safe behind him he counted out two thousand dollars. "For you, for Kelly." Pocketing the cash I shook his hand and went out to the bar. I asked Piper if she could look after Angel for me.

"Mo, I kill house plants. I stay out all night, sleep all day. Do you really think I'm the poster child for adopt-a-pet?" She said.

"No, I guess not."

"You take care of yourself," she said in a wistful tone. "You come back to me in one piece." She ran her hand gently across my cheek, then put on her stripper's smile and turned away. As she swished off, I realized she meant it.

CHAPTER 7

I hit Helen up the next day while our dogs tore up the park. "I'd love to watch Angel for you. Maybe she can work the extra ten pounds off of Bruiser for me." I didn't tell her where I was going. If this thing went south, the less she knew, the better. I left Angel playing with Bruiser. Good-byes weren't really my strong suit. I sold my bike for six grand to a guy who owned a shop that specialized in Nortons over in North Hollywood. I left him drooling over the flawless black paint and perfect chrome, I had bigger fish to fry. I took a bus ride over to Jason B's, a wanna be actor who paid the bills by buying cars at the police auction and re-selling them over Ebay. He had a '05 Ford Crown Vic police Interceptor I bought for his cost of twenty-three hundred dollars. It was big and black with white doors which I spray painted to match the body. With an old school V8 and computer driven fuel injection, the bitch was built for fast takeoffs. It had heavy-duty four-wheel discs to stop on a dime, and a suspension tuned for ripping around corners at max speed. With a twenty gallon gas tank, it was a long range road beast built to take down the bad men. A gaping hole in the dashboard spoke of a missing radio and computer terminal. She wasn't pretty but she would blend in on most streets and she was mine. For an extra fifty bucks Jason B tossed in a set of prop Nevada plates, they were hand-painted to look punched out. Although they wouldn't hold up to close eye-balling, if the cops got that close I was screwed anyway. I had him transfer the papers on the car over to Johnny Stahl. He was a clean identity I'd built over the last ten years, with just enough of a paper trail to make him legal. Johnny owned a legally registered .45 automatic, a Visa card with a five hundred dollar limit and a library card. Johnny was twice the square I was. He was almost human.

Back in East LA I had a neighborhood kid hook me up with a car stereo for forty bucks and a six pack of tall boys. If I was going to be rolling long and wide I needed tuneage. He cut a piece of plywood to fill the gaping dash and bolted it in. Like everything else in the Ford it was all go, no show.

My house felt empty with Angel gone. Silly, I hadn't had her that long but I missed her wagging tail and sloppy face. This is no time to go soft and cuddly so I loaded a Mossberg twelve-gauge riot gun, a Colt .45 1911 automatic, my S&W .38 and boxes of shells for all into the trunk of the Crown Vic. I didn't know where the trail would lead, but I knew I should pack heavy just in case it turned ugly. I filled a gym bag with jeans, tee-shirts and socks. I took out my one and only nice suit. It was gray gabardine with black piping on its country western yoke. I added a white western shirt with pearl buttons, a scorpion bolo and a pair of black Tony Lama boots. Packed and ready, I was almost out the door when I noticed the Marilyn cookie jar with the charm bracelet wrapped around the handle on its lid. If I found Kelly's sister, she might know what to do with Kelly's remains. I set her in the back seat and rumbled out of town.

Joe Strummer and the Mescaleros kicked a beat to my retreat from the city. Fuck Mick Jones, Strummer's drunken growl will always be the heart and soul of the Clash. The only blessing in his death is the world will be spared an embarrassing oldies tour. I almost threw up when I heard Johnny Rotten and a less Vicious Sex Pistols played Trump's place in Atlantic City. In case there was any doubt that the go-go 80's had killed punk, that show put the nail in the coffin.

The Crown Vic took to the freeways like a duck to water. It was still early enough so that the quitting traffic hadn't clogged the road. In San Berdo I took the I-15 toward Vegas, up over the mountains and then a gentle sweep down into the desert. I had made this run enough times in my life, I probably could have done it with my eyes closed. Vegas had been my Camelot, the land where all the rules were clear and fair. Less than a tank of gas from LA and I was in a whole 'nother world, one full of beautiful women who brought you drinks, lit your cigarettes and laughed at all your jokes. One good run at the blackjack table and I drove home with shiny new boots and two months rent. And if I lost, I'd had one hell of a time doing it. The main difference between Bob the bookie and a Vegas pit boss was, Bob would let me lose more than I had, in Vegas when I was broke, I was broke. I might have to hock my watch for gas money, but that was the worst it could get.

Pushing the accelerator down an SUV full of college kids pulled over to let me fly by. One of the added benefits to driving an ex-cop car is when the other motorists see that familiar silhouette in their rear view, they get instant guilt and slow down to let you pass. Cruising along at a safe eighty miles an hour I had plenty of time to think. I had lived my life to this point without direction, letting the currents take me where they would. I was a ship without a rudder, and a questionable moral compass to guide me. My childhood was something I didn't like to dwell on. A violent father who had skipped when I was six, and a mother who mixed equal parts gin and televangelism, she could quote all the parts in the Bible that made you feel shitty and small. Most afternoons she would fly into rages and tear the house up, by night she would pass out in front of the TV set while some preacher droned on about the cash he needed. My older brother Luke and I mostly raised ourselves. It wasn't all bad, we had nothing to judge it against so it seemed like our lives, nothing more nothing less. We didn't know that other kid's moms tucked them in at night, or that their moms didn't wake up every day with bloodshot eyes and sick headaches. We lived in a small two bedroom bungalow in a court of other paint chipped bungalows up on the sad side of Altadena. The court was populated by the retired, the recently rehabilitated and those like our mom, who lived on permanent disability. Luke and I were the only people under thirty so we kept to ourselves. In school we had a reputation as wild boys, probably well earned but it kept most of the parents from letting their progeny hang with us. That was fine by me, screw the squares if they don't want to be with us. Luke and me were a tribe of two, or we were until he grew hair on his nut sack and discovered that being a bad boy got more girls to lift their skirts than driving a BMW or living in a mansion up on the hill. So he deserted me for gash and I waited alone for the mystery to take hold of me. At fourteen I lost my cherry to a thirty five year old pro who had gentlemen callers as she called them into her bungalow across the brown patch of grass from our front door. Right after I came I had two contradictory ideas, what was all the talk about? Getting laid wasn't all that big a deal, in fact it was kinda nasty. At the same moment I heard a much deeper voice saying when do we get to do this again? I spent the whole summer doing odd jobs around her place, working on the barter system.

My brother left when I was sixteen. He just packed up his '56 Ford and moved to Texas. He said it was where our roots were, our old man had been a Texan, and I guess that was all the excuse Luke needed to put three thousand miles between himself and our childhood. Whatever his reasons were, he left me alone with the care and feeding of the monster. I still haven't forgiven him for that. She was getting crazier by the day, bouncing between DT's and liver meltdown. Her skin had taken on a greenish yellow color and a dull shine like wax. Her hearing was shot so she always had the Bible Boosters on full blast overdrive.

I stood it for two long months, believing Luke would roll up with a beer in one hand and a Texas cheerleader in the other, and our life would go back to the dull crazy I had always known. But he didn't, so I lifted his birth certificate and an old driver's license and enlisted in the Marines.

Six weeks later, I graduated boot and was shipped out to Lebanon. President Ronny that actor fuck sent us a televised message. He was proud of us upholding the Marine tradition of protecting the innocent. Our mission as he outlined it was to show the world our support of the legit Lebanese government. How that translated into a battle plan was a bit sketchy. They posted some bullshit called the ROE, rules of engagement, we were never to carry a round chambered in our guns, we were only to fire if in direct and imminent danger. Under no circumstances were we to give chase or fire upon the enemy unless they were firing on us. It was pure political bullshit and we knew it.

WELCOME TO THE ROOT, was chalked in tall uneven letters on the landing strip where our transport chopper landed. The Root, Beirut, or what was left of it stretched out before us, the night sky lit up with green tracers and the city rocked from mortar fire.

Me and a twelve-man squad were assigned to checkpoint 79. It was down in an East Beirut ghetto we called Hooterville. The first time a sniper fired on us I about shit myself. Rounds burst open our sandbags and we dove for cover. Most of the time they were bad enough shots so that it became more of an irritant than any big danger.

I had only been in country about a week when the Shiite militia drove a truckload of explosive into the American embassy killing 17 Americans. The press blamed the marine guard, but what the hell were they supposed to have done? By the time they saw what was happening and chambered a round it was too late.

That's when we decided to change the rules of engagement. The Gunny had us rake a 50 caliber machine-gun across an apartment building where ten or so snipers had been harassing us. The big bullets ripped glass, curtains, plaster, wall studs, whatever came into their line of fire. Me and two other sharpshooters lay on a rooftop across from the building. When the Muslim fighters came running out into the street, Gunny blew a whistle. We rose up and tore the surprised sons of bitches to shreds. Blood and bone chips and pieces of cloth flew in all directions. One of the militia spun trying to aim up at us, through my scope I could see the stupid shock on his face as my bullets ripped him apart.

There was movement at the front door, more were coming out, I sprayed them down before I noticed it was a young mother chasing her panicked child out of the building. Miraculously the child was not hit, but his mother hadn't been so lucky. A line of my bullets had stitched across her chest. She fell face first down the stone steps, her arm outstretched, reaching for her son.

Afterwards the Gunny said it couldn't have been helped, it was the cunt's fault for running into a fire zone. That night I discovered peace in a glass. Six boilermakers and I couldn't even remember what I was crying about.

Our misguided adventure in that red shit pile came to an end after a suicide bomber drove his truck into a barracks killing 270 sleeping marines. One flash of light followed by a pillar of fire and every friend I had in the corps was dead. 270 KIA in one day, the only thing even close was Iwo Jima. It was a few too many body bags for Prez Ronny and his cronies to stomach so we got our orders to ship home. It would be a lie to say we left that place any worse than we found it, but we sure didn't do it any good.

Back stateside, my head was filled with the smell of burnt Marines and the face of a dead woman. My C.O. got word that my mother was in the hospital, he offered me hardship leave to go to her. I told him it must have been a mistake, I was an orphan.

I spent my off hours in the base club drowning my head in beer and whiskey. To their credit the officers understood that what we had been through over there had taken its toll, but even they had their limits. My almost constant drinking and general insanity led to a medical discharge. I didn't fight it, I was sick and tired of their rules eating into my drinking time.

I was waiting for the paperwork to clear when I got word that my mother had died. I should have felt guilty for not going to her, but I didn't. I only felt free.

The drive was giving me way too much time to think. Sometimes I wish I could contract Alzheimer's so I could start every day with a fresh slate. Once, in the joint this lifer, who had discovered AA six dead bodies too late, had told me that my mind was a dangerous neighborhood and I shouldn't go in alone. I could see the wisdom in that but the truth was if I invited anyone into my head they'd lock me down and toss away the key.

At Baker I pulled into Bun Boys for a burger and a cup of coffee served by a waitress named Dolly. I think she had the last beehive in captivity. Back on the road I headed for the Nevada State line. Out on an empty section of highway I decided to keep my mind occupied by seeing what the Crown Vic could do. Mashing down the gas pedal it leapt from eighty to one-twenty like a racehorse. Slamming on the brakes it skidded to a stop in a relatively straight line. It proved to be a good solid piece of Detroit iron. I knew that if they took this battle to the roads I could trust its moves.

About five feet across the state line Buffalo Bill's casino stabbed up out of the tan dirt desert floor. In a nod to the family fun theme of it all, they have a roller coaster running five stories up above the place. Come on down and bring the kiddies, let them ride the whopper while mom and dad get hammered and spend the rent check. Oh yeah, that has family fun written all over it. I pulled in to fill the tank. Standing in line to pay, the ping and ching of slots clattering around me in the service station, I looked out the window to the welcoming face of the casino across the road. I had a roll of cash, hell a couple lucky hands and I would be square with Bob the bookie and maybe with just a little more luck I could put my ex-wife finally behind me. Just a few quick hands and then back on the road, no one would ever know I had stopped.

"That's right where it happened." I turned to see a greasy haired clerk watching me. "I saw you staring, we get a lot of that. It was all over the news. I was working that night, saw them pull her out, even got myself on the eleven o'clock news."

"What?" I said in total confusion.

"That little colored girl that got raped and murdered in the men's room, it was right over there. That boy did it while his friend watched or some shit." The story came back to me, it had been all over the airwaves a few years back. A little girl of six or seven had been raped and strangled by this nice looking freak in his early twenties, his pal had seen him starting to do it and had walked out, didn't try to stop him. Her mom was right outside in the restaurant the whole time, not fifty feet from where her daughter was being dragged through hell. I wonder if that woman ever got another peaceful moment's rest; what does she see when she closes her eyes at night? The kid who did it, he was broken beyond repair long before he dragged that scared little girl in there. I know what they do to short eyes in the slam, so he is getting his daily, but the fuck who really needs to be taken off the count is the punk who saw it start and walked away. In my book that's the worst of all, because at some level he knew better and wasn't man enough to act.

I shoved my change into my pocket and cranked the beast over. I made a friend a promise and gambling wasn't part of the deal, so I pulled past the casino and onto the highway, dodging that bullet one more time. At Sin City I took a left onto highway ninety-five. The Cock's Roost was sixty miles from Vegas, just outside the Clark County line. Back in the sixties when prostitution was made legal the mob boys and the state struck a deal to keep it out of the gambling capitals of Vegas and Reno. The sex trade is small potatoes compared to the real cash cow, the twenty-four-hour hum of slot machines. The gaming business, with its stage shows and roller coasters was after all good clean all-American fun. The smaller counties were free to license brothels, it helped their tax base and hurt no one. They had strict health codes and the girl's safety was protected. In a world that always had and always would have hookers, it seemed sane to regulate it. Not that anyone ever asked my opinion. The same hypocrites who screamed to outlaw all "deviant" sex acts were no doubt banging their interns behind closed doors. Power attracts creeps, that's just the fact of the world.

It was about ten thirty when I started to see signs with a cartoon rooster and hens inviting me to stop on by for a good time. Pulling down the long driveway I discovered the Cock's Roost, a squat, spread out complex of interconnected single story houses. The slapped together additions looked like sorry afterthoughts. An eight-foot cyclone fence surrounded the property. The fence was to keep the girls in. The way the rules worked is that while the girls were employed, they couldn't leave the compound, they didn't want them going to town and freelancing. The large gravel parking lot was only a quarter full. I parked the Crown Vic and slipped the .38 into a boot holster. At a gas station along the road I'd changed into my suit. Pulling up my bolo tie, I rang the bell. The gate opened with an electronic click and I walked the thirty feet up the path to the door where I was greeted by the floor manager, a professional looking older woman who piled her gray hair on top of her head in a tight bun. She smiled pleasantly and invited me in.

Twenty-five girls stood in a line waiting for my approval. They were all dressed in skimpy outfits, from lace baby doll nightgowns to short shorts with bikini tops. They each held out a hand and demurely said her name. "Lacy," "Shayla," "Daisy," "Mercedes," "Bianca," "Trinity," "Pleasure," "Sunset," "Savanna," "Dallas," "Phoenix," "Cherri," "Shanda," "Jessie," "Ginger," "Kiki," and "CoCo". Their names like their breasts and their lusty smiles were all counterfeit. Not that most men would care, not as long as they knew how to make him come, which, by the way, ain't really rocket science. All the dancers I knew had two fake names, a stage name and one to tell a big spender so he could feel like he really knew her.

At the end of the line of names I would never remember, the floor manager asked me to make my choice. It was all so cold and businesslike, devoid of any of the romance one might expect in a whorehouse. No old black man playing piano, no men playing cards and laughing with the girls. This was a place you bought sex clean and cold. I acted nervous, said maybe I needed a drink first. I moved to the small bar and the line broke up. The girls lounged around the lobby, some trying to catch my eye. Others wrote me off and sat chatting with their girlfriends. I ordered a rum and coke, sipping it while several young lovelies came by to see if I wanted a party. I told them maybe later and they drifted off. "Party," that's their classy way of saying "fuck," it made it sound so clean and fun. "I would like an oral party followed by a you-peeing-in-my-mouth party?" Oh yeah that sounds so much better. Jessie, a woman about my age sauntered up and leaned against the bar, resting her thigh against my leg.

"First time?" she asked.

"Yes... truth is I'm looking for a friend of mine." I casually set a hundred dollar bill on the bar. "Her name is Cass." Jessie looked at the hundred then up at me. Her eyes flitted to the floor manager who was watching me like a hawk.

"Why don't we go back to my room and have a party?" Jessie said, "I think I know just what you need."

Her room was small, enough space for a bed, dresser, and a small writing table. She had a bathroom that she shared with the girl next door. Through the walls came the squeak of bedsprings and a man moaning. "Now, what kind of party would you like?" Jessie said, pointing to a small microphone in the corner of the ceiling.

"I don't know, you're the pro, what do you think?"

"How about we do a half and half for two-fifty?"

"Sounds fun," I said, trying to sound excited.

"Drop your pants, I have to check your tool, health code." I did as told and stood like a piece of meat for inspection. She raised an eyebrow when she saw all my scars. "You've had a rough life," she said, then lifted my limp penis and inspected it closely. "Ok. I'll be right back. Make yourself comfortable." She took my bills and went out to pay the cashier. The girls split the money fifty-fifty with the house. In the bathroom I found a bowl of cotton balls and some Band-Aids next to an industrial size bottle of Betadine. Stepping up on her chair I bandaged a cotton ball over the microphone. When she returned I said I'd like a little music, to get in the mood. She turned a small radio on and tuned in a country station. Willie Nelson was singing about an angel flying too close to the ground. I pointed to the job I'd done on the microphone and Jessie smiled. "You're one smart cookie. Not that it matters, but are you a cop?"

"No, just a man trying to find a friend." Pulling my pants down again she kneeled between my legs, letting her bleached blonde hair fall over my lap.

"Just in case someone comes in," she said. From the door it would look like she was taking care of business. "Cass was a sweet girl, tough as nails but not catty like the others. She didn't hit on other girls' regulars or any of the other crap most of these skanks do."

"How long was she here?"

"About two months. I remember she was here for a big Easter party we threw for a busload of Japanese businessmen. She and I did a double for this one skinny dude. You sure you don't want me to relieve a little tension while we talk? I mean, you paid for it and all."

"Don't do that."

"What, stroke you? You like it, I can tell."

"I'm not a John. I really just need help finding Cass."

"You sure?"

"Absolutely."

"Thank heaven for small favors." She sighed looking up at me. "I get so tired of dick. Dick for breakfast, lunch and dinner. And sometimes dick for a midnight snack. On my day off I can't even look at a hot dog, swear to god." Her eyes sparkled with good humor.

"Rough life."

"It isn't digging a ditch, but sometimes it feels like it."

"Are you going to tell me about Cass?"

"Ok, you're not with the mob and you're not a cop, I can tell, want to know how?"

"How?"

"You didn't fuck me first and then ask your questions. Power boys always have time to get their nuts off. So here it is, a week or so ago, two guys in classy suits showed up, Cass took one look at them and slipped out of the lobby. Ditching lineup is a firing offense, but some girls do it, say they had to pee or some bullshit. They picked Venus and Gwen, two young girls with monster fake tit jobs. Afterwards, Gwen said the whole time the guy was fucking her, he was asking about Cass. She played dumb like she had never heard of Cass, she figured he had big bucks and maybe she could become his regular. She said he liked it rough, slapping her ass while he pumped her. She also said he had a gun in his jacket."

"What did these guys look like?" I asked.

"Goombas, Vegas mob boys, dark hair, Italian features, you know the look. We better move on to the bed." I took off my shirt and lay back on the bed. She slipped out of her dress. She had a strong tanned body with flesh in all the right places, she lay on top of me. Our naked bodies pressed together, she raised up onto her elbows, bouncing her hips so the bed squeaked softly. I knew there was no love, not even very much attraction between us, but put a body on a body and the blood wants what the blood wants. I could feel myself stiffen as her beasts rubbed against my chest.

"What happened to Cass?" I was fighting for concentration.

"The next morning, she wasn't at breakfast, and that was weird because as skinny as she was, that girl could eat.

I went to her room to check on her but she was gone. She must have slipped out in the night. Maybe the night manager would know, but when I asked her, she said it was none of my business. You building a house?"

"What?"

"You're packing some serious timber. Sure you don't want me to handle it?" She said dully, it sounded like she was offering to fix my drywall.

"No, really. Do you have any ideas where she might have gone?"

"If I was to guess, I'd say she went up north. She had heard from some of the girls about a house in the mountains outside of Reno. The Eagle's Nest, a much smaller place, off the beaten track, serves mostly locals."

Climbing off her, I thanked her for the information and got dressed. She told me with a laugh that leaving a man stiff hurt her professional pride. She also told me if I found Cass to send her her love. I walked back through the lobby and none of the girls even looked up. Whatever cash I had was spent, so I was of no use to any of them. Back in the Crown Vic, I took a long breath. I wondered what had kept me from screwing Jessie, it wasn't like me to pass up sexual favors. In the rearview mirror I caught Marilyn staring at me with her pouting red lips. Was I keeping myself pure for a dead girl? Had the talk around the club about us bugged me because it was true? Had I waited too long to discover what I really felt for Kelly wasn't just friendship? I slammed the Crown Vic into gear and spun out of the parking lot, spraying gravel in a fan out behind me.

Down the road I found an open liquor store and bought a half pint of Seagrams and a bottle of ginger ale. I mixed the drink in a paper cup in the car. The booze quieted my brain down. All those unanswered questions weren't going to help me find what I was looking for. I had to keep focused. I crunched a white crisscross with my teeth. I'd bought a bag of cheap, homemade speed from Billy the DJ before leaving town. It tasted bitter and nasty but I knew it would get the job done, so I crunched another. Unfolding a map I discovered that Reno was three hundred and forty miles up Highway 95. I settled in for a long night's cruise.

The timing on the suits showing up at the Cock's Roost was right. Maybe they found an address book, or maybe they made Kelly talk. The speed kicked in, giving me that rough jangle I knew so well. If the suits were looking for Cass, it meant I was on the right track. The sun rose over the barren countryside. On the dirt shoulder I poured the last of the Seagrams into a cup and chased two more tabs with it. It wasn't enough to get me drunk, just enough to take the edge off the speed. In a pasture beside the road a bunch of lazy cows watched me. Driving on, I bypassed Reno taking highway 80 toward Battle Mountain. I followed the signs up a small county road to the Eagle's Nest. Just before the brothel I turned up a dirt road and parked in the tall pines. Dressed again in my jeans and tee-shirt I climbed a small scrub covered hill. Laying on my belly, I looked down at the Eagle's Nest through a pair of army surplus binoculars. A tall chain-link fence surrounded a two-story farmhouse that looked like it might have been built at the turn of the century. The dove-gray paint was peeling. A large porch covered the front. It was around eight in the morning and I couldn't see anyone moving inside. The sun felt warm and good on my back as it filtered down through the pine boughs. An hour later, I watched a muscular young man water the lawn and pull some weeds out of a rose bed up against the front porch. He pushed a hand mower across the grass. It was all so Norman Rockwell.

Four hours later, I awoke to a large crow cawing in the tree above. The sun overhead burned into my eyes, sending sparks exploding into my brain. There is nothing quite as much fun as a speed hangover. My entire nervous system felt toasted and I could taste something like burned wires in the back of my throat. I focused on my watch, it was one o'clock, I struggled to get my bearings. I was on my back on the hard packed dirt, I could feel pine needles in my hair. I had been in the middle of a dream I couldn't shake, as if it was still overlapping the waking world. Kelly and I were riding my Norton in the Mexican countryside. I could feel her arms around me, the warm air rushing past us. As I continued to wake the dream broke down into fragments too small to hold onto. Kelly and I played in the surf on an empty beach. In the sand she turned to kiss me, but somehow she changed into a young Lebanese mother. Blood rolling from her chest she fell into the surf.

The only cure for this sort of craziness was forward movement. Popping a couple more whites I rolled over and scanned the brothel. A few cars were in the parking lot, a late model Toyota, a couple of pickups, and a Jeep. Blue-collar cars, transportation for the working class. An hour later, a red 1971 Cutlass convertible pulled in and four teenagers piled out, laughing and horsing around. They rang the bell and waited with nervous glee. To call the older woman who opened the door for them buxom would be an understatement. She was opulent. Even from a distance I saw she had the kind of curves that little boys dreamed about and grown men sighed thanks watching her sway by. A short time later a man in a khaki gas company uniform left in the Toyota. Two cowboys arrived in a bondo patched pickup. Whenever a new car arrived I could see movement behind the curtains, but I couldn't see any faces. The sun set behind the mountains and the temperature instantly dropped. I shivered, waited and ate some whites to keep my edge on.

At eight o'clock I climbed into the Crown Vic, put on my suit and headed down to the parking lot. There were more pickups than sedans in the small, half-full lot. Buzzed in I walked up the pea gravel path. Under a propane heater in a porch swing a young girl in a teddy was drinking and talking to an equally young cowpoke. I was met at the door by Mrs. Altman in all her curvy glory, up close I could tell she was pushing sixty, not that it mattered, she was timeless and knew it. Instead of a lineup, she took me around the parlor, introducing me to the girls. It was a wide pleasant room, with club chairs and overstuffed sofas. As I looked from face to face, I realized I had no idea what Cass looked like. She could be any one of these lovelies, maybe not the Chinese girl, unless she was adopted. I suddenly knew with certainty that my mad rush to find Kelly's sister had one gaping flaw.

After I met all the girls, Mrs. Altman led me to an old oak bar stretching the length of the room. A cute gal in jeans and a shirt tied just under her breasts poured me a stiff bourbon. Around the room there were several other men, some at the bar drinking, others sitting chatting with the girls.

"So, big feller," Mrs. Altman said, "you see any fillies that strike your fancy? No need to be shy, we run a nice friendly house."

"Actually, um, I was looking for a girl a buddy told me about..." effecting my nervous first-timer act.

"Well, you tell me her name and I will make sure you're taken care of," she said with a big easy smile.

"I think her name's Cass?"

Her smile remained but I could see a steel door slam shut behind her eyes. "I've never heard of a girl by that name, are you sure he said she worked here?"

"Yeah, but to be honest he drinks a bit and may have gotten it wrong."

"Guess he did. What sort of girl are you looking for, maybe I can find some one to fill your desires. Do you like young? A girl-next-door blonde? Black widow brunette? Wild redhead?"

I looked at the floor, feigning shyness. "I don't even know what I'm doing here. My wife left me last year and I..." I gulped my drink.

"Why don't you just have another drink, get comfortable. You decide on a girl, you just let me know. Or go talk to her, they won't bite, not unless you ask them to."

In the mirror behind the bar I saw her talk to a weathered-looking working cowboy. He glanced over to where I was standing and then disappeared up the stairs. If I had unlimited funds I might have taken one of the girls upstairs to find out what I could. But I knew she was there, I could feel it. I finished my drink and decided to come back when the place was empty, plead my case then and hope they believed I was a friend not foe. As I walked back down the path I felt eyes on me, turning I looked up, the porch was empty. I scanned the windows on the first floor, I could see movement in the parlor but no one looked out so I moved up to the second floor bedroom windows. A lace curtain fluttered and for the briefest of moments I saw her. Dark curls framed a round lovely face that I knew so well. Kelly was looking down at me, the ghost of a dead friend, her eyes calling me to come for her. Then she was gone leaving only a small ripple in the curtain. Logic and the desire to have it be her fought in my head. I stumbled back, it was as if the ground under my feet had gone to jello. I wanted to run back into the house. I wanted to find Kelly there safe, but life doesn't work that way. The dead don't rise up to greet you.

Too much speed and not enough sleep will twist your mind. I knew a trucker once who was driving in the fog, he hallucinated a ship sailing in front of him. He kept driving and plowed into a yacht that had fallen off another rig. I guess the moral of that story is don't trust your eyes except when you need to. Trick is, knowing when that is. Was I so fixated on finding Kelly's past that I was seeing her in the shadows?

My headlights pierced the silky blackness of a moonless night. As I rounded a corner I saw headlights speeding up behind me, bearing down on me. I mashed down the gas pedal. The monster V8 roared to life. I took a corner in a four-wheel drift, sliding across both lanes, then punched it and the Crown Vic straightened out. Behind me the lights came on, unrelenting. Suddenly they disappeared as I flew over a small hill. The asphalt was pocked with potholes so I dropped down in speed. No need trashing my suspension if they'd given up. Suddenly, in front of me a red Chevy pickup truck bounced up onto the road. It locked its breaks and stopped, blocking the road. In a squeal of burning rubber I skidded to a stop inches from the truck. I was scrambling for reverse when my driver's side window exploded showering me with chunks of safety glass. Before I could react the weathered cowboy had my door open. With a mighty pull he had me dragged out and on the ground. A younger man stood by the truck aiming a hunting rifle at me. Trying to get up, my shoulder rippled with pain as the cowboy hit me with the axe handle he had used to bust out my window. A powerful blow struck my gut and I went over, my face grinding the pavement. I curled into a ball, hoping to reach the .38 in my boot holster then I heard a rush of wind and rolled just in time to have the hardwood miss splitting my skull. Reaching my pistol I pulled it and rolled up onto one knee but before I could aim, he hit my arm with a blow that made it go numb. The .38 skidded across the pavement and under my car. He swung again at my head, I ducked quick enough to take the force on my neck. Pain racked my body. I fell onto my side and threw up. The axe handle touched my face, twisting it so I looked up at the cowboy.

"Give me one reason not to kill you and leave you out here for coyote bait."

"I just...I wanted to meet a girl," I mumbled.

"Maybe, but I doubt it." He slapped the wood against my cheek, hard. I could feel a warm trickle of blood.

"She's a friend of... a..." My brain was struggling to rise above the pain to think of any words that would keep the axe handle from causing any more agony.

"Horse shit." A thud sent my left leg screaming. "Forget you ever heard that girl's name. Go back and tell the mob boys you couldn't find her. Tell 'em she's dead, tell 'em any damn thing you want. But don't come back. We clear?"

"Yes... I won't..." I said, feeling the bile back up in my throat.

"Next time we meet, you die." He accented his words with another strike to my gut. Puke of rotten whiskey and green gut slime flowed past my teeth and down my chin. From the ground, I watched the boots walk away. I heard the truck start, then they drove past my crumpled form and the world went dark. I lay there covered by a blanket of stars. I hurt all over, I couldn't imagine standing up. My brain had betrayed me when I most needed it, it had left me to flop like a landed fish under his blows. I was that little kid cowering under an adult's power. Defenseless and stupid.

My old pal anger reached down and pulled me to my knees. Fuck that corny cowboy bastard. Fuck him and his axe handle. Tomorrow was my day, and if I could stand up, his ass was mine.

On my hands and knees I crawled over to the Crown Vic. I found my .38 and pulled myself into the driver's seat. Small cubes of glass were scattered everywhere. In the mirror I found my cheek was purple and cut but it wasn't deep. The blood had already stopped flowing. Peeling off my shirt, my belly was mottled red and swelling but my ribs had been spared. All things considered the old guy had gone light on me. Not that that made me feel any better about him. Driving with my lights off I turned down the dirt road and parked hidden behind the pines and scrub brush. I lay in the back seat, forcing the pain down until I finally drifted into a nightmare filled sleep.

CHAPTER 8

I awoke in the grey predawn light and although it was cold in the car I was covered in sweat. Unfolding from a sitting position my body screamed in protest, my muscles had all turned into bruised and painful lead overnight. Pulling on a pair of shorts I dropped my ripped and stained suit into the trunk. Lacing up an old pair of hi-tops I assessed the damage reflected in the car window. My cheek had a new puffy lump and large purple bruises patterned my shoulders, neck and gut. All in all I looked like shit, not that I'd ever been a beauty queen but I sure wasn't getting prettier since I'd left LA.

Stretching was painful, but necessary. Gripping a sturdy tree limb I let my body weight pull down on my arms and shoulders, then breathed deeply through my nose and hung until the stiff muscles gave up the fight and relaxed. Slowly I pulled myself into a chin-up and thanked my Viking ancestors for strong bones. Jogging slowly at first I moved through the pines, down a small animal path. Building in speed I started to run full out. I could feel the toxins flowing out of my pores. Slowly my body started to loosen up. After a mile I turned back. Fifty push-ups and a hundred painful stomach crunches later I was ready for the day.

Pulling on a clean pair of jeans and a black tee-shirt I drove down the highway and found a small diner. In the bathroom I removed most of the crusted blood and evil smelling sweat with a whore's bath. It made me feel almost human. Powering my way through a plate of steak and eggs and a mug of strong coffee, I planned my next move. I didn't know what Cass looked like or even what stage name she was using. What I had were bruises and a fist full of nothing. I ordered two ham sandwiches to go and filled up a thermos with coffee. It was late afternoon when I returned to my perch. Around eight, the red Chevy pickup pulled into the parking lot. My good friend, the cowboy from the night before, got out and went into the house.

Slipping my .45 into my belt, I put on my leather jacket and moved off on foot. It took forty minutes of scrabbling down the steep incline, but finally I hit the fence that surrounded the house. Moving in the shadows I made it to the parking lot without detection. Crouched down in front of the red Chevy pickup I waited.

Men came and went. Some laughing, some nervously looking around. They reminded me of the men who came into the club. All looking to make a connection, all willing to believe a whore's promise, that contrary to every shred of evidence, the girl really liked you for more than the cash in your pocket. Some left the Eagle's Nest with heads down, telling themselves that this was the last time. The last time until night fell, and loneliness settled down on them. The reason men fall in love with strippers and whores is simple, they are the perfect date. They laugh at all your jokes, if you feel fat they tell you that you have big bones, and that they like big men. They make their living making men feel special. If you fall for the trick then no real woman can ever fulfill you. Outside of the clubs and whorehouses you were just you, another slob trying to make it through the day, but for a few hours you could be anything you wanted. I'd heard of men who saved girls from their lives as prostitutes, set them up in apartments, paid all their bills. The girls would bleed them dry, and once the mark was bankrupt, they would return to the whorehouse and look for their next sugar daddy. Life is simpler once you realize all relationships are commerce. Jen, my ex-wife, had fallen in love with my outlaw ways, and for six painful years she tried to change me. I got my one and only straight job, working for a roofing company with a group of Samoan ex-cons. Every night I'd come home stinking of tar and try to be her version of a husband. I may have been in love with her, but the toll was too high.

What is the price of love?

Ask her lawyer, he had an exact figure and I'm still paying it off.

It was just past midnight when the weathered cowboy came out. I waited until he had his keys out and was unlocking the truck's door. Pulling my .45 I bolted up, he turned at the sound but I was on him, shoving the pistol's barrel into his ribs. "Remember me?" I said in a soft even voice. He nodded slightly. "Let's do this nice and easy, cowboy, my nerves are frayed, this thing may go off all by itself." I got in the truck and slid across to the passenger seat. "Get in, slow and calm." He drove us out of the parking lot, and down the road. I had him pull off on a dirt road. "Kill it," I told him. The Chevy dieseled twice then was silent. I leaned against the passenger door, aiming at him. "Keep your hands on the wheel."

"Boy, if you're going to kill me, let's get to it," he said, looking over at me with steely gray eyes. I placed him at maybe fifty, with leathery skin and the strong muscles that only hard work brought.

"I may. First we talk, unless you're in a hurry to die."

"Nope, but I ain't afraid of it, neither."

"Cut the John Wayne bullshit." Slapping the .45 against his knee, I snapped the thumb safety off.

"Whoa, ease up a bit, son. This don't have to get stupid."

"Not afraid to die, but you don't want to be crippled, that it?" I tapped his kneecap with the pistol barrel. "What's your deal? If you were a bouncer I'd be dead or in jail."

"I just help out from time to time. Look after the girls." His eyes stayed on the pistol. "You want to point that cannon elsewhere?"

"Nope. What about Cass?"

"Now she's something special." His eyes went soft when he spoke of her. "If I was a younger man, and she'd have me, I'd probably marry her."

"Sweet, you're making me go all misty," I hissed through clenched teeth. "Why did you think I was connected?"

"Cass told me you mob boys were looking for her. You all may own Vegas and Reno, but this is my country out here. So maybe you best shoot me or move it on down the highway before you wind up dead."

"I'm not with the mob, you dumb hick. Do I look like any mob guy you ever saw?"

He looked me over slowly, "Well, you're uglier than most, bigger than many, but yeah, you look like a criminal."

"I didn't say I wasn't a criminal, but I'm not with any mob, they've got a dress code. Or haven't you seen the Sopranos?"

"Don't think I know them, they some of your Vegas friends?"

"If I was with the mob, you and your pal from last night would both be in a shallow grave. And Cass, she'd be following you by daybreak."

"If you say so." His stoicism was starting to really piss me off.

"Do I have to shoot you to convince you I'm not a mobster?"

"Possibly. You decide to pull that trigger, just let me know." Slouching back in the seat he lowered the brim of his straw Stetson down over his eyes.

"Do you really think you can keep her safe?"

Lowering the gun, I clicked the safety on and stuffed it into my belt. "Cards face up time. Some greaseballs took down Cass' sister. If they're coming for her you won't stop them. Right now, I'm that little girl's only chance." Slowly he tilted back his hat and looked at me, searching for the truth. "You owe her the choice."

He stared at me for a long moment. "You're either one hell of a liar, or I made a mistake last night." Taking out a bag of Bull Durham he rolled a cigarette. Striking a kitchen match on the dash he let out a long plume of blue smoke. Looking me over one more time, he smoked for a long moment. "You got any proof of what you say?"

"Give Cass this." I handed him the charm bracelet I'd taken from Kelly's apartment. "If she doesn't want to see me after that, I'll blow on down the road."

"Son, you hurt that little girl, you better say your prayers and get ready to meet the devil, 'cause I'll be sending you to hell." His tone was quiet and firm, as if it wasn't a threat just a fact. He dropped me off at the Crown Vic and drove back down the dirt road. I can't say I liked the son of a bitch but I had to respect his willingness to die for a whore. I thought I was the only man stupid enough to ride that train wreck.

I parked in the Eagle's Nest parking lot, and put all my firepower in the trunk. I had agreed to come in clean and I meant to keep my word. If it was a trap, they could have me. I was tired of chasing my tail and ready for whatever came my way. Fifteen minutes later the old cowboy came out of the gate. "The lady said she'd see you.

That trinket's got her all shook up," he said and led me around the back of the farmhouse. We entered a large kitchen where a rotund gray-haired woman was stirring beans. She didn't look up as we passed through and climbed a small back stairway. The narrow hall on the second floor was lined with doors, each one numbered in flowing red paint. The cowboy tapped twice fast, then three times slow on lucky 13, then opened the door and sent my world spinning sideways.

As the door swung slowly open it revealed... Kelly very much alive, sitting in a sea of crimson satin on the big brass bed, dressed in a black satin and lace merry widow, her dark curls falling down over pale sunken shoulders. She fingered the charm bracelet in her small hands, almost as if it were a rosary. One tear rolled down her cheek. I had to grab onto the door jamb to keep from falling over. She blinked, wiped the tear away, and looked up at me. As she straightened her shoulders and backbone, all sign of regret vanished, her face hardening with a strength I had never seen in Kelly. Reason flooded into my confused mind. Cass was not just Kelly's sister, she was her twin. Except for a small crescent-shaped scar by her right eye and a firmness in her jaw line she was an exact replica of Kelly, punched from the same flesh mold.

"You gonna be alright, darlin'?" The cowboy clearly loved this girl, it was tearing him up that he wasn't the man to save her.

"I'll be fine Ned, thank you." She blinked her eyes slowly and the cowboy closed the door leaving us alone. I was sure he stayed in the hall just to be certain she was safe.

"You're Moses, aren't you?" she asked in a quiet

voice.

"Yeah. Kelly wrote you about me?" My voice sounded hollow and strange. I dropped into a chair by the bed. I wanted to reach out and touch her, she looked so much like her sister.

"She said you were a good man, a rare thing in this world. I told her I thought you probably just wanted to get in her shorts. Was I right?" She was talking about anything but her sister's fate. If she needed time I would give it to her. So we chatted, almost like it was about the weather, but the weather hadn't killed this girl's sister and the weather wasn't out there hunting her right now.

"We were friends. That's all."

"You were in love with her. Otherwise, why are you here?"

"I owe her... or maybe I just had nothing better to do with my Friday night than traipse across two states. Either way, I'm here now, so maybe you can tell me what you girls got yourselves into."

She let out a sad laugh as she looked me over. "Are you my knight in shining armor? Proving God really does have a sense of humor?"

"I can't slay your dragons unless you tell me what they look like. Baby girl, what's going on? What'd you two do?" Her smile faded. Her eyes dared me to try and drag the truth out of her. Then she broke contact to look down at the charm bracelet wrapped around her delicate fingers.

"Was it painful?" she asked.

"Death is always painful. You really want the details?" It came out harder than I intended.

"Yes," she said, still not looking up. She set her jaw, preparing for the punch to come. She looked like a girl who had taken her share of hits and would take a few more before her run was done.

"They made her suck on the barrel and blew her brains out." She nodded slightly, her breath coming in shallow gulps. Her eyes were focused away from the room seeing the scene in her head no doubt. "Cigar burns, pliers, rape, they did a full bore lock down number on your sister and I suspect they did it to get to you. But I doubt she talked. The way you're running, my bet is she took a ride that was meant for you. I also think you know who did it." I wanted to hold her and tell her it was all going to be ok. I wanted to slap her for what she did to Kelly. I wanted her to be Kelly and this to be a bad dream. Before she could speak a knock came on the door. The cowboy leaned in.

"Cass, two boys in suits are downstairs looking for you, they don't look like they're going to take no for an answer," he said. Out her window, I could see a Cadillac in the parking lot with a mobbed up thug leaning on the fender.

Cass' face went cold and firm. "You want answers, get me out of here, now."

"Let's jet," I said. When she got up from the bed, I noticed she was five foot nothing. Just like her sister, these girls would always stand taller in your memory. She grabbed a small suitcase and filled it quickly with her meager belongings. From a drawer she pulled a picture, her and Kelly laughing in a wheat field. They looked to be about sixteen in the picture and full of all the hope and life teenage girls are meant to have. She stepped into a pair of six-inch spikes and pulled on a long red velvet cape, then slid the hood up over her head. For a moment I thought of Little Red Riding Hood and wondered if I was the wolf or the woodcutter? Then we were running down the hall. The cowboy went down the front stairs to try and slow the mob boys down. We went out the back. I knew we had thirty feet of open space between the house and the gate. I cursed myself for leaving my gun in the car. I hooked Cass' arm around mine and told her to follow my lead. Moving out of the shadows, I let out a loud drunken laugh. I stumbled toward the gate. I could see the thug on the Cadillac watching us. Hitting the gate I pulled her into a kiss, or at least that's what it would look like, past her I could see the house. No one was coming out the door. Pushing open the gate we swayed toward the Cadillac. I let go of Cass and rolled up on the thug.

"Hey buddy, I'm getting hitched! What do you think about that?" I slurred. Cass let her cape float casually open, suddenly his attention was on her creamy flesh. Swinging a powerful right cross I dropped him, sending his sunglasses skidding across the gravel. As he fell I kicked him in the head and he flopped over on his back, his eyes fluttered once and he was out. If the girl was sickened or scared by my sudden burst of violence she sure didn't show it. Taking her arm I lead her to the Crown Vic.

"This is your car? What are you, a cop?" Cass asked.

"It runs. Now get in."

From the trunk I pulled my guns, slipping the .45 automatic into my waistband and dropping the riot gun into the back seat. Cass looked from the shotgun up to me.

"Get your head down, this may get messy," I said in the voice I reserve for drunks and new girls at the club. It did the job, she stared at me defiantly for a moment then ducked down. I fired up all eight cylinders of Detroit magic and jammed the Crown into reverse. Spinning around I heard a car horn. The punk had been playing possum. The Cadillac had been moved and now it sat between us and the exit. Hitting the emergency brake I spun the Crown Vic in a 180 sending up a fantail wake of gravel. We stopped facing the Cadillac. Out of the side window I spotted two cats in dark suits running from the house. Both had ugly little automatics in their hands. The thug at the Cadillac pulled a shotgun out of the driver's side window, aiming it at my windshield. I pushed Cass down onto the floorboards and stomped on the gas. The blast tore a hole in my windshield and I felt a sharp pain in my neck as the buckshot and safety-glass sailed past my face. I watched in syrupy slow motion as bits and pieces floated around the car, the thug's face distorted as his mind locked in on the fact that I wasn't going to stop. He had given his best and it wasn't enough. With a blur and a rush the thug rolled over the hood of my car as I careened into the side of the Cadillac. Sparks flew and my side view mirror went sailing into the air. Straightening out the Crown Vic, I leaned hard on the steering wheel, fishtailing out of the parking lot. I heard two small pops and the thud of lead hitting the trunk. Then, only the comforting purr of the beast.

I redlined the engine, slid around the curves. Cass clambered up into the seat, gripping the door to keep from landing in my lap. As we rounded the mountain I caught a brief glimpse of headlights behind us, coming on fast. The road was flattening out to a long sloping straightaway. Punching it up to a hundred and twenty, the scrub brush beside the road blurred by. The headlights rounded another bend behind us. Soon they would wind down onto the straightaway and then it would be an all out run for cover. No way we would make the highway in time to lose them. If we got pulled over by troopers, there would be way too much to explain. On the left a rutted ranch road intersected the pavement, locking the brakes I killed the headlights and spun the wheel. The car slid sideways down the road, the rear tires fighting for traction. When we hit the dirt road I was driving blind. A tall pine appeared in front of me, wrenching the wheel I fishtailed past it, the rear end smacking into the trunk. Next we hit a bump that sent Cass tumbling back onto the floor. I hit my skull on the roof hard enough to leave a dent, and my head ringing. I eased on the brakes, pulled to a stop and killed the engine.

"Now that was fun..." Cass said without a hint of a smile. I motioned for silence. In the distance I could hear the deep roar of the Cadillac coming on steady and strong. They were almost past us when I heard their brakes, they must have seen the dust trail.

"Hold on," I told Cass, revving the Crown Vic to life. The road was a tore-up nasty piece of turf, full of dips and dives that would destroy the strongest suspension. Their headlights bounced wildly in my rearview mirror now. There was a pop as someone leaned out trying to fire, but with all the bumping and jostling I didn't have much fear they would hit anything. We flew over a hill and suddenly the road fell away from below us, airborne we sailed for fifteen feet, landing with a splash in a wide riverbed. The rear tires spun but couldn't gain purchase. We were stuck in the gravel. "Hit the brush!" I yelled at Cass as I rolled out of the door. Kneeling in the icy water, I leaned against my car, aiming the .45 back up the road. First headlights came over the hill then the grill of the Cadillac. I sighted in between the headlights and fired four quick shots into the engine block. As jacked rounds ripped metal it seized and the car lurched to a stop, steam jetting from its radiator. Staring into the headlights fucked my night vision for the moment, so I emptied the clip into the body of the car without much hope of hitting anything. Grabbing the Mossberg I ran for the bank of the river. Jacking a shell into the shotgun I crawled toward the Cadillac. Through the brush I saw the driver stepping out. I jumped up and pulled the trigger, the blast hit him in the middle of the chest with a load of double ought buck. He flopped back against the car and went down. From over the car the other two boys let fly. I dove and rolled away, the dirt around me exploded with their bullets. Crawling behind a pine tree I leaned out firing. They ducked and fired back, blowing chunks of bark out of my only protection. I was pinned down.

"Yo Bubba, why don't you give us the girl and we all part friends?" one of them yelled.

"Why don't you pencil dick grease-balls come get me?" Cass yelled from the brush behind them. As they turned I jumped out from behind the tree, zigzagging across the rough terrain. They spun and fired at me, sending powder burning into the night and shots whizzing past my head. The muzzle flash of a gun sparked behind them. Cass had joined the party and apparently she brought an automatic friend. Trapped, they ran from the cover of the car. I caught the first in the gut, he spun to fire but I hit him again in the chest. He was dead before he hit the ground. Leveling my shotgun at the last punk, I pulled the trigger only to hear a quiet click as the firing pin fell on an empty chamber. He leveled his automatic on me smiling, enjoying the turn of events. Without warning the side of his face erupted in a spray of blood. Cass stood like some comic book geek's wet dream in her merry widow, cape flowing behind her. She held a 9 mm in a classic pistolero single-hand stance, her left hand outstretched behind her for balance. She emptied the clip into the last punk as he crumpled, twisted and rolled with the impacts. It was over as quickly as it had started and silence fell over us. My ears were ringing from the gunfire and the acrid burn of spent powder stung my lungs. Checking the thugs I confirmed what I already knew, they were all dead. Looking at their useless corpses I felt a sick pride. The fuck-heads had tried to take me down and I showed their asses.

Cass walked up to me, the shiny little pocket 9 mm still in her hand. Her face was alive, electric with the rush. "Did you see that punk?" Cass was running on a full tilt motor mouth adrenalin high "Bam! Our old man was a cop, taught us to shoot rats at the dump. He used to say you had to practice until it became automatic. That was the one true thing he told us. Bam! That's one scuz who'll never fuck with me again. Did you see that?" Was her pride real, or covering for fear?

I don't know. Whichever way, it scared me. I had seen something like it in the Root, newbies first kill, all glory and pride. That soaring moment before the ghosts start knocking at your door. Then, there were those who never sweated the death they brought. Freaks who saw only a target, not the living flesh beyond it.

"What's wrong?" She searched my face, seeking out my mood and how she should respond to it.

"Everything's copacetic, baby girl." I could feel her eyes on me as I walked away, rather than explain all I knew about life-taking. In the trunk of the Cadillac I found a shovel and a bag of lye, intended, no doubt, for Cass. The sweaty hard work of digging their grave made me feel good, human. I was built for hard work and had spent too many days on my ass. Dragging their bodies over it sunk in. This wasn't a game. These men were dead, whatever else they were going to be wasn't going to happen. No more Christmas dinner with their families. No more shooting the shit around a pool table. No more anything. Perhaps the sickest thing about battle is how good it feels when you're in the middle of it. I had helped send three young men into the silky blackness from which they would never return. Then again, it's not like these rat fucks were worth getting all misty over. Me or them, that's the game. These young fucks came to put the old man down and were found wanting. I win - they lose. I am the king of this bend in the river. Thus it has been since the dawn of time thus it shall ever be, sooner or later the talking stops, the bullshit walks and the Viking puts the hammer down on these motherless bastards. Them or me.

Patting the earth smooth over them, I walked back to the Cadillac. Their pockets had produced two driver's licenses, one from California with a SF address, and the other a Nevada with a North Vegas address. I had little hope that the addresses were much more than mail drops, these boys clearly weren't living the straight life. I also came up with one Rolex (good for 5k cash anywhere in the world), six hundred and fifty dollars in greenbacks and an LA phone number. The Cadillac was registered to a corporation in Vegas. I was fairly sure the VIN numbers didn't match any records on this planet so I put a match to the registration card, grinding the ashes out with my boots. I clicked the Cadillac into neutral and stepping out I let it roll over the edge, crashing through the brush, burying its nose in the river. With any luck it would rust away undetected. Even if they found it, I was sure I could trust the folks at The Eagle's Nest to keep their mouths shut.

Cass sat up out of the water on the trunk of the Crown Vic, her body was vibrating but her eyes locked solid on me. In the dirt I set out a clean handkerchief and field stripped my .45. Wiping the barrel clean of any prints I tossed it and the firing pin out into the water. From my gun bag I got a spare barrel and firing pin and re-assembled the gun. It was a clean gun duly registered to Johnny Stahl, ballistics can trace a barrel but not the gun. So now I had a clean piece again. A blind ex-hitman had taught me that trick in the joint, amazing what you learn if you're willing to shut your yap hole and listen once in a while.

"This registered to you?" I said, taking Cass' 9 mm. She looked at me like I must be joking. I stripped it and wiped it clean and then scattered the parts into the flowing water.

"Hey, that was mine. Are you nuts?" she called.

"Just keeping you out of jail. You mind?"

"No, but you owe me a pistol," she said with a cute

smile that let me know she forgave me. In the beam of a flashlight I policed up the spent shells and after wiping them, they too went into the drink. There was nothing left to tie us to the crime scene. That was a joke, there is always something, you just do the best you can and hope for some O.J. style, a sloppy cop fucked up the key evidence type of luck. Cass kept watching me, she looked half afraid of what I might do next, half excited. Popping the trunk on the Crown Vic I pulled out an army surplus GI jungle machete.

"You planning to kill me with that?" Cass said.

"Not unless you really piss me off. Or you lie to me, that's probably a killing offense at this point."

I turned toward the bank and found a small tree with limbs about two inches around. Hacking away I soon had wood chips in my hair, and stuck to the stubble covering my face. At my feet was a small stack of five foot long staffs. The river water was icy cold, my legs and hands started to sting then go numb as I dug the front end of the Crown Vic out of the river bed. Giving it a more or less level launching pad I moved to the rear tires. In the fight for traction they had buried themselves in deep sandy grooves. Kneeling in the cold, bone chilling goddamn water, I worked the tree limbs down under the tires, one by one building a ramp up out of the grooves. The hope was to get enough speed by the end of the limb ramp that we wouldn't get bogged down, otherwise I was back in the water laying logs.

"Ease the gas down, one fluid motion all the way to the floor and keep the wheel dead straight. Ok?" I said to Cass as she slid in behind the wheel.

"No sweat, chief," she said, realizing I'm sure that if she screwed up it wasn't her going back under the car in the icy river. Placing myself at the center of the trunk, I hunkered down, my shoulder against the steel, one hand on either side. Knees bent I started to push, applying tension before she hit the gas, wanting to be sure of my footing. "Now," I yelled. The engine roared as the RPM's climbed the scale. The rear tires started to spin, then caught traction and the Crown Vic shot up out of her hole like a rocket set free. With no car to push against I fell face down into the river. In a spray of water and sand the Crown Vic bounced across the river. It must have been doing forty when it hit the other bank, with one powerful leap it was up and out of sight. Pulling my soggy ass up the embankment it occurred to me that I was taking it on faith that Cass would be there waiting for me. It wasn't like I'd really been her good luck charm so far or anything. And the truth was, push come to shove most people split. Apparently push hadn't come to shove yet or she still figured she needed me because when I cleared the rim of the river bank there was Cass, leaning against the Crown Vic with a shit eating grin on her face.

"That was fun, daddy, can we do it again, can we huh? Can we?" she said.

"Get in the goddamn car."

"What crawled up your ass?" she said, her smile gone to stone.

"Who the fuck were those suits I just put in a ditch?"

"I don't know, they came with you, so maybe you could tell me." Her eyes had gone hard, her armor in place.

"If that's how you wanna play it, then get in the goddamn car. Or walk out of here, I really don't give a rat's ass anymore." Climbing behind the wheel I powered up the beast and fought the shivers that were hitting hard. Cass slid into the passenger seat, pointedly looking out the window away from me. She was a piece of work, but at this point I was too battle fatigued to even begin to try and figure her out. Survival was what mattered now. Run and gun and make sure we don't get caught, stumble you die or wind up back in the joint which is worse. It wasn't pretty but at least it was a game I was raised to play and I knew rule one, learned it at birth...Trust no one.

With a sliver of a moon and stars above, we drove out into the rock-strewn landscape. Wind whistled through the hole in the windshield, in the distance a lonely train wailed out into the night, but we were silent, each alone in our own private battlements. Working my way through a series of dirt roads, I finally rejoined Highway 80 as the sun splashed golden light out over the land. An hour later we were in Reno. I got us a room in Sugar's Motor Lodge. It was a small court of quaint bungalows on the outskirts of town. I paid cash and the rummy clerk didn't ask any questions when I signed in as Shane MacGowan. He spent more time checking the twenties for counterfeits than looking at my face.

The room was last decorated in the fifties in hunting lodge style, the dark wood paneling held decades of grime. Prints of grizzlies and mountain men hung on the walls. A wagon wheel lamp lit the room, dimly, which was a good thing, the cleaning crew appeared to have lost interest in their jobs sometime around when LBJ left office. In the maroon and white checkerboard tiled bathroom, I assessed the damage. I stripped off my shirt, my trip into the river had washed me clean of dirt and blood, making it easy to spot several new bruises from rolling around in the brush. The shotgun blast through the windshield ripped my neck up pretty good, embedding chunks of safety glass under the skin. They hurt like hell and when I tried to dig at them with my fingers, a little blood oozed out of the holes. I pulled the buck knife out of my pocket, as I snapped the lock open I heard Cass laughing. Tilting the mirror I found her watching me leaning in the bathroom door jam, one hip cocked out.

"You planning to slit your throat?" she said.

"Seems like it would save a lot of people the trouble of killing me."

"Yeah, but a knife to the neck? Real messy. Then I got to clean it, and to speak the truth, I am bone tired, so why don't you let me fix you up?"

"Go to it little girl," I said, handing her the buck knife. She cocked an eyebrow and took a pair of tweezers out of her bag. She reached up on her tiptoes to get to my neck.

"Ok, we have established you're a real tall guy, now sit down so I can fix your goddamn neck and get some sleep," she said. I sat on the tub and she started to dig the tweezers into my wounds. My jaw locked as the pain burned up to my head. Hiding the pain I looked stone faced up at her eyes. She showed no more emotion than if she was carving a steak. She noticed the fresh tattoo image of her sister on my shoulder, tracing a finger over the healing skin without comment. Her eyes followed the scars running up into my scalp and down to the ragged bullet scar in my chest. "This ain't your first time at the rodeo," she said with a little admiration, and went back to digging. To keep my mind away from the pain I let my eyes roam, down her neck, down to the lace and satin, and creamy soft skin spilling over it. What is it about cleavage that makes me lose my mind? Makes me want to get lost in those soft curves and never return to my life. One, two, three, she popped the chunks of glass out of my flesh. Noticing where I had been looking, she didn't chastise me or feign modesty, she just gave me a slight smile. She dabbed a washcloth in vodka from a flask in her purse and cleaned the wounds. Man she knew how to travel, never leave home without a flask, an automatic, and a medical-grade pair of tweezers. She was my kind of girl.

"You'll need to get some bandages, but I don't think you'll die, not from this at least," she said, taking a short snort off the flask. I left her with the shotgun and instructions not to open the door. After a quick stop at a small drug store for bandages and extra strength aspirin, I went searching for a junkyard. Bullet holes tend to attract attention from the law dogs. At Trading Post Bob's Junkyard, I found an old Crown Vic, it was rusted and dented, the engine was gone, but the glass was in useable condition. It also had a pitted but serviceable side-view mirror. Taking my toolbox out of the trunk I worked to remove the windshield and side window. With sun came heat. I took off my shirt, enjoying the sweat as it ran down my back. It was simple work, no moral judgments to make, no instant life changing decisions. Removing the chrome trim, I used a screwdriver to pop the rubber gasket surrounding the glass. Sixty-seven dollars and several hours later I was back on the road. At Pep Boys I bought a small tin of bondo and some black spray paint. I filled the bullet holes in the parking lot, and painted them over. Scanning the Crown Vic, it looked as if nothing had happened. Our trouble in the mountains was a whisper of a memory. Just one more nightmare waiting to wake me up.

I pawned the Rolex for half its value, with no questions asked and no I.D. shown. Driving back the flashing lights cut though the sunshine. "Off Track Betting!" "Best Odds In Town!" "Be A Winner!" I had a fat roll in my pocket and no reason I could think of not to double it. Looking down I saw my knuckles white on the wheel. Things are fine when you want them, it's when you need them you better look out. Marilyn pouted from the face of the cookie jar on the floor. I knew there would be no happy gambling today.

I let myself quietly into the motel room. Cass was asleep, the covers pulled back exposing her long muscular leg. Brown curly ringlets haloed her face. Asleep she looked even more like Kelly. Sitting in a comfortable chair I couldn't take my eyes off of her. Her heart shaped face with those full lips, lips built for kissing. Cass' eyes fluttered then opened, she looked for a moment at me, then spoke. "What the hell are you staring at?" she asked without a smile.

"You...I was staring at you. Just wondering how the fuck I got in this mess," I said hardening. "You wanna tell me who those punks I buried were?"

"I don't know," she said.

"Not good enough."

128

"It's the truth." Climbing off the bed she moved to me, her face forming a sultry smile. "I do know you saved my life, if there is any way I can repay you, let me know." Her hand went up, resting on my shoulder. Every cell in my body screamed for me to take her to bed, forget my troubles and get lost in her flesh. Standing up I looked straight into her deep brown eyes.

"Listen little girl, I'm not a John. The pouting coquette bullshit doesn't do squat for me, got it?" I lied. "My dick don't even get hard when I'm on the run. Now, I just killed some men, I don't give a fuck about them. What I do care about is who sent them. If I'm going to be looking over my shoulder I need to know who I'm looking for." Her smile faded, and she sat back down on the bed.

"I need some coffee."

"And I need some answers."

"Then go get me some coffee, cream no sugar."

"And let you slip out the back door? I don't think so."

"I wouldn't."

"Maybe, maybe not. You're good at running, why don't we see how you are at sticking." After a long pause she finally got I wasn't budging an inch. She sank back into the bed.

"A few years ago Kelly and I moved to San Francisco..." she said, speaking to the ceiling. "We had nothing but the clothes on our backs and a few dollars we'd stolen from the old bastard when we split Indiana. Kelly always dreamed of San Francisco, she called it the Emerald City by the Bay. But if the all-powerful Oz lived there, we never found him. We got jobs dancing at the Barbary Coast. I didn't want to at first, but my wild sister said it would be fun. What the hell else could we do that would bring in instant cash? She was a natural, from the minute she hit that stage she seemed to know all the moves. They'd pay extra if we danced together, something about naked twins made the dollars come flying. It wasn't so bad. We'd smoke a little boo, cover each other in whipped cream and have a pajama party, and they would throw money at us. We had plenty of offers to sleep with the customers, seems most men fantasize about doing twins. We could have gotten rich if I had been willing to cross that line." Confusion rained down on me. The Kelly I had known was too shy to ever strip, but I didn't say anything, afraid if I did Cass might clam up again. "Kelly told me it was just like what we'd already had done to us, but this time we'd get paid. But I couldn't do it. Kind of funny considering where I wound up. Anyway, Kelly started dating some old guy she met at the club. She said she wasn't fucking him but I could tell she was lying. That innocent hick act of hers didn't play with me. He would shower her with expensive jewelry, which we hocked for cash. It was a sweet deal, and if she didn't want to call it prostitution, who was I to judge her. One night, she came home late from a date with the guy. She was in a panic, she had blood on her shirt. She said she had seen a bad thing, the less I knew the better. She said we had to leave town, fast. That we should split up, twins would be too easy to track. We had to change our names. From that day forward we were Cass and Kelly. She said when I got settled to send a letter to the LA post office general delivery under the name Lotta Love. The last time I saw her was in the SF airport. She hugged me and promised we'd be back together soon, then I headed out to Vegas. When I heard two mob boys were looking for me at the Cock's Roost I took off..." Rolling onto her side she looked at me, "That's the truth Moses, every sad part of it." I nodded my head slowly, then stood up and walked out. I had to get away from her story. If it was true, then everything I'd known about Kelly was false.

I walked down to a corner liquor store. On the street cars cruised happily by, the sun was shining and all was right in their world. My world on the other hand was crumbling. Kelly had played me for a chump, here I thought she was the one pure thing in my life and I was just another squid to be played. Had any of it been true? Were we even friends? I bought a fifth of Seagram's and a bottle of ginger ale. I sat in the Crown Vic and poured myself a stiff one. I picked up Marilyn hoping to find some answers in the ashes. So what if Kelly had been less than honest, maybe she wasn't the angel I had made her out to be. I had loved her, that was true. Maybe loving someone meant you accepted who they were. She had accepted me with all my dark crap, or was she using me as a shield, a dark knight to protect her? If so, she'd chosen the wrong man. Maybe I should have put the key in and driven away, left Cass behind me and never looked back. But I had given my word. With Marilyn and whiskey in hand I went back to the motel.

Confronted with the ashes of her dead sister, Cass lost it. Tears rolled freely down her cheeks. Now it was concrete, Kelly wasn't going to pop out of the bathroom and say it was all a big joke. I wanted to comfort her, give her a shoulder to cry on. Instead I sat in the chair and poured a fresh drink. I placed the bottle on the nightstand. If she wanted a drink she could get one. She curled up, holding Marilyn to her chest murmuring quietly to it. Grief was a solo act, we all did it in our own private way. I was sullenly working on my third drink when she got up and took a shower. She left the door open a crack so I could catch glimpses of her through the pebbled glass. I turned my back on her. Someone had done a real job on these girls, someone convinced them that sex was the most they had to offer men. It was hard-wired into their systems, a default setting that had to have been placed there at a young age. It played on like a ghost in the machine, overriding grief, fear and even love. Maybe the bastard I should be hunting was farther back in their past. The dead end street Kelly was traveling on started way before I met her. But the punk who pulled the trigger was going down, he ended any chance for her to ever recover.

"They have to die," Cass said, drying her hair. It was as if she'd been reading my mind. Her tears were gone now, replaced by a set jaw and cold hard eyes.

"Yes they do, but we have to find them first, what's his name?"

"Whose?"

"The rich cat Kelly was fucking." I said with more edge than I intended.

"Gino T, Ter-something. He was old school Italian, diamond pinky ring, gold chains, hairy chest and the manners of a pig. He looked at us girls like he was judging a piece of beef. Torelli! Yeah, that was his name, Gino

132

Torelli."

"Then he's where we start." Images of a fat Guinea sweating on top of Kelly flooded my brain. The whiskey and lack of sleep washed over me like a warm rain. It all suddenly felt too big to handle. I wanted to climb into bed and pull the covers over my head. I wanted to be back at the dog park watching Angel play. I wanted to be anywhere but here. Crunching down six whites I gulped the rest of my drink. Locking the bathroom door I took a long cold shower. It felt like needles on my skin but I could feel my blood rushing to warm me. The speed and cold water evaporated my sluggishness. Putting on a clean pair of jeans and fresh tee-shirt I was ready for action.

"Let's roll," I told Cass.

"To where?" she asked.

"San Francisco, I want to get clear of Nevada in case they find those graves."

Driving out of Reno I winked goodbye to the glittering gambling dens, free from their draw for the moment. I could hear them laughing, they knew I'd be back sooner or later. Cass told me she thought the blood on Kelly was sugar daddy Gino's, and that he was probably dead. It wasn't much to go on, a name and a city, but it was all we had.

In Walmart she bought some hair bleach and a pair of scissors. At a truck stop she went into the ladies room, twenty minutes later she came out as a different girl. Her curls were now cut to shoulder length and honey blonde. I was stunned by the transformation, she looked like

Marilyn's twin sister.

"What, you don't like?" she said pouting her lips.

"No, you did fine, nobody will recognize you," I said turning for the car. She caught my shoulder turning me to look at her.

"Do you like it?" she said, a twinkle in her eye.

"I said you did fine, now let's roll." After that we drove for a while in silence. She was still putting on the pout. We purred down Highway 80, through the Sierras. We crossed the state line without any problems, no we didn't have any fruit or vegetables, did I forget to mention we left some corpses in Nevada? Well they didn't ask, so I didn't tell.

"Were you one of her lovers?" Cass asked, breaking the silence as we pasted Truckee.

"No, I thought I was her friend." I kept my eyes on the road. But she saw through me anyway.

"You were in love with her. You still are, I've seen the way you look at me. But trust me, I'm not her. She always had the way with men, it was like she could sense who they wanted her to be and that's who she'd become. In high school she could have had any boy she wanted, but she wound up screwing the gym teacher. He was a burly bear. Yeah, you were her type," she said with a wry smile. "Big, strong, a bit too old and a lot too dangerous. I'm just surprised you weren't lovers. Maybe she saw you needed a friend more than sex." I flinched, forcing my face into neutral. "That's it, isn't it?" I didn't answer. I couldn't believe Kelly had played me like that. Was I that transparent? As I thought about it I realized I was kin to these sisters. We were all children of the battle zone. Growing up in violence you learned to duck and weave, you learned how to read the signs and become whoever you needed to be to keep from getting whacked. At Donner Pass I pulled into a rest area to make a fresh drink; Cass arched an eyebrow, but I didn't care. I needed the whiskey to take the edge off the speed I was popping like Altoids, and I needed the speed because it had been too many days without sleep. Crunching a few whites I sipped the drink.

"Boy you have more bad habits than a convent." She said with a grin.

Pulling out onto the highway I noticed a stone pillar commemorating the Donner Party. They were a true testament to the American spirit, push forward at all costs and eat the dead when necessary. Wasn't that the American dream in a nutshell.

CHAPTER 9

At midnight we crossed the Golden Gate Bridge, Cass was asleep and I was in a drug driven haze. Somewhere around the Sacramento delta the lines between real and surreal had blurred. Fog swirled dancing in the beams of the headlights. Orange cables and girders dripped and bent at impossible angles, like a giant braided steel spider web it waited to catch low flying dreams. The bridge under our tires beat out a steady tip tapping rhythm counter punching to Iggy's Afro Idiot CD. Where would I be without music? It had been my one true friend. From my first Stones LP, music always filled the empty void I swam in.

Through the fog and steel, jewels sparkled calling our names. The city lights drawing us in like so many sailors before us. Calling us to crash on their rocks, this city of sirens. San Francisco, with its historic promise of magic and wonder. Built to fleece the gold miners coming and going to the fields up north, back then it had more brothels than churches and more saloons than schools. Destroyed by earthquake and fire it rose from the ashes, bigger and grander than before. In the sixties it called the youth of America to crash on its rocks, what started in peace, love, and LSD ended with heroin and STD's. In the sixties the kids took to the streets and said fuck you to the government. In the seventies the government took the belt to them, and we've been paying the price ever since. War on drugs, war on music content, war on all that was strange and different. The tragic truth is, start a war with your kids and you wind up with drive-bys and Columbine. Just like two plus two equals four, it's simple old school math.

The Detroit beast cut through the fog, rising up over the near vertical streets, then swooping down past neat rows of meticulously painted Victorians. San Francisco was the closest thing to a European style city we had in the states, but its underbelly wasn't elegant or quaint, it was pocked with strip clubs and junkies, pimps and sailors, drug dealers and dot com fast money artists. God I loved this city. The new media money may have caused the property values to skyrocket and driven out the artists, but it fed the world I swam in. The more money they got, the more sex, drugs and rock-n-roll they bought. And when the bubble burst my people bought their shit at five cents on the dollar, cash these soulless geeks needed just to keep the party going one more day.

Floating across Market Street I saw a skinny hooker stumbling up the sidewalk. Her blonde wig had slipped sideways showing the stubble of her shaved head, her arm was possessively wrapped around a drunk business guy sporting a goatee and a badly rumpled suit. Watching them, I knew I was home. Like Tom Joad said, "Wherever there's a young girl selling herself to a fat old man, wherever there's a bad drug deal going down twisted look for me and I'll be there."

I found us a room at a flophouse on O'Farrell, across the street from the Barbary Coast and several other strip clubs. If you were in town on shore leave and wanted to see some tits, O'Farrell was your street. Unlike in LA where strip clubs dot the map and piss off the neighborhood improvement folks, up here they concentrate them all on one strip and turn it into a tourist destination. The night manager was a pimply kid with the bone thin body of a long time friend of Sister Morphine. He barely glanced up when I carried the sleeping Cass into the elevator. I tried to wake her in the car but she was out cold, in the small room I put her into the bed. I knew I should sleep but my heart was still hammering away from the speed. Objects in the room seemed to glow with their own interior light source. Through the cheap woven curtains the neon called to me with its candy land colors and its promise of a good time. Oh yeah, this was a town that would love you long time G.I.

Ten minutes later I was seated in the Barbary Coast, slamming down shots of Jack with a beer back. It was bigger, older, and classier looking than Uncle Manny's club but the game was just the same. A tall Black girl was strutting her rather wonderful stuff on a large stage. She pressed her breasts together creating a soft brown valley of cleavage. Legs spread, ass stuck out, hips rocking to the beat, she sucked on her finger in mime fellatio. She used her moist fingertip to stiffen her half dollar sized nipples. A brass rail surrounded the footlights at the base of the stage, where businessmen sat waving dollars, hoping to get an up close and personal look at her titties. Change the location, change the player, the moves remain the same.

I sat at the bar, next to an old fisherman and a fat cat

who was being hustled by a redhead in a short neon blue lycra dress that might as well have been spray painted onto her plump frame. As the room swam around me, I told myself I was looking for traces of Kelly, the truth was...when I was lost, I returned to what I knew, or some psych bullshit like that. Maybe the speed and booze and death had made me horny, who the fuck knows how this fucked up brain worked, not me that's for damn sure.... A skinny Asian gal swirled out of the haze, her small naturally proportioned breasts were a real turn on in this sea of monster ta-tas. She aimed toward me, dancing up swaying her hips. From a distance she looked like a lithe wood nymph, all legs and arms and the promise of unbridled sensuality, just the ticket for these weary bones. But the closer she got the younger she got, a baby at best, but her eyes were old and cold. She was the walking wounded, one more victim of the life. Sliding up, she latched herself onto my thigh. "Want a nasty, grab-your-cock-suck-on-my-tits lap dance? Come on, big guy?" Behind her smile lurked those dead eyes. "Don't worry 'bout the bouncer," she leaned in whispering into my ear, I could smell cheap perfume. "I know a dark corner in the lap room, I will rock you so hard, baby, I really want to make you come. I want to feel your cock in my hand, between my legs. Come on, baby." Her tongue licked my ear to show she really meant it, I guess. I decided this was one lonely ride I didn't need to take. Handing her a twenty I walked out.

I could feel the speed crashing out of my system as I stumbled across the boulevard. I made it to the room before I puked into the toilet, I washed my face and fell into the bed beside Cass. She stirred once then went back to softly snoring. With neon lights blinking on the ceiling I drifted in the deep warm blackness of sleep.

Tijuana is baked hot, close buildings in the centro district make the air pungent with the stink of humanity. Cheap bars and strip clubs line Avenue of the Heroes. After the Root I spent my leave time down here, drinking and fucking and trying to find that blissful play of pure numb. Now it all feels different, gaudy and tarnished. A long snaking line of marines stretches down the street. Some of the soldiers are in their dress whites, others wear sweat stained flack jackets and soiled olive drabs. Many have rifles strapped over their shoulders. Every few minutes the line shuffles forward a few feet, then stands waiting, bored. I move down the line, studying the faces, looking for anyone I might know.

Sergeant Tibs, a jolly Black Marine from the Root, is standing in the middle of a busy intersection. MP's block the taxis from crossing. Horns blare. I touch Tibs' arm. He turns his face and I see the hole in his forehead. He took a round from a sniper two days before ship out. His eyes are milky and lacking any shine. He opens his mouth to speak, red dust drifts out past his cracked lips, but no sound.

I run away from Tibs, up the line. In the shacks by the river the head of the line disappears into a tin walled building. A young Muslim woman in a black burka stands guard on the door, her hand tightly grips an AK47.

The line snakes past the front door and down an ally. They are lined up to a back door. I move past them like a ghost. Through a curtain, men are standing around a table, they all have dollars in their hands. Moving through them I see a young soldier pumping away on some girl. I can't see her face, but I get a queasy feeling when I see her brown curls. The young grunt finishes and the others cheer him. As he climbs off her I can see her face... it's Kelly.

"Hey baby, how are you," she says smiling up at me.

I try to speak but my throat closes off.

The next in line climbs on her, covering her face with his chest.

I run out into the street, only now it's Hooterville, the Lebanese ghetto. Towel-heads point and laugh at me. The crowd parts and I see the little boy kneeling over his dead mother. She sits up and reaches out a bloody hand. She points an accusing finger at me and lets out a high-pitched wail.

I jerked up in bed, my body covered in sweat. The late afternoon sun flooded the room with its painful radiance. Where the hell was I? The dream still felt more real than this strange hotel room. Slowly the last few days came back to me like flashes from a fever nightmare. A rank odor wafted up over me. It smelled like something had died in the bed beside me. Sniffing around I discovered to my shame and disgust that the smell was coming from me. All the poison I had put in my body over the last few days seemed to have leaked out of my pores. My body reeked like a barroom floor on Sunday morning. Flicking my eyes around the room I noticed something was missing, Cass. While I'd slept she must have skipped out. I wasn't really sure how I should feel about that, pissed or relieved?

A shower, a cup of coffee and some food in that order, and death to anyone who tried to stop me. As the warm water soothed my muscles I thought about Cass. Maybe I didn't owe her or Kelly anything. Maybe I should drive home and forget I ever met either of them. I made a promise to my fantasy of a girl who never existed. In the only movie ever made worth watching, "The Wild Bunch," Sikes asks why their friend is hunting them so hard, and Pike says, "He gave his word." But Sikes says, "To a railroad!" and Pike roars, "It doesn't matter who you give it to." Words I lived by I guess. Walking away wasn't an option, at least not one I could live with.

The first thing I noticed when I stepped out of the bathroom was the wonderful smell of hot coffee. Cass sat on the bed. She flicked her eyes up and down my scar tattered naked body, a smile forming on her lips. I quickly pulled on my jeans. My white belly hung over my belt line, I don't know why I was shy in front of her, but I was. I pulled on a tee-shirt. On top of the old television set were two large coffees, some bagels, lox, thinly sliced tomatoes, and onions.

"I figured you drank it black, if not you can have mine."

"Black's fine." The food tasted good and the coffee even better. Mid-bite I realized I was glad Cass had come back, as dark and twisted as it was, she gave my life direction.

"So, big boy, when you're done wolfing down the fine food I brought you, where do we start?" Clearly she was enjoying watching me tear into the food.

"We start by buying you some new clothes. Something that doesn't shout hooker quite so loud."

"You don't like the way I look?" she said with a coy pout.

"I just don't want to spend my time beating off the dogs."

"But you like the way I look?" She struck a pose meant to send me drooling. She had on a silver leather miniskirt and a purple tube top, no bra, so her nipples were giving me a weather report. I turned my attention away from her. Lacing up my Doc Martins I clipped the .38 into my boot holster. "Come on say it, you like the way I look." I let my eyes travel from her feet, up her body to her eyes.

"You're alright."

"Alright? You and I both know you'd give your left testicle to hit my fine stuff."

"You are one classy broad Cass, now let's roll."

Down on Market Street I bought her a nice Donna Karan knock off, she said it was too big, she wasn't used to dresses that didn't hug her every curve. The dress made her look sweet and a bit innocent. Truth is she would look great in a potato sack. Next stop, a shoe outlet to trade her seven inch spikes for a nice sensible pair of Bass walking shoes. Sure she could move quick in the new shoes but I had to agree with Fred Astaire, "God makes legs, but it takes a pair of heels to make a gam." In flats she barely came up to the scar above my nipple. She looked more like my daughter than my partner in crime. I bought myself a casual un-constructed tan suit. I was going for middle level exec but looking in the mirror I realized I looked more like a Viking killer in a suit. Most people don't look past the outlines, they see a suit and read businessman, they see a tattoo and leather jacket and they read trouble. Someone should tell them Hitler and his crew wore real nice suits. At a quick glance Cass and I could pass for tourists or dot commers on a break, as long as they didn't look too deep into our eyes.

Our first stop was the main branch of the San Francisco Library, they stored back issues of the SF Chronicle on a database. An officious young clerk pointed to a bank of computers and told me to look it up. I stared at the screen for a long painful moment. I hated computers, they made me feel stupid and old. I was an analogue man living in a digital age. My hands hovered over the keyboard, my eyes flicking over the screen, it was all garbled gibberish to me. I could feel rage growing, it was like when I was in school, Moses the dummy. It took all the self-control I could muster not to grab the monitor and throw it across the room.

"Move over sport, let me show you how it's done." With a rapid flurry of keystrokes she was into the system. She winked at me, clearly proud of herself. I shrugged, like it wasn't a big deal. We searched back to the week they had left town. After two hours we hadn't discovered any dead men or any links to the mysterious Mr. Torelli.

Leaving the library no wiser, we went down to Fisherman's Wharf. I bought a steamed and cracked crab, a loaf of French bread and a couple of bottles of Bass ale. In a park down by the bay we sat looking out at the water. It was a clear day, we could see all the way to the Golden Gate Bridge. There is no graceful way to eat crab, it is a messy, dig your fingers in the shell kind of food. Cass laughed, her eyes sparkling as she fought with her meal, it was the youngest I had seen her look. She picked a piece of crab meat off my beard and popped it in her mouth.

The sun glittered off the wake of a ferry, returning from Alcatraz. The rocky prison sat peacefully in the bay; it had been Al Capone's last home. How many ghosts roamed those pain filled iron halls? I'd done a four-year stint in Chino, for a joyride in a stolen Mercedes. I was twenty-two and all alone. I hooked up with a Chicano cat named Tommy, he wasn't in a gang. The Aryan brothers called me a race traitor, the blacks hated us because of our skin. Inside you either joined or fought, so we watched each other's backs, lifted weights and kicked ass when called to. Tommy taught me to go insane in battle, the crazier the better. Let them know you don't give a fuck, laugh and howl when you attack. I learned to become a berserker, that was the Viking term for the first wave of soldiers they sent in, wild men who went insane on their enemies. I remember this skinhead coming after me in the yard. I let him hit me, felt my blood rising, let him hit me again until somewhere deep down I snapped. I let out a wild war cry, wrapping my arms around his trunk I lifted him off the ground, slamming his body into a light stanchion. Pushing his neck into the crook of my arm I crushed down on his throat. I could see his brothers moving in and I felt his body go limp in my arms. I was outside my body watching it all go down. If Tommy hadn't arrived I would have killed the man. Tommy let out a wild laugh, setting himself for battle he danced between me and the Aryan brothers, a skinny shiv in his hand. Letting out a screaming laugh I dropped the gasping punk to the ground. I scanned the group, looking for my next victim. The skinheads let us walk, gave us a pass that day. What do you do with crazy bastards who don't give a rat's ass what you do to them; how do you threaten the insane? I wondered where Tommy was now, did he ever make it out of the life, was he living in the suburbs with a wife and the kids he dreamed about? Was our time together just a bad dream he finally woke from?

Cass tossed pieces of French bread to a building group of seagulls. She laughed as they caught the bread in midair. For a brief moment, the scars that made her seem so old were erased and I could see the girl she would have been if the world were fair. I was filled with the desire to make her world safe and just, a world where men didn't fuck little girls and make them old before their time. A world I knew didn't exist for people like us. Ok, that was only half of what I was thinking, deeper down in my shadow self I wished I was one of the men who got to fuck her. The sun fire in her hair, the way her firm body showed through the demure dress. She's Kelly's sister, how fucked am I.

"You're doing it again," she said.

"Doing what?"

"Staring at me."

"What, I'm not supposed to look at you now?" I said looking back out at the water.

Tossing the crab shells into a trash can we headed back to the Barbary Coast. Strip clubs were an addiction for most men. If Kelly had met Gino there odds were he'd come back. The Coast was quiet, a few early birds sat at the bar and chatted up the day girls. I ordered a Gimlet, a gin and Rose's lime juice and promised to pace my drinking. Cass had a diet coke and a bowl of pretzels. Jane the bartender was a stout girl, she had on low-rise jeans and a short shirt, showing off her sweet fuzz dusted round belly. She reminded me of a juicy peach, inviting you to take a thirst-quenching bite. When I asked her about Gino, she put a finger to her temple, pretending to think. "Your friend Benjamin Franklin might know a Gino," she said with a cute smile. I dropped a hundred on the bar. She lifted it to her ear. "Oh really, no…" she said talking to the bill, then looked over to me. "He told me, Gino used to come in here, but he hasn't been around for a while."

"Does our friend know what he looked like?" I asked.

"Um," she said listening to the bill again, "He said Gino was pushing sixty hard, with a bad dye job. Always wore nice suits, and tipped well." With that she dropped the bill into her tip jar.

"Do you think your friend Grant might know anything else?" I said dropping a fifty on the bar.

"You don't look like a fed, and you sure don't tip like a fed."

"Is that a bad thing?"

"Only if you like cheap suits and a lousy pension."

"I'm just a guy, looking for a guy, hoping you can help."

"You are not just a guy." She flashed me a smile. Cass looked from Jane to me, then got up and headed for the ladies' room. "I don't think your girlfriend likes me."

"Do you care?" I asked.

"Hum, no, I guess I don't." She let her fingers dance along my hand. Something about being with a pretty girl made other pretty girls want you. It's like you have a seal of approval. They want to know what the other girl sees in you. I caught her finger in my palm and pulled her closer to me.

"Tell me about Gino, why are the feds looking for him?"

"What will you give me if I tell you?"

"My undying appreciation."

"I was hoping for something a bit more, um, concrete. But that will do, for now," she said with a meaningful grin. "He used to come in every Friday night, eight o'clock on the dot. He was into some kind of internet porn, but in the boom days, who wasn't? He hired some of the girls to work for him. They said he paid good, even better for rough stuff. Four or five months ago he stopped coming in, I just figured he moved back to Chicago. But then the feds came sniffing around, so who knows what happened. Did I do good?"

"You did great."

"Are you going to give me some candy?"

"Which girls worked for him?" I said with a slight chuckle, god, she was cute.

"Shelly and Crystal, maybe others. Shelly moved to

LA, but Crystal is on the schedule for tonight. She may even surprise us all and show up."

"Thank you," I said, putting the fifty into her tip jar.

"You'll be back."

"How can you be sure?"

"I saw the way you looked at me." She traced her body with her finger, circling her belly. "You will be back, and not just to talk to Crystal."

"Time will tell." I said and walked away. I caught Cass coming out of the ladies' room and together, we walked out into the street. With the last golden light of the setting sun banks of fog rolled up over the tall hills, blanketing the Victorians in softness. We walked down to Chinatown.

"One of the dancers came into the bathroom, she just stared at me."

"Maybe she was coming on to you."

"I don't think so. I think she recognized me."

"Damn... I shouldn't have taken you in there."

"That bitch Jane would have been happier if you hadn't, could she have been any less subtle? And what was that shit with the talking to the bill?" she said, setting her jaw. I would be flattered if I didn't know I was just a prize the girls were fighting over. I didn't have any value until they noticed someone else noticing me. Kelly had got it right, my only value was as a protector, like a big mean dog. We ate at a small Chinese restaurant. I had no idea where she put it, but Cass could pack the food in. Half my size and she matched me bite for bite. We had greasy pork fried rice, broccoli beef, lemon chicken, egg rolls, pressed duck, fried wontons and a gallon of green tea. Well fed and feeling comfortable we walked back toward the hotel. Cass slipped her arm into mine, the fog swirled around us haloing the streetlights in the mist above. To any passers by we looked like lovers on a romantic date. "Moses?" Cass asked in a soft whisper.

"Yeah?"

"If we met, on the street, or in a park... Would you like me?" I knew what she was asking, the question we all asked. If we met in the straight world, would we be of worth.

"Yes, I think I would," I said. She smiled and snuggled her blonde head against my ribcage. The fact was I'd have liked her anywhere. But if things were different, I doubt she would have noticed me.

Back in our room she jumped onto the bed. "Want to play tent, big boy?" She flipped the blankets up, letting them drift slowly down. I shook my head fighting to hold down my grin. I washed my face and got ready to go back out. We had agreed it would be best if Cass stayed away from the Barbary Coast.

"Why don't you stay in tonight?" she purred from the bed.

"Clock is ticking, we have to find them before they find us."

"If you fuck that bitch, I'll smell it on you," she said,

hard and cold.

"Stay in the room. And…"

"I know, don't open the door for anyone." I gave her my .45 with no doubt she would plug anyone stupid enough to break in on her.

It was ten o'clock and the club was starting to fill up with men from all walks of life. All searching for something, most shallow enough to think they could find it here. Jane let out a small laugh when she saw me at the bar. "I see you dumped the skirt," she said setting down a gimlet.

"Yeah, she was cramping my style. Did Crystal show up?"

"Hell must be freezing over, she's in the back room giving some drunk a lap ride. So I guess you're stuck with me, at least for a couple of songs."

"Lucky me." The gin felt warm in my belly. It took the edge off the pressure building inside me and that was good, so good I ordered another.

"I'm not a tramp you know," she said "I don't throw myself at every hunk of man stuff that walks through that door. But there is something about you… ummm. Something different. This town is full of millionaire stock option babies, or at least it used to be, but real men are hard to find."

"You want the truth?"

"Yes."

"It's not going to happen between us."

"And yet here you are, without the skirt."

"It isn't going to happen with her either, if it did you'd both realize I'm nothing special. Just one more brother swimming for shore," I said. She shook her head with a slight smile. I was drinking my third gimlet, starting to feel the comfortable buzz when Jane pointed out Crystal. She was a statuesque blonde in an emerald green evening gown. Her hair was piled up on her head, with tendrils framing her face. She was walking a grinning sailor out of the back room, he left her side and ran over to his buddies at the rail, slapping them five.

"Hi, handsome," she said in a raspy sultry voice as I walked up to her, "Do you want a private dance?"

"I just need some information," I said, her smile dropped instantly.

"And I need to make a living." Her eyes roamed the room. I snapped a fifty in front of my face. The sound got her attention. In a flash the fifty disappeared into her hand. She led me to a booth, sliding in next to me. "You have my undivided attention."

"Tell me about Gino."

"Who?" she said, with a blank expression.

"Torelli. Let's not dance around it. You did some cyber work for him. Ringing any bells?"

"Oh that Gino, sure I did a gig for him, down in

South City, he had a studio set up, he and some tech geek. It was a scam, they had me pose in different positions, strip, touch myself. Later they rigged it so guys thought they were talking to a live girl. They had some kind of program that would play the sections that linked to what the guy was typing. Isn't technology grand?"

"You have an address for this studio?"

"Gino drove, sorry."

"Could you find it again, if the price was right?"

"Much as I'd love to take your cash, I'm afraid it would waste both our time. Zanax and champagne you know? It's all a happy blur." She looked away from me, scanning the room again.

"One last thing, do you have any idea where I could find Gino?"

"Only thing I ever saw was his big comfortable BMW." At the bar she noticed a lone man in an expensive looking suit. Without even a goodbye she stood up and headed for the man. She was like a graceful shark who had just smelled blood in the water. I hung around the club watching the cash driven mating rituals. I don't know what I expected to find out, maybe I hoped Gino would walk through the door, sit down and tell me what the hell happened. He didn't so I kept drinking gimlets and watching.

"You met Crystal, mission accomplished. And there you sit, your fine ass still on my bar stool. What is a gal to make of that?" Jane said giving me a sideways over the shoulder smile that could melt the polar caps and drown

Malibu. The DJ was spinning Robert Cray's "Back Door Man", and I don't know who I figured I was cheating on but the song seemed to fit my mood just right.

"Don't make nothing of it little girl, just a fool having a drink in a bar," I said.

"There is nothing little about me," she said, stopping to look into my eyes. "And I haven't been a girl since I started to bleed. But you got one thing right. You are a fool, if you walk out that door without making a date to take me out later."

"Have you ever been at a moment in your life when it's all falling in, a tumbling shit storm and you can't see up or down? Just struggling to keep moving forward and not step on a land mine. You ever feel like that?"

"Baby, I'm tending bar in a strip club, what do you think? This is not the career choice one makes when life is all peaches and cream," she said ignoring a drunk pounding his beer mug at the other end of the bar. "But you have to learn to roll with it or it rolls over you."

"This one's bigger than that."

"Bigger than what?"

"Bigger than whatever you were imagining," I said. She looked at me, wide eyed. Rising up on straight arms she looked over the bar and down at my lap.

"Really, um, I was imagining pretty big," she said with a smile that got me grinning. "First smile I've seen big guy, I like it." With a wink she went down the bar to service the waiting drunks. While her back was turned I got up to go. I left a fifty for a tip. I was going through the dead greaseball's cash like it was stolen, which it was. Maybe I thought when the cash was gone I would forget their decomposing bodies and their pals that were sure to come hunting us. Or maybe it was like the song says, you should spend it like you got it, drive like it's stolen and love like they'll love you back. Sometimes even country music has wisdom if you listen.

Cass was sleeping when I got back to the room. I sat up for another hour looking down at neon, blinking through the fog. I was running down a blind alley chasing a ghost who was always just out of my reach. I searched the phone book, but found no listing for Gino Torelli. His being Italian was one more nail in my coffin. I had found a way to piss off the mob. Once they caught wind of me, there would be no place safe to hide. No place in the world they couldn't reach out and swat me. And here I was trying to find them. Maybe Gino wasn't connected, maybe the boys in the desert being Italian was a coincidence. Maybe, but I doubted it.

CHAPTER 10

"It's simple, hit search, type in stripper and bingo," Cass said, we were in a cyber coffee shop called Java Enabler down in the Haight district. It was once the epicenter of the flower power explosion, full of hippies and junkies and free love. Now it was just another quaint gentrified neighborhood. Gone are the runaways whose lives were forever changed by that long cool summer. Gone, the valiant peaceniks who faced the riot police with flowers against batons and mace only to see their dreams crushed under the wheels of the coming corporate dream of a Coca-cola USA forever world. Gone, the hippies who tuned in and dropped out then discovered heroin and died… all reduced to a footnote in the cable-car-tour-bus ride, come see where it all happened, come see it from the comfort of your air-conditioned Trail-ways seat.

The kid behind the counter at Java Enabler told me that before the bottom dropped out of the dot com stocks, this place used to be packed twenty-four seven. A flick of the eyes and I saw the small shop was near empty. Along one wall, it had a row of iMacs with overstuffed chairs in front of them. While Cass started to bang away in a blur of meaningless clicks and clacks on the keyboard, I ordered her a latte and a black house coffee for me, say what you will about yuppie scum they have improved the quality of coffee for all of us and for that I bless them. Cass found 157,263 sites listing the key word "Stripper". I had her add the word "Live" and that got us down to 42,637. She started clicking on addresses and a flurry of porn sites flashed on. I was flooded with embarrassment to be looking at these pictures in broad daylight with Cass at my side. It wasn't like this was anything we hadn't seen before. Hell, I reminded myself, her last place of employment was a brothel. Still it felt odd. After an hour of mind-numbing bad porn I had her add the word "Crystal" to the search. The top web site listed was called Hot-horny-strippers.com. When she clicked on the address I nearly spit out my coffee. There on the welcome page was a picture of Kelly. She was naked, on her hands and knees, ass to the camera. Her face stared back at me over her shoulder, it was animated so she winked at me. On her left butt cheek I noticed a tattoo of Tinkerbell or some other fairy who's name I didn't know. Fact is, all fairies look alike to me. It had never occurred to me that Kelly would have a tattoo, not that she should or shouldn't have had one. It was just that I didn't know she did. It was one more in the growing list of things I hadn't known about Kelly. And there she was kneeling on the screen forming her crude, "come fuck me" wink.

"That bastard," Cass said more to herself than me. We both stared at the picture for a long moment, as if we could make her real if we watched long enough. "Give me a credit card number."

"Do I look like the kind of guy they give credit cards

to?" Fact was I had one hidden in my car, but it was clean in John Stahl's name and needed it to stay that way. It was my get out of jail, I'll be in Paris 'cause there are too many dead bodies in this room to cover up, security card.

"We need one to see more," she said.

"I don't need to see more, I need to see where this is coming from." Looking around, the shop was now empty. The clerk was sitting at one of the iMacs tapping away on the keys. I decided to take a wild shot in the dark. I caught Cass' attention and then looked over at the clerk. She smiled, this was her area of expertise. In the few steps it took for her to reach him she completely transformed herself. She stood up a hardened woman but by the time she reached him she was the girl next door. Meryl Streep had nothing on this girl.

She slid into a chair next to him and flashed the kind of smile that made you forget your troubles, your wife, even your car keys. Caught in her crosshairs he never had a chance.

"Hi," she said.

"How's it going," he mumbled, unable to keep eye contact he looked down, then found himself staring at her breasts. He gulped and quickly looked up, a slight rosy tint forming on his cheeks. "You need something?"

"You're good with computers, I can tell by the way you whip around the keyboard." She let her fingertips brush against his hand resting on the keys.

"I know a thing or two," he said with false modesty, still glowing from her briefest of touches. Yeah, she was that good.

"My uncle and I were trying to trace a web site."
She nodded at me. "It was pictures, bad pictures of his
daughter, he wants to know how to find the server it's on. I
love computers but I'm in way over my head on this one.
Could you, no I don't want to bother you."

"It's no big deal, piece of cake really." The clerk
smiled, this was his turf, his moment to shine.

"Really?" She looked like she was in awe of his
prowess.

"If you have the IP address, I can find out where the
data is hosted."

"IP address?" Unconsciously she ran her thumb
over her lower lip acting confused.

"Sorry, do you know the site's name?"

"This is embarrassing." She said pursing her lips
into a heart shape and looking down. In her flower print
day dress she looked like an innocent college student. "I
don't know how Betty got into this, she was always a bit
wild but after her mom died she just went crazy. It's tearing
Uncle Travis up."

"I'm sorry."

"I just want to help him. The site is called, um," she
stammered, ashamed to say it out loud, she whispered,
"Hot-horny-strippers.com."

The clerk looked down at the keyboard and typed in
the address. He paused for a moment, embarrassed by the

picture in front of him. Cass studied the floor. "Damn, she could be your twin, except the hair, yours is, you know..."

"Blonde," Cass said eyes still downcast. "Please turn it off."

"Sorry, I, um, just, you know, need the address." He tore his eyes from the naked picture and quickly wrote down a series of numbers, then clicked out of the site. "Every IP address has five numbers, they give the country, region, municipality, city block and real world address." He was relieved to be back on a subject he was strong in. Cass rewarded his returning confidence with another brilliant smile. "The phone company keeps records of all the addresses. Their firewalls are some of the weakest on the net, I wrote a program to hack them."

"You're amazing. Where did you learn all this?" Cass said with admiration.

"I've been messing with computers since before I could walk," he said proudly. He slipped in a disk and typed in several commands. Numbers and letters flashed across the screen in rapid succession. "This is going to take a couple of minutes, you want another latte?"

"That would be nice." As they moved to the counter, Cass moved close beside him, giving him a comfortable sense of familiarity. He was a small boy, I don't think he was ever chosen first for stick ball, but next to Cass' petite body, he looked almost full size. Looking down at her, he beamed with pride. I'm sure at that moment he wished someone he knew would come in and see just how cool he was.

I couldn't hear what they said but they seemed to chat happily. Watching them was like seeing an alternate path Cass could have taken. A nice girl on a date with a nice boy her own age. He could walk her home to a house where a good mother and father waited. Maybe he'd take her to the movies and get up the courage to slip an arm onto her shoulder. I knew it was all an act, but if I was her Uncle Travis, it's the life I would want for her.

Back at the computer, she sipped a fresh latte while they watched the blinking screen. "And we are in," the clerk said proudly. He typed in the IP address and then scribbled something down. "It's down in Palo Alto, not one of the big servers, may even be a private home," he said handing her the paper.

"You are fantastic." She kissed him on the cheek. We left him glowing, at least for a moment he was somebody cool. On the street, her happy smile dropped instantly and she transformed back into her twenty going on forty year old self.

"Nice kid," I said.

"I guess, if you like nice." She gave me a look that told me she didn't, she liked bad men like me.

"Come on, he seemed like a good kid." We were walking down the steep street, leaning back for balance.

"A real saint. Did you see the way he was drooling over Kelly's picture? He was easy to play, I liked that about him." We walked on in silence. At the bottom of the hill she turned to me, suddenly serious. "I did good right?"

"Yeah you did swell."

"And you couldn't have done it without me?"

"Not without spilling some of that kid's coffee and or blood. And I hate to waste good coffee. Who's Uncle Travis? He the one?"

"He's from that movie, you know, the old time one about the guy who drives the taxi?" she said searching for the title.

"Taxi Driver?"

"Yeah, that's the one, sometimes you remind me of him." For her it was a compliment. And oddly enough that's how I took it.

"With or without the mohawk?" I said with a grin.

"With, most definitely. You're whacko, straight up crazy. But in a good way," she said as we climbed into the Crown Vic. The address was down the bay in Palo Alto, in the heart of Silicon Valley. We took the 101 out of the city, out of the fog and out past Candlestick Park, or at least that's what it was called for forever until some corporate bandits bought the rights to name it after their crap. Everything is for sale in America, you just have to know the price. It was a forty minute drive, traffic was light, the sun was on the bay, seagulls circled in the air and everything was right with the world except for all the parts that were fucked up. Like mob assassins trying to whack you for no good reason, and little girls posing naked on their hands and knees when they should be going to junior college and dating Biff the track star. I wondered what else I would have to find out about Kelly. With every step I took, I knew her less and less. Or maybe I knew her better. But she wasn't the girl I had cared so deeply for. She had been an actress playing a part that should have been her life. That guileless country girl I shared Chinese food with, the girl who loved her puppy and went to the dog park, that's who she should have been. Who she could have been if the world had kept its hands to itself and let her grow up.

"Was it your father?" I asked Cass.

"Was who my father?" she said, looking out the window.

"Who put the scars on you two. Was it your father?"

"Oh you think you have it all figured out, do you? You think you know me? Forget it," she said, her voice turning cold. "Keep your mind on who killed Kelly, ok?"

"What ever you say." I let it lay. I didn't really need the details, the names changed but the facts remained. Girls of the sex trade all came from the same mold, shaped by a world that sexualized them at a young age. They all yearned for the good daddy, but looked for him in bad men. They searched to master what they couldn't control as children. I had spent my adult life in their world and only seen a handful make it out. The rest put scars on scar tissue and kept moving on, getting colder and colder. In the end cynicism replaced hope and they lived their lives in rigid resignation.

We got off the freeway at University Avenue. It was a broad street canopied by deep-rooted trees. The homes were large yet still cozy, with eight mile long unfenced front lawns stretching to the curb. Palo Alto was a rich man's small town USA. Kids played on lawns with a

JOSH STALLINGS

Frisbee, others rode bikes and skateboards. If Dennis the
Menace ran out chased by Mr. Wilson, I wouldn't have
been surprised one bit. It was just that freaking quaint a
town and it made my palms sweat just to be there.

The address we had turned out to be a two-story
Tudor on Hamilton Avenue, a quiet residential
neighborhood that stunk of both old money and new dot
com cash. It was early evening so I cruised past the house,
in the driveway was a late model Volvo station wagon and
a BMW sedan five series. With something like ninety plus
grand in rolling stock, and a mil plus house, whoever lived
there was doing ok, I kept going.

On University, I found a fifties style diner. The
place looked about a week old but everything had been pre-
aged so it had the feeling of a real greasy spoon, in a creepy
Disney-land sort of way. This was a town that had real
history, which they tore out and replaced with fake history,
just because they could. As we walked in, four Stanford
boys craned their necks to watch Cass walk by. They
looked at me and I could hear the laughter at some joke
being told. I moved us to the counter with our backs to the
boys, I knew if I had to look at them it would get ugly and
that wasn't why I was here. If Cass noticed any of it she
didn't say, it seemed she'd become immune years ago to the
bullshit her looks brought out in men, unless she was using
it for a purpose, then she knew how to turn it on like a light
switch. We ordered and Cass powered down two double
burgers and an order of chili fries. I still had no idea where
she put it, but watching her eat I forgot about the college
boys and beating the crap out of them and I laughed.

Drinking some of the best diner coffee I'd ever had

from a to-go cup I watched the house. At around ten the lights upstairs went dark. "Let's do it," I said to Cass. At the door I leaned out of sight against the wall, my .45 hung in my hand. Cass rang the bell, we could hear it echoing into the house followed by footsteps. An iron port in the door swung open spilling a square of light onto Cass.

"Sorry to bother you, but my car died, well it didn't die, it ran out of gas and I left my cell phone at home, and well... I wonder if I could use your phone to call my husband?" she said.

"Sure, just a minute." a male voice said. I heard the deadbolt click and the door opened. I moved into the light, aiming the pistol at his chest. He was a tall skinny man of about thirty, he had gold rimmed glasses and a ponytail. "What the hell?" he squeaked.

"Shhh, why don't you invite us in," I said, clicking the hammer back on the .45.

"No, my wife and kids...." he blurted out.

"...Will wake up when they hear me shoot you if you don't do what I say." I pushed him into the house. Cass closed the door behind us.

"I don't have any cash," he stammered.

"And I don't want any. Play this straight and an hour from now we'll just be a bad memory. Fuck with me and you better hope your life insurance is paid up. Got it?"

"No... what do you want?"

"Hot Horny Stripper, you prick. Does your little wifey know where you get your cash?" Cass said.

"Who sent you?" he asked.

"Unimportant. Fact is we are here now and we want answers," I said. From upstairs a woman's voice called out.

"Jerry, is everything ok?"

"Fine honey, go back to bed." At gunpoint, he led us out the back door, through the backyard, past his kids' redwood jungle gym and into a detached garage. The garage had been converted into a triple insulated, windowless, high-tech bunker. The door closed with a swoosh behind us and all sound from the outside world disappeared, replaced by the low hum of computer fans. The room was climate controlled to a chilly sixty five degrees and clean of all particles of dust, every surface was shiny white, even the floor. A row of computers flashed and blinked into the night. Cass wanted to know which server held the porno site. He pointed to a terminal, she sat down and started typing.

"Where is Gino?" I asked him.

"I don't know who you are talking about." I whipped the barrel of the automatic down across his cheek, he stumbled back holding his face. I could see a slight smear of blood where the front sight had cut him.

"Let's be clear, porn-boy. I don't like you one bit, so splattering you will be a pleasure. Your only value is what you know." I smacked him again and he started to cry, his face growing pale. The reality of his situation was sinking in.

"Stop, please, I'm just a provider, it was Gino's idea. He came to me. I didn't want to do it but when Apple laid

166

me off I had to do something," he said through his tears.

"How did he find you?" I wanted to smack him for crying, tell him to be a man.

"I met him at a club in the city," he sniveled.

"Barbary Coast?"

"Yes," he said, looking down.

"Moses." Cass was trembling and pointing at the computer screen. Moving to her side I looked and saw Kelly on the screen, she was being held by an anonymous fist. His fingers were laced into her curly hair, he was forcing her to give him head. The faceless figure pulled her mouth off his cock. He struck several hard slaps across her face, a trickle of blood ran down from her nose. He forced her bloody lips back down onto his erection. Her eyes were wild, like a trapped animal. I felt my stomach clench, bile backed up into my throat. Blood pounding in my brain, I grabbed the monitor ripping it off the desk and hurled it at the skinny man. It caught him in the chest and he tumbled back into the wall. Cracking the plasterboard with his back he fell to the floor. I let out a pain filled cry and jumped on him, with my knees on his chest I shoved the barrel of the pistol into his forehead. I had to fight not to pull the trigger and rid the planet of this weasel.

"Did you film this?" I hissed through clenched teeth.

"Yes...but I didn't know what he was going to do. He just lost it."

"Gino?"

"Yes."

"Anyone else involved?"

"No… He went crazy on her."

"And you kept filming. 'Cause you lost your job and all?"

"Yes." He was gasping for air as I bore down on his chest.

"Kill him." Cass stood over us. Her jaw set, her eyes devoid of life.

"Not yet, baby girl," I said, then turned back to his tear and blood stained face. "Where is Gino? No bullshit or I'll give her the gun and leave the room."

"I don't know, we always met in different restaurants … Every week I'd give him his cut… He hasn't called in several months… I don't know where he is, really I don't, I swear I'd tell you if I knew." He was telling the truth, he didn't have the balls to lie to me. Standing up, I handed the gun to Cass.

"No! What are you doing, I told you all I know!" he cried out. I turned and walked out of the garage. Cass had paid dear for this moment. In the backyard I found a box of sports equipment. In it was just what I was looking for, a Louisville slugger, America's favorite solid oak baseball bat. When I reentered the garage the ponytail boy was curled up in a ball, I could smell the rank odor of urine. A yellow stain spilled out onto the white linoleum beneath him. Blood flowed from several fresh cuts on his face, she must have given him a pistol whipping. If that was all he got that night he would be a luckier son of a bitch than me. Cass looked down at him in disgust. I put a firm hand on her shoulder and spoke quietly.

"He isn't worth it," I said.

"No he's not..." she said turning away from the crumpled waste of a man. Swinging the bat I let all my rage out on the computer towers. The plastic and metal exploded across the room. I broke them to pieces and then broke the pieces into pieces. Wires and circuit boards scattered across the floor. I handed the bat to Cass and let her go wild on the monitors. Glass shattered with a pop, she screamed, her face contorting with the fury she felt. She was ugly and marvelous, clear for the moment of the guise of beauty she wore so well. She screamed and kept swinging. While she vented on the equipment I searched a tall file cabinet, it was mostly tax information, receipts for computer gear, warranties we had just voided. In the back I found an envelope with four small cassettes, DV videotape. Each was labeled as Girl One through Four. I slipped the tapes into my pocket. Cass stood, panting over the wreckage. The punk was sniveling in the corner. I leaned down, rolling his limp body onto his back so he could see me.

"One day I'll be back. You will pay for what you have done. You won't know when, you won't see it coming, but you will pay the price." We left him there and walked down the driveway out onto the peaceful street. A street full of happy families, all sleeping comfortably, all unaware of the pain merchant in their midst.

I got on the 101 and headed south. It was time to go home, back where I had the connections to find out what the hell was going on. "How did you know I wouldn't shoot him?" Cass asked.

"I didn't, but I figured it was your choice to make."

"I could have."

"I know."

"Thank you," she said. In San Jose I pulled off and bought a bottle of whiskey and one of ginger ale. This time Cass drank with me. It was the first time since I met her I'd seen her drink anything harder than diet coke. Purring over the 152 past Casa de Fruitas we rolled into the mountains. Billowing clouds drifted past the moon, casting huge moving shadows across the landscape, obscuring and illuminating the steep hills that climbed around us. Sharp rocks stabbed up out of the smooth brown grass and a grove of oak trees dotting the mountainside looked like monstrous skeletons reaching out their many arms to grab wandering strangers.

"You're a good man, Moses," Cass slurred after her second drink. "Really, you are a good man...fuck 'em all that's what I say... She was just a sweet little girl, why'd they do that to her?"

"I don't know, baby girl, I don't know."

"Fuck all men... All but you, Moses, you're a good man."

"Ok."

"I mean it Moses, you are a good man..." Cass was out cold by the time we reached the 5, she fell asleep curled up in the seat with her head on my lap. I had tenderly stroked her hair until she had finally let go and drifted off. I wished she hadn't had to see her sister like that, I wished I could protect her from all the ugliness in the world. But the best I could do was hold her head and let her sleep.

Highway 5 stretched out before us, a long dark ribbon that ran in a straight line to the horizon. All around us was an endless expanse of nothing, flat dirt broken up by small scrub brush and then more dirt. Few cars were traveling at this late hour. I blew past a tractor trailer pulling a load of onions, the scarecrow driving the rig shot me a thumbs up. My guess is he was glad to find out the Crown Vic wasn't a cop car. Then I was out on this lonely stretch of hell, I saw no lights for over an hour. I was left by myself, just me and my dark thoughts. Whoever killed Kelly was out there somewhere, by now they would have figured out what I did in the desert. Could they be hunting me at this moment? In the rear view mirror a pair of low-slung headlights flew up out of the horizon. I was doing a clean eighty but they were quickly closing the gap. I eased the hammer down and let the beast roar. The speedo' read 120 mph, but the headlights kept coming on, burning up the miles between us. I left my guns in the trunk out of fear that we might get stopped by the cherry tops. But now I would have gladly dealt with a cop just to have my trusty .45. I could start to make out the silhouette of my pursuer, it was a sports car, either an Audi TT or Porsche. I pushed it up to a buck forty, but couldn't gain any ground on them, it had to be a Porsche. White light engulfed the interior of the Crown Vic, I flicked the mirror up to keep from being blinded. In a rush of wind a deep purple Porsche whipped past me. As they passed I looked over expecting to see the barrel of a shotgun, what I got was a glimpse of a salt and pepper haired man with his bimbo girlfriend. They were both laughing and bouncing along to what ever music they had ripping on their stereo, they didn't even look over. I wasn't a blip on their radar. Dropping back down to a less cop attracting speed, I noticed my knuckles were white as they gripped the steering-wheel like it was a life preserver and I was drowning. Maybe I was, and I was just too simple to know it. Just because some old fuck in a purple Porsche made me paranoid didn't mean I wasn't being hunted.

After a pit stop in a rest area, to piss and make myself a fresh cocktail, I rejoined the road. My pulse was back down to its normal speed driven thump. I slipped Joshua Tree into the CD player and let The Edge's guitar licks take me away. Bono sang about how he had climbed mountains and ran through fields and still had not found what he was looking for. I knew the feeling only too well.

At the end of the central valley the highway snaked suddenly up the Grape Vine into the steep mountains. In only a couple of miles the road gains two thousand feet in elevation, the incline forces lesser cars and trucks with trailers to slow to a crawl. The Crown Vic purred up the incline at a steady 80 mph. If only I could trust the woman I was rolling with like I trusted this car.

CHAPTER 11

It was five AM when I dropped down out of the mountains and into LA. The sky was the palest of blues in the dawn as we passed the old WPA bridges that cross the LA river up and over the freeway. They were built a long time before the twisted web of concrete we call a freeway system scarred up Los Angeles. This town was like that, look at it from the proper angle and you were transported back to a time when Humphrey Bogart ruled the silver screen and instead of paying folks to stay at home and worry, they paid them to build wonderful stone bridges.

I carried Cass into my house. She stirred once when I laid her down in the bed, she reached out and touched my stubbled face and then went back to sleep. I unloaded the Crown Vic, and placed Marilyn on the kitchen table. Curling up on the couch I held my .45 to my chest. I still had phantom feelings of the highway moving under me. Sleep seemed many rumbling miles off. My brain was a jumble of fears and plans. What I should or shouldn't do, who I should talk to, what wrong step might get us both killed. I blinked and an hour and a half had disappeared off the clock. I sat up, not much more rested but a little less blurry. I brewed a pot of coffee and sat on the back stoop drinking the rich black brew. My backyard was small and tangled, weeds had taken over the lawn and the orange tree was in bad need of pruning. The three roses had grown into wild bushes. The rent was cheap, my landlord was a widow who had moved to Oregon to be near her grandchildren, so I was left to do as I pleased. I hadn't noticed how small and shabby the house was, but I'd never had a guest in it before. An hour later I checked on Cass. She was sleeping the sleep of the innocent. The hard edges from her face erased, she looked like the young girl she was. I left her a note and a loaded .45 and headed for the dog park.

Angel saw me as soon as I cleared the double gates. She let go her grip on Bruiser's neck and galloped across the grass. Going to my knees I let her lick my face and nibble on my ears and nose.

"She missed her Daddy," Helen said, offering a hand to help me up. She had a firm strong grip. "How was your trip?"

"Rough."

"Looks like it. Getting any sleep?"

"Some. How's the writing going?"

"We're on hiatus, I should be working on a spec script, but life is short and I'm lazy." While we talked, Bruiser came over and tried to get Angel to play, but she wouldn't leave my side. She leaned into my leg, keeping contact. "Your girl can eat!"

"No, really? She's always so demure at home," I chuckled. We chatted about nothing important, new plans for the park, the city was tired of watching the trees it planted die from dog piss, everything but where I'd been. They were planning to build a lattice structure for shade and there was talk about replacing the struggling grass with ground up concrete. Five hundred dogs a day used the park, making it one of the rec. departments most used spots. Helen told me about her show, it dealt with vampires infiltrating the Mob, it had been picked up for a second season, so Bruiser wouldn't starve this year. After the last few super charged days it was good just to chat. As I went to go Helen caught my arm, looking me square in the eyes.

"Are you ok, Moses?"

"I will be…"

"Kelly?"

"Among other things, yeah," I said.

"If you need to talk, I work weird hours and don't sleep much, so call me." I wondered if she knew the truth about me, Kelly, the dead men, would she be so ready to be available? Maybe when it was all over I'd test her out, then again maybe she didn't need this crap rattling around in her brain. Let Kelly remain pure in her memory, if no place else.

Picking Angel up I went back to my crib. She liked the Crown Vic, jumping from the front seat into the back and then up front again. To her it was a big rolling playpen. From the floor she watched my foot flexing on the accelerator, dropping onto her forepaws her eyebrows scrunched up and her butt wiggled as her body tensed. As I rounded a corner she leapt like a wild beast, all forty pounds of her landing on her prey, my foot, driving it to the floorboards. The Crown Vic gained velocity as it lurched forward toward the stalled traffic in front of me. Racking the wheel to the left I skidded across the path of oncoming cars and up a small alley. Picking Angel up by the scruff of her neck I sat her on the seat. After all I had survived it would be a real bitch if I died in a car wreck because of a puppy.

Cass was still sleeping when we returned with a bag of pan dulce. Angel curled up at my feet while I called Lowrie. "How are you, son, you doing ok?" he asked after telling me he had no news on Kelly's case.

"Can I buy you a cup of coffee?" I said.

"I'm booked full up, narcotics pulled three detectives from our division, new mayor has the war on drugs on the brain. So we're pulling doubles. I haven't seen my wife in a week."

"I need to see you." There was a long pause on the other end of the phone. He finally let out a sigh.

"You know the Denny's on Santa Monica?" he said.

"Yeah, off Cherokee?"

"Be there at eleven." He hung up without even saying goodbye. Angel's head popped up, I turned to see Cass standing in the doorway, wiping grains of sleep from her eyes. Angel jumped up and ran to Cass, leaping at her bare legs. It was the first time she had left my side since I had picked her up.

"Who's your friend?" Cass asked, scratching Angel

behind the ear.

"Angel, she was Kelly's."

"And you took her in? You're not a big tough guy after all, are you?"

"No, I'm a big sissy, afraid of the dark, my turn-ons are puppy dogs and long walks on the beach, my turn-offs are cheeky girls who sleep in my bed without so much as a thank you." I said with a grin.

"Thank you, Moses, you got anything to eat?" I poured the Mexican pastries onto a plate and got her a mug of coffee. She ate four of the crumbly treats in big bites. Angel danced around her feet, hoping to catch falling crumbs. A dark cloud drifted across Cass's eyes. It was as if for a brief moment she had stepped out of her life, and now memories had sucked her back in.

"I have to go into Hollywood."

"Can I come with you?" Fear shadowed her face.

"Not this time, baby girl. I'm meeting a cop who might see it as his duty to ask you questions neither of us wants to answer."

"Come on, big boy, I can handle some cop."

"No. You're safe here. Just don't…"

"Open the door for anyone, I know the drill." Like a petulant teenager she sulked out of the room to go take a shower. Again she left the door open, and made sure the curtain parted enough so that I could get a good eye full of her as water splashed down over her firm young body.

Maybe she hoped her nakedness would be enough to keep me from leaving. It almost was.

The Denny's was a few blocks from the Hollywood police station. It looked like every Denny's in the world, purple, orange and ugly. I slid into a bright naugahyde booth and ordered coffee, it was weak and bitter but I needed the caffeine. At eleven on the dot Lowrie walked through the door. His eyes were ringed with dark circles. "Son you look as tired as I feel," he said as he sat down. He ordered a fried egg sandwich and a cup of coffee, decaf. "Doctors orders, no more coffee, no cigars, what is the world coming to, huh?"

"Do you know anybody in the FBI?" I asked.

"Paulson, he's the liaison with our department, good man, bit too by the book like most of the feds. Why, you in trouble? "

"Yes, but not how you think. I need some answers and I don't know where to turn."

"This about Kelly? I told you to leave it alone."

"Yeah, you also told me you'd stay on the case, but what do you have? Nothing right? Well nothing doesn't cut it with me. So I did some digging."

"Do you know why they gave me a gold shield and a gun? Because I'm a trained investigator. My job is to build a case so that when I take down the bad guys, they stay down. Now when you go running around tainting evidence, muddying the water it just makes my job that much harder.

Not to mention, you up your own odds of winding up as an unsolved homicide. Another case I have to handle."

"You want to hear what I found, or do you want to keep running your mouth?"

"Do you know the most common phrase said before a victim is killed? No? Well I'll tell you. It's 'Go ahead and shoot me then.' Or some variation on the theme. And you run through life like it's your mantra. That said, what have you got?" The waitress delivered his sandwich but he didn't touch it. I told him the whole story, leaving out the dead soldiers in the desert. I told him about Gino and my suspicion he was mobbed up. I knew the feds were looking for him and that he had dropped off the radar. When I told him about the web tapes, he pushed his plate away, his appetite ruined. "You destroyed the evidence? Damn it Moses what were you thinking? There's no way to bust the prick now."

"He won't be peddling his crap on the web anymore, I saw to that. Plus I sent his wife a letter and one of the tapes. By the time I'm done he'll dream about the fine and slap on the wrist the court would have given a straight squid like him."

"If you don't believe in the system, why the hell did you come to me? What do you want, absolution? You want me to say you did the right thing? You didn't, you let this scum skate, and there's nothing I can do about it."

"I think the guys trying to kill Cass are mobbed up."

"Bring her in, we'll put her in protective custody."

"You mean jail her? We both know the mob can

reach in there with the snap of a finger. No thanks Lowrie. I'll keep her safe, I just need to know the score."

"Why should I help you?"

"Because it's the right thing to do and you know it."

"No, it's not. But you'll go ahead with or without my help... I'll make you a deal, I'll look into this Torelli matter, but you have to promise that if you find the mutts who dropped the girl you'll let me take them down. I want your word."

"I can't promise how it will play out."

"Then I can't help you," he said starting to rise.

"Wait, my word, if at all possible I'll let you have these pukes. That's the best I can do Lowrie." I stretched out my hand, he looked at it for a moment then shook it.

"I'll be in touch." And he was gone. I paid the bill and headed for home. Lowrie was a good cop, better than most but he was out of touch with the streets. If I had waited for his system to work Cass would be dead and buried by now, and I'd be left with my thumb up my ass wondering if I could have stopped it. I would be true to my word, if I saw a way to have Kelly's killers busted I would. I also knew I wouldn't hesitate to drop a hammer on them if that's what was called for.

Walking up to my crib I was afraid Cass would be holding a grudge for leaving her behind. Instead I found her smiling, curled up on the sofa with Angel's head on her lap. She had cleaned up the house, it looked nice. She even cut a rose from the garden and put it in a water glass on the coffee table. She had draped one of my Mexican blankets over the sofa, two or three little touches and it almost looked like someone could live here.

"Hi dear, how was your day?" Rising up onto tiptoes, she gave me a peck on the cheek.

"Still going on. You want some lunch?" Her eyes sparkled at that.

"Always." We went down to a small taco stand, she ate three carne asada soft tacos, a plate of rice and beans, and a diet coke. I told her about Lowrie and his offer of police protection.

"Are you trying to dump me? Did you make a deal with him?" Fear flickered down deep behind her eyes.

"No, just giving you your options."

"I'm staying with you," she said firmly taking my hand in hers. "I'll be a good girl, I'll do just what you say. I promise." I was her lifeboat and the storm clouds were brewing all around us.

Walking up the block toward my house I spotted a dark sedan parked across the street, a G-man in a cheap dark suit and Raybans was leaning against the front fender.

I pulled Cass back around the corner before the fed could see us. "Go in the back, through the alley, ok, baby girl?" I said, she started to say something then caught herself and complied. I crossed the street and walked up to the G-man. His partner sat behind the wheel, reading a file. They both looked bored. "You looking for me, or do you just like my house?"

"McGuire?" he said in a clipped voice.

"That's me."

"What do you know about Gino Torelli?" He didn't waste any time on formalities.

"Who?" I kept my expression neutral.

"You're a two time loser McGuire, want to go for three strikes? Interfering with a federal investigation, resisting arrest, threatening a federal officer with an unlicensed firearm. Oh yes, I can make it stick, who do you think the court will believe? "

"Is that your best shot? I reached out to you, remember?"

"You may have fooled your LAPD buddy, but I know who you are. Now, what do you know about Gino Torelli?"

"Fuck you," I said and started to turn away, he grabbed my arm and spun me back. Suddenly he had his Glock in hand, pointed at my gut.

"As long as you asked me so nicely." I strained to look calm. A pat search would reveal the .38 in my boot and then I would be dry lube fucked. "Like I told Lowrie, the name Torelli came up in connection to a murdered friend. I don't know anything about the man, except he has something to do with internet porn and that you boys are looking for him."

"That's it? Everything?" He slammed the barrel of

the 9 mm into my gut and almost got a face full of my partially digested taco. "Don't think about holding back on me."

"Look, that's it. You want more, you're going to have to find another sucker."

"Alright for now. Do yourself a favor and stay out of San Francisco. You pissed in my stream, and I will warn you once, but only once. Walk away. Don't look back and forget you ever heard the name Gino Torelli." I hung my head in what I hoped passed for defeat. He holstered his piece, climbed in the sedan and left me standing in the middle of the street.

My face felt cold as I tried to stuff down my feelings of rage and impotence, fact was the fed could drop me any time he wanted, put me in a cage and say goodbye to daylight. He was right, who the hell would take my word over his. I knew the score and so did he. In the straight world I was nothing but a two time loser with a penchant for violence. And he was a shining star of valor.

"Who was that?" Cass asked as I walked past her to the kitchen.

"A couple of government pricks on a fishing expedition." I poured myself a tall glass of Scotch and sat down at the kitchen table. Angel curled up around my legs laying her head on my foot, and went to sleep.

"What's the plan, Ace? Get drunk and hope it all goes away?" Cass said.

"You got a better plan? Me, I'm fresh out of ideas."

"Then let them skate. Put me on a bus out of town, they will find me sooner or later but you won't have to worry about it. You can just get drunk and forget you ever met my sister or me. Is that what you want?" I didn't answer her, instead I took a long warm drink. The McCallans tasted like liquid smoke warming its way down to my soul. Standing with the bottle in hand I walked past Cass and her reproachful eyes. Falling into bed I took one pull off the bottle before sleep swept up over me and took me down under.

I'm back in Chino, out on the yard, but the place is completely empty of human life. The guard tower is manned by a guy in a black suit and dark glasses. He is following my every move with a scoped rifle. Men just like him stand on all the walls, none move. Except for the wind rustling their suits they could be statues. I try to move but a cage has formed around me, closing in getting tighter with every second. My breath is ragged as the bars push against my chest.

It was dark when I woke, Cass had taken the bottle from my hand while I slept and Angel was curled up on my chest. In the shower I let my mind unwind. Somehow I'd been looking at this thing from the wrong direction. Kelly's killers had something to do with this Gino Torelli. The boys in the desert were mobbed up, I was sure of that. Two from Vegas and one, a James Grasso, his driver's license told me, was from San Francisco with an address on Post Street. Had they whacked Kelly? If so, who sent them? I knew who would know.

It was ten o'clock when I pushed through the door of Figueroa's. An older square headed muscle man stepped into my path as I moved for the back room. "Sorry, we're closed."

"It's me, Eddy. Moses, remember?"

"I know who you are, and we're closed."

"I need to see the old man."

"Make an appointment, he's busy."

"Eddie!" The metallic chirp of the Pope's voice box called out.

"Don't move," Eddie the Mechanic said as he headed for the back. He was once one of the most feared enforcers in LA. Pushing sixty he still put a chill in my bones.

Don Gallico sat at his table, drinking an espresso while a mousy young nurse stood beside him drawing blood. "Moses, word is our Armenian problem is walking with a limp, I owe you one for that. The vig is stopped, the principal is all you owe us," he said spreading his hands out with benevolence.

"I've come to ask for more than that, I need your help." I said keeping my face neutral.

"You owe two large and I haven't taken your spleen. I'd say we were even. What the fuck are you trying to do shish-kabob me? " he squawked at the nurse. She didn't bat an eyelash, she just kept pulling blood from his wrinkled arm.

"A girl I know was killed up in Silver Lake."

"It happens, LA is going to the dogs."

"She was hit, pro." I shot the nurse a glance but her full attention was on her job. "Is it ok to speak around her?"

"Say what you want, she's deaf as a tombstone. Now, what the fuck makes you think I know anything about some dead girl?"

"It came out of San Francisco. Gino Torelli is involved. It's got mob stink all over it." I looked in his eyes, not a flicker or a flinch.

"Mob stink? That's nice, you got the manners of a wart hog. And you're ignorant to boot. Read the papers, there hasn't been any family business in the Bay Area since 1988 when Milano bought a Rico charge."

"Who is Gino Torelli?" I said, and still saw no reaction.

"Other than he sounds Italian, I got no clue." If he was lying he was good, but then again you don't get to be his age in the game without being good.

"James Grasso?"

"Sorry, are they connected to the dead girl?"

"Yeah. Look sir, you know me, I don't want to make trouble for anyone. Live and let live. I just need to know what I'm dealing with so I don't step on any toes."

"Take my advice kid, walk away. Shit you don't need to know about, shit I don't need to know about. Forget you ever met these girls and get back to earning the cabbage you owe me."

"You're right. Fuck it. Italian don't make it mob. Thank you for the time."

"You going to take a hike on the matter, let dead dogs lay?"

"Maybe..." I let out a long tired sigh.

"Do." Even through the squawking box, the edge in his voice was clear.

"Alright, I will."

"Good boy." His face relaxed. "Now you want me to have Charley make you an espresso? You can tell me who's winning at the track?"

"I'd love it, but I have to get to work or Manny will have my ass." I walked out shooting Eddy a smirk and a wink, he shook his head scowling.

Two blocks away I found a phone booth and called home. Cass picked up on the third ring. "Get your things, grab my dog and get out of the house, now!"

"What? Moses what's happening."

"Do it. Wait for me at the panaderia."

"The what?"

"Mexican bakery down on the corner. Now move." Sweat was running down my back in a cold stream. I hung up the phone and jumped into the Crown Vic. I hadn't told the Pope about Cass, but he told me to walk away from those "girls". I should have known, if there was a hit in his town, they would need his approval. I skidded up onto Los Feliz almost smacking a mini van full of kids in dirty soccer uniforms. The mom flipped me off as I sped past them. I raced around the Griffith Park fountain and slid onto the freeway. Traffic was at a crawl. Half a mile up I could see the flashing lights of emergency vehicles. I pulled over onto the shoulder and punched it. I jumped off at Fletcher and took side streets into Highland Park. The whole wild ride took only twenty minutes, I just hoped that wasn't too long.

Looking through the front window of the panaderia I could see the entire shop, Cass wasn't there. A bell rang over the door when I entered, past a rack of bread and tortillas I found her sitting on the floor with the owner's granddaughter, playing with Angel. Letting out a long sigh, I grabbed her suitcase.

"Let's roll," I said picking up Angel. Cass followed me without question. In the car I told her about my meeting with the Pope.

"You told him I was with you?"

"No, he put it together when I asked about Kelly. My place isn't safe anymore." I said flicking my eyes to the rearview to make sure I wasn't being followed.

"Who ever is after me, now knows you're involved." She said.

"Or they will soon."

"So, I guess you're stuck with me now." She was right, walking away was no longer an option, if it ever truly had been. Sooner or later they would find out I took out three of their soldiers, and they would want me to pay the freight. My only chance was to find them first.

"Where are we going?"she asked as we snaked onto the freeway.

"I have to hook up a place for you to stay."

"Us. A place for us."

"You have to trust me, baby girl, I have things I have to do that I can't do if I'm worrying about keeping you alive. When it hits the fan I have to know you're safe if I'm going to be any good to either of us." She didn't like it, but she knew all the cute pouts and coy eyes weren't going to change my mind.

I parked behind Club Xtasy. "Is this where Kelly worked?"

"That's the place."

"Kind of shabby."

"It's alright." I left Cass in the car and went inside. Piper was sitting in a booth with a man in a baseball cap and a tee-shirt that proclaimed he was a party animal. Piper's face formed a broad grin when she saw me approach. "Hey buddy, wait your turn, I'm talking to the lady," the guy said.

"I'm not your buddy, pal. I'm with the health department and this 'Lady' has tested positive." The guy instantly took his arm off Piper. "Come with me miss," I said. Piper stood up and stalked me into the back.

"You crazy bastard, he was good for sixty bucks,

minimum." Her eyes were sparking with mirth.

"I need you to slip out the back and take a friend of mine to your house."

"Can't do it sweet cheeks, this is my big night. And momma needs to make rent."

"I'm jammed up Piper. I really need this."

"And I look like a pushover, is that it?" she said, crossing her arms over her chest, pressing her breasts together creating a mountain of cleavage. It was a power move, half defiance, half seduction, designed to confuse the poor male brain into doing her will.

"I don't have any options here," I said honestly.

"You sleep in my bed but you won't fuck me, you leave town and you don't call. Now you want me to leave my money night to help a friend of yours. When did we get married?"

"Fuck it, you're right. I'm out of line. I'm sorry I asked," I said and started to turn away.

"Slow down, big guy. Have I ever refused you anything, have I?" Leaning up she gave me an almost sweet peck on the cheek. "There's something about you, I don't know what it is, but you got me. Now let's go before I change my mind and have Turaj kick your ass out of here." That image was enough to make me smirk. Grabbing her bag from the dressing room locker we went out the back door, then down the thin staircase and into the parking lot. Piper stopped cold at the foot of the stairs.

Across the parking lot she saw my car with a pair of

clearly female legs hanging out of the window. Piper spun on me, her face hardening, "You want me to take in your strumpet, you got some balls Moses."

"It ain't like that Piper, she's a friend, and she's in trouble," I said.

"A friend you're fucking? Huh, Mo?"

"No baby doll, I ain't fucking anyone. Getting fucked pretty hard." I shot her a feeble wink. She stared hard at me for a long moment, then a smile crept onto her face and I knew I was home free.

"God damn you, Mo." Hooking her arm into mine we strolled through the parked cars to the Crown Vic. Cass sat up, looking at Piper and her arm on me, it was subtle but I could see her eyes flicking back and forth.

"Piper, this is Cass, she needs looking after," I said. Piper studied Cass' face with growing shock.

"Kelly?" she whispered.

"Her sister," I said.

"It's like looking at a ghost."

"I'm not a ghost. Ok?" Cass said climbing out. "This your girlfriend?" she looked Piper up and down. I was saved from answering by Angel jumping out of the car and bouncing up to Piper.

"No, no no no, Mo! I told you how I feel about dogs," she said.

"Just one night, that's all I'm asking," I said, flashing

some uneven teeth.

"Fine, whatever. But if it pees on my carpet I'm making it into slippers. That's right little fur ball welcome to Cruella DeVil land." Whoever said all women loved puppies had never met Piper. Getting Cass into Piper's powder blue '65 Ford Falcon I sat Angel on her lap and told her to keep the pup out of trouble. As they drove away, Cass watched me through the window. Somewhere in her heart she believed every goodbye might turn out to be permanent.

When I got back to Highland Park the streets were quiet. I parked around the corner from my house, jumped the fence and entered through the back door. With my .45 in hand I moved through the kitchen, bedroom, bathroom and then the living room. Content that I was alone I pushed my club chair into a corner. From this position I could cover the front door and the kitchen. I left the lights out, waiting with the Mossberg riot gun on my lap. Patience was never my long suit, I would rather rush forward then lay in wait. I could hear the treads on every car as they rolled past along the pavement. Around midnight the neighborhood dogs began to bark, first one then joined by many. I tensed, ready for the door to fly open. One of the dogs let out a painful yap. A slight odor of a skunk drifted through the window. Somewhere down the block a dog had been sprayed. I drifted off sometime after midnight.

In my dream, Cass and I are living in a house on a Mexican beach. She is dressed in a flowing kimono with

*gold braid dragons climbing up her breasts. She is feeding
me slices of mango while we watch Angel playing in the
surf. She kisses the back of my neck. Someone is knocking
at our door. I hope they will go away.*

I was awake in time to hear the second knock. The
street light glowed through my shabby curtains, silhouetting
a hulking man on my front porch. I hefted the shot gun to
my shoulder and aimed at the door. I could hear the scratch
of metal against wood. A quick crack and the door jamb
gave way as the door popped open. Two shadowy men
stood outlined against the streetlight. I held my breath.
They moved into the dark room, pulling the door closed
behind them. I racked a shell into the shot gun and watched
their eyes pop.

"Sorry, wrong house," a beefy man in a jogging suit
said.

"Right house, wrong day." I aimed at his gut. His
buddy wore pressed jeans and an argyle sweater vest.
"Kick your guns over here, before I get nervous and bad
things start to happen." They weighed their odds and came
up short. They might have been able to drop me, but one of
them was going to lose his life in the transaction. Slowly
they dropped their pistols and kicked them over in my
direction. Sweater boy kicked short so the chrome
automatic lay on the hardwood between us. He was a leap
away from it. Getting up I kicked the gun under my sofa.

"Now comes the real fun part," I said, drifting the
shotgun barrel from one to the other for emphasis, "the part
where I ask you who sent you, and you play it tough, so I
start blowing off parts of your body. And one of you plays
it real tough so I kill him and the other of you looks down at

his missing leg and ruined arm and decides it can still get worse so he talks." If I was getting through to them it wasn't clear from their black eyes. "Now we can skip all that messy bullshit, or I can go to work. Honestly I don't give a fuck which way you want to play it." I heard a rush of wind behind me, and felt the thud of a black jack hitting the base of my skull. The world went sideways. My knees buckled and I fell, I waited for the impact of the floor but I just kept falling into a big black hole.

CHAPTER 12

Tumble and twist, drifting down through oblivion. No guilt for those I'd hurt. No guilt for those I couldn't save, just rich warm black rushing past... Memory was a foggy distant thought lost in the haze...There was something I was supposed to do but it was all behind me now, lost... out of the black cotton came a growing pain. A pin point at first, then it sped at me, trying to catch me like a cop car in hot pursuit. Bam! My head exploded into sixteen different colors. I could feel pain so I wasn't dead. Pain equals life, it's a shitty conclusion to a fucked equation but there it was. My eyes fluttered and rolled open only to find more darkness surrounding me. My arms were pinned behind my back and bound by duct tape, ghetto cuffs also taped my ankles together. My rather large frame had been crumpled and folded nastily into a small dark space. My tiny prison bumped and rumbled with a rhythm I couldn't place but knew was familiar. I tried to sit up and hit my head on padded sheet metal inches above me. It snapped into focus, I was in a car trunk, and that was a freeway rumbling beneath me. Muffled rap music thumped from the interior, keeping beat with my pounding brain. I was being taken for a ride, as they say in the gangster flicks. Only these were real gangsters and it wasn't going to end with a pretty fade-out or the cops rolling to the rescue. Dumb bastard, I'd let them take me and now I was going to pay big. Odds were these were the same punks, or ones like them, who had done Kelly. And now it was my turn to go down ugly. One more useless corpse. One more unsolved murder for Lowrie. And like a big death machine they got to keep rolling along, unthinking and unstoppable. Fuck them. I squirmed onto my back. The speed shifted, we were pulling off the freeway. With every bit of strength I had I kicked at the side of the trunk. "What the hell!" came from the cab of the car. I kept kicking, it was an outside shot, but maybe someone on the street would hear me. Suddenly the car ground to a stop. I heard the doors open and kept on kicking like my life depended on it, which it did.

The trunk popped up, flooding me in the yellow light of a street lamp. The beefy guy in a jogging suit jumped in on top of me. I flailed and tried to fight, but with my hands behind my back and legs jammed in I couldn't have bested a crippled midget. The thug grabbed my hair, covering my face with a sweet smelling rag. I twitched and jerked but couldn't get free. When I could no longer hold my breath I inhaled... The world blurred, growing soft at its edges. The pain in my head evaporated into a descending fog and I was lost once again to the darkness.

From a great distance I could smell someone barbecuing. A searing pain came with consciousness. A thin cigar tip pressed into my chest. The burning I smelled was me. A scream crawled its way out of my throat.

"I'm sorry, did that hurt you?" The preppy boy in his argyle was kneeling down pressing the ember into my flesh. Lifting the cigar to his lips he sucked in, the tip glowed red. He jabbed the ember back down. I clenched my jaw so tight I almost broke a molar. I squashed the building scream down into my gut and forced a smile. "Tough it all you want, sooner or later you'll beg to talk."

"You haven't asked him any questions." An older man in an immaculate suit moved into view. "What do you expect him to talk about, the weather perhaps?"

"He knows what we want, trust me he knows."

"Please, go see if you can find me a chair. I'll have a little chat with Mr. McGuire." Following orders, sweater boy stood up. He gave me a quick loafer to the ribs and walked away chuckling at my torn gasp.

"This is building up to be a very long night. Now I'm sure you have no desire to prolong this little dance, so why don't you tell me where the girl is."

"What girl?" I wheezed.

"Please, tell me or not, but don't infer I'm stupid."

"Perish the thought mother fucker!" I said. His kick landed hard to the side of my head. I rolled away, trying to protect myself from the next blow. Instead I heard him stepping out of the room and down what sounded like wooden stairs. Rolling over, I scanned my surroundings. I was in a small bare room, through grease streaked windows I could make out the tower of the downtown train yard. From the view I could tell we were on the second floor, probably of a warehouse, not that this information did me a damn bit of good.

The two younger grease-balls clattered into the room dragging an office chair and a gym bag. While the man in the running suit lifted me into the chair his young friend opened the bag lifting out a cordless drill.

"Hey, you ever see that show, This Old House?" sweater asked his partner.

"Yeah that Bob Villa is one smart wop. He must've saved me a grand around the house, you know, doing fix it myself stuff."

"You think they'd want to do a show on me and my use of tools?" he said fitting a drill bit into the head and keying it down. "You want to pick which leg I start on?" he asked me with a stupid smile. I locked my jaw and grinned up at him. "Ok, left it is." He revved the drill up several times like a street racer getting ready to launch. With a slow arc, he moved the spinning steel down into my thigh. As the bit dug into my flesh I jerked my legs up knocking the drill from his hand. I kicked out at his chest with a strength meant to kill. Instead of knocking him over the force sent me speeding backwards on the chair's castors. They both looked shocked and amazed by what they saw next. I felt my back slam into something solid that gave way with the sound of glass breaking. I tilted violently back and saw the stars above as I fell through the night. Wood snapped against my back shattering the chair as I landed on a pile of discarded pallets, breaking their cross braces like they were matchsticks. A sharp spear of broken board pierced my leg.

Pieces of the broken window rained down around

me. Somewhere above me the greaseballs were screaming. The familiar pop of small arms fire echoed just before the wood around me started to splinter from wild rounds. I had darkness on my side. But even idiots get lucky sometimes. Reaching out behind my back I found a long piece of glass and sawed at the tape binding my wrists. The glass cut my fingers but it also sliced off the duct tape. Freeing my ankles, I pulled the wooden spear from my leg and ran limping for the cyclone fence surrounding the warehouse.

A square of light spilled out of the warehouse as the door slid up and three silhouettes charged out. I jumped onto the fence and started to climb. As I hit the top a pistol cracked and a bullet whizzed past my head. I pulled myself up and over, falling hard on the other side. I was on a thin strip of pavement on the bank of the LA River.

The dark forms hit the fence as I rolled down the embankment, bouncing over the moss slick cement I splashed down into the river. Above me the mob boys topped the fence. Pulling myself up I fought the current and ran for cover. I lost my footing on the rocks, went down, got up and kept going. I pulled myself onto a small sand island covered in bamboo and scrub brush. Hunkering down in the brush I lay silently. Past the branches I could see Sweater Boy and Running Suit on the top of the bank looking down. They walked back and forth, searching. After several long painful minutes they turned and disappeared back towards the warehouse.

I lay still for another half an hour just to be sure. I stayed in the river working my way north for a couple of miles before moving my way up the bank. I was wet and cold, my body ached and my left leg was having trouble holding my weight. I pulled myself up onto the street. I was in frog town, a small Latin neighborhood tucked between Riverside Drive and the River. Luckily this is LA, where people are used to seeing torn and battered homeless people, a town full of averted eyes and empty hands. I stumbled into a gas station on Fletcher. I thought I would call Piper, but I didn't know her number. A gang-banger in a slammed Impala looked me over while he filled his tank. "You don't look too good, ese," he said.

"I've been shot at, beat up, burnt, drilled and almost drowned. So whatever you're going to do, just get to it and put me out of my misery." I slid down to sit on the pavement.

"Shit, homes, what do I look like to you? I ain't going to rob you. I thought you was a drunk. I was going to take you to a meeting." He leaned down to look me over. "You need to have a doctor look at that leg, homes."

"No doctors."

"Too many questions, eh, ese? Too many cops at the ER?" Leaning down he started to lift me up.

"What the..." I tried to resist but his grip on my shoulders was massive. This man was prison buff and I was weak as a wet kitten. Looking down at the arm that clamped on to me I saw his history in prison ink. Tattoos ran all the way up under his muscle shirt. Pancho Villa stood on his arm next to the Virgin de Guadalupe, in blue ink a low rider rolled and a sad man stood locked behind bars... On his shoulder hands intertwined in prayer while a dove flew from them up into his tee-shirt. Helping me walk he led me to his Impala.

"Why are you doing this?"

"Ese, I leave your ass out here, the piranhas will pick your bones clean in two minutes flat." The car doors had been shaved and filled leaving a clean line with no apparent way of entry. He clicked a remote and the door opened with a deep pneumatic whoosh. It was all rich brown tuck and roll, I could see the marks my muddy pants were tracking onto the seats as I sunk in.

"Sorry," I said looking down at my boots on the shag carpet.

"Relax, this is only stuff, it cleans," he said and meant it. "Now where am I taking you?" I told him a cross street near Piper's place. As we drove he glanced over at me. "I been where you are, guns in my face, guns in my hand. Done a lot of shit I'm not proud of loco, but you don't have to keep running so hard. There's an easier softer way."

"Yeah? Move to Jamaica and forget this crap ever happened?" I said.

"No, you'd just make a mess there, trust me I tried pulling a geographic," he said sliding smoothly though traffic. "Ten years ago I was doing a stint up at Pelican Bay, best thing ever happened to me."

"Main line, huh?"

"Yeah, crazy right? I met this old time drunk, he showed me a new way to live. You ever hear of the Big Book?" he asked.

"You think I'm a drunk?"

"Normies don't get into the kind of shit we do, ese, know what I mean?" he said with a slight smile.

"Look pal, I don't need a fucking meeting unless it's a Psycho-mob-hit-men-are-trying-to-kill-me Anonymous meeting, you got one of those?" I said.

"Not yet," he said with a laugh, "but this is LA so who knows, we got every other kind of meeting, shit I heard they even have one for owners of co-dependent pets. Look, straight up, if I'm wrong no problem. But if not, I'll save you a seat, down front."

I had him pull up two blocks away from Piper's place, sure he seemed on the up and up, but trust no one fully and you don't get burned fully. As I got out he passed me a simple card with his name and phone number, he said to call if I ever needed to talk or whatever, and then with the deep rumble of glass packs he motored off down the street. I started up to a stranger's house until he was around the corner, then backtracked to the sidewalk and stumbled up to Piper's. Every step took my full concentration. Don't fall or you may never get up again.

Slipping into a warm bath I felt a million years old. Piper sat on the lip of the tub, a worried expression on her face. She had almost bit my head off for waking her, but when she saw my condition she kicked into mother hen mode. "Are you sure you don't want to go to the emergency room?"

"Be the first place they'd look. First place I'd look." She washed away the dirt from around the cuts, and bathed them in hydrogen peroxide. Cass had been asleep on the couch when I came in.

"What the hell have you gotten yourself into?" Piper asked, scrubbing a bit rougher than necessary.

"Same old, same old," I said, trying not to wince too bad.

"Bullshit, what has that girl got you tied into?"

"You don't want to know about this one, sweetheart, trust me. When it's cleaned up I'll tell you all there is, but 'til then forget you ever saw her. Got it?" I looked into her deep green eyes holding them, letting her see into mine, past the shield and into the real danger of the situation. After a moment, she gave me a slow blink of agreement.

"You're the boss, Mo."

"That's all I want to hear."

"That little girl is in love with you," Piper said as she started to bandage my leg.

"That little girl is very confused."

"She'd have to be, to be in love with a tore up old man like you," she said with a deep throaty chuckle. "Now let's finish getting your tired ass patched up and in bed. Momma still needs her beauty rest." She helped me into her bed and lay down beside me.

"I'm sorry I brought this to your door..." I said, starting to fade.

"What the hell are friends for? If not to complicate your life, now shhhh." Piper was gently stroking my back as I finally let go and drifted off.

I'm on the beach in Mexico, Cass is splashing in the surf. Sun dances on the water. The sand is cool and soft on my back. For miles the beach is empty, sand dunes run up against a jungle. Palm trees burn green. Cass drops down beside me, her warm lips press against my chest. She softly kisses her way down my belly...

My eyes drifted open, Piper's blackout curtains kept the room in complete darkness. Cass lay on top of me. She was naked and her smooth skin pressed down against me. Her supple body felt warm and comforting. She gently placed her soft full lips on mine. Her hair smelled of bleach and spring rain as it brushed across my face. Her small tongue darted into my mouth. I ran my tongue across her tiny teeth, she bit it playfully then invited me into her mouth. I had forgotten how good a kiss could feel. Girls in my world would lap dance a man to orgasm but never kiss him, even prostitutes drew the line there, that was too personal an act to sell. Lost in her lips I couldn't remember the last time I had kissed a girl. Running my hands through her hair I pulled her face off of mine.

"I know you want me," she said.

"No question about it, but..."

"You still don't get it. I could have any man I want, and I choose you." Whatever else I had to say was lost in her kisses. Logic lost the battle against hunger. In the dark I explored her body like a blind man. My hands felt rough on her supple flesh as I ran my fingers down her back, feeling every ridge and valley of her finely toned muscles. I tapped my fingertips down her vertebrae until I came to the tip of her tail bone. Cupping her succulent tush, pulling her tighter into me, the blood rushed out of my brain in a steady exodus down south. Licking small strokes around her areola, I sucked her nipple into my mouth and felt her swelling with desire. Sitting up, she straddled me, her thigh hit my wounded leg. Hot pain roared up.

"Oh baby, I'm sorry," she said with real concern. "Do you want me to stop?"

"No, never." I clenched my jaw and let the pain subside. Rising up onto her knees, she wrapped her fingers around my penis and led me inside her. Lowering herself slowly down onto me she let out a small gasp, paused and then took in a little more.

Gently rocking back and forth she settled all the way down on me. Gripping her hips I found she was light enough for me to lift her up off the bed, then pull her back down onto me. Wildly she pressed down in a quickening rhythm. "Come on Baby," she called out, willing me to come. She pressed her wondrous body against mine until I could hold back no more. In a rush of release I roared and whimpered, filling the room with my strangled animal sounds.

Leaning down she brushed tears from my face. Tears I didn't even know I'd cried. "Now you're mine," she said, kissing my tears. I couldn't stop the tears from flowing, pulling my head into her chest she stroked my hair and let me cry. The weight of my life rushed through me, all that I had lost, all that I had never had. I lay in the darkness, unprotected and safe.

CHAPTER 13

"You're a pig," Piper said. I was dressed and drinking a cup of coffee in her breakfast nook with Angel curled up at my feet when she came in. From the back of the house I could hear Cass in the shower. "You fucked that little girl. In my bed. Don't you have any shame?"

"I guess not," I shrugged, not able to meet her eyes.

"God damn it, Moses, she's a baby. She can't even legally drink yet. What the fuck are you thinking?" Her eyes bore into me, killing the glow of the morning.

"I wasn't, it just happened." She was correct, I had broken a cardinal rule; don't eat the young.

"No, flat tires, runs in my stocking, those are things that happen. This you did. So you finally got to fuck Kelly, or at least her proxy. So how was it? Everything you dreamed of or just another lay?"

"Come on, Piper."

"Does little miss fine ass know you like to dry hump me when you're horny?"

"I need a ride to my car," I said.

"Fine." She shook her head and picked up her keys off the table. We left without another word, what could I say. I was sorry I hadn't lived up to some picture Piper had of me? I was just another guy like all the others?

In Highland Park Piper dropped me off around the block from my house. "I want her and that dog out of my place by the time I get off tonight," she said.

"Done." Somehow I'd stumbled over a line she had drawn in the sand. She drove off without looking back. Limping around the corner of my street I spotted a Lincoln Town parked in front of my house. No goons leaned on the hood with tommy guns waiting for me, they were probably in my house frying eggs and playing Frank Sinatra on my stereo. Keeping low I slid into the passenger side of the Crown Vic. Purring it to life I drove off like just another neighbor going off to work, thankful that out of a paranoid habit I always parked two doors down. I drove over to York Boulevard to a small clinic. Dr. Pikia, a compact older woman with a thick Indian accent, ran it. She accepted cash, and never asked too many questions. I was sitting on the table with my pants down around my ankles as Dr Pikia unceremoniously ripped off the blood soaked gauze bandage Piper had put on my thigh, taking the fresh scab and a patch of hair with it. The gash from the wood spike was angry and oozing blood. She swabbed it out with iodine, then cleaned the wound left by the drill bit. I closed my eyes fighting to think of anything else. Cass' fine body filled my head.

"You will be needing stitches," the doctor told me, injecting a syringe full of Novocain into my leg. With numb detachment I watched the needle thread my flesh wondering how many times I had sat here or in another room getting myself patched back together. Rolling on my side, she spiked my rump with a tetanus shot and told me to keep the wounds clean and come back in two weeks. We both knew I wouldn't be back unless I got ripped up again, I knew how to take out my own stitches.

Cass and Angel greeted me at Piper's door. Cass started to give me a big kiss but I pulled away. Crouching down I let Angel lick my face and ears.

"I came out of the shower and you were gone," Cass said, trying to get a read on my mood.

"I had to get stitched up."

"Do we have to have that awkward moment where we pretend we didn't make love?"

I couldn't answer her. My mind and groin had very different opinions on what my next move should be.

"Piper told me to watch my step with you, said I could trust you with my life but not my heart."

"She could be right."

"She's jealous."

"No, she's looking out for you. Now get your things and let's roll." When she left the room I called Helen and told her I needed a favor.

"You want me to watch Angel? Bruiser missed her

at the park this morning. That fat slob laid around pining for her."

"It's bigger than that, can I come over?" She gave me her address in Silverlake. I started to leave Piper a note but could think of nothing worth saying. I loaded my strange little crew into the Crown Vic and purred across town. Cass slid across the seat, slipping her head under my arm. Angel wanted to be in the middle of the affection, she crawled onto Cass' lap and put her head on mine.

"I have to go back to San Francisco, take the war to them."

"Good, it's time we made them pay."

"Baby girl, this whole deal is about to go sideways. And I don't want you on board when the wheels come off."

"You're dumping me again?" she said quietly. "Is this about this morning, didn't you like me?"

"It sure as hell isn't that. I have to put you in a safe place, I told you I can't do what I have to and worry about you at the same time."

"I can take care of myself. I can help you."

"No, look, you're the only hold card I got. They find you, and I'm screwed."

"I'm not leaving your side," she said, setting her jaw.

"You don't have a choice. I'm not taking you."

"I'll follow you."

"Look, bitch, you have got us both on the fucking

chopping block," I spat out. Angel crawled onto the floor to get away from my rage.

"You love me, I know it." Cass searched my eyes, seeking the truth beneath my words.

"I don't know what I feel. Right now, I'm going to make this shit right. Then we'll see what we see."

"And if you don't come back?"

"Then pack your bags and hit the border."

"I'm your girl. Tell me I'm your girl." Her eyes pleaded, "Tell me."

"You're my girl," I said and I might have meant it.

"Then I'll do what you say. But if you die on me I'll haunt your ass into the next life. I'll go to New Orleans and have the chicken man turn you into a zombie. So you better not die."

"That's one hell of a threat," I said with a laugh.

"Laugh if you want, but I'll do it."

"I bet you would." Nuzzling her head into my chest we drove on. She was an amazing girl, a mixture of contradictions. Hard and soft, old and young, hot and cold. She touched me deep down inside, maybe I could live up to the man she thought I was, maybe when this was over I could take her down to old Mexico, rent a house on the beach and find out who we were without the threat of death hanging over us.

Helen lived in a terraced house in the steep hills

overlooking the reservoir, it was designed by Frank Lloyd Wright with classic flat roof lines, clean boxes stacked into the hillside. When Helen opened the door, Bruiser bounded past her and me, dropping to his forepaws he barked at Angel, egging her into a game of chase. Helen let out a high whistle and Bruiser bounced into the house followed by Angel. When I introduced her to Cass Helen stared at her face.

"She's Kelly's sister," I told her.

"No, really? You look more like Kelly, than Kelly did. We were good friends, I miss her too much for words."

"She wrote me about you, she loved talking to you," Cass said, I knew she was lying but it lit Helen's face up, so I let it pass.

"Can I get you two some coffee, the goddess caffeine is my one true love."

"No, listen, some really bad men are after Cass. I need a safe house for her until I can straighten it out. I know it's a lot to ask."

"What sort of bad men? Moses?"

"Bad enough."

"The less I know, the better, is that it? What the heck, is this one of my screenplays come to life?"

"I won't be any bother, I promise," Cass said, with a coy smile that almost sent Helen giggling.

"Of course you won't. I have a guest room I never

use and I'm on hiatus so I can use the distraction. But it's all so mysterious, you sure you don't want to tell me more, Moses, so I don't have to drag it out of this sweet girl?"

"Let it lay, and when it's all over, I'll tell you about it," I said.

"Every gory detail."

"You got it." Cass followed me out to the car for her suitcase. Wrapping her arms around my waist she hugged her head to my chest. I could feel her trembling in my arms. Leaning down, my lips met hers, we stood there kissing, as the sun sparkled on the water below us. Pulling myself away from her I kissed her forehead, got in and drove away. In the rearview mirror I could see her standing in the street, shoulders slumped, she stood there until I rounded the corner. I had to shake her from my head. No room for soft memories where I was going.

On Hillcrest I pulled into a liquor store and bought a pint of Seagram's and a bottle of ginger ale. In the car I mixed a drink and pulled my whites stash out from under the seat. I needed the jangle and the edge, I needed to wash Cass from my mind. I wanted to run back to her, fall into her arms, make love until dawn and then drink rich coffee while we watched the dogs play. But that was a dream. And I had work to do.

I hit the Pony Express gun shop just before closing. They were out in the sweaty end of the valley, it was a large shop with stuffed dead animals hung across the ceiling. They supplied most of the black powder shooters and re-enactors, folks who liked to dress up as cowboys and play shoot 'em up. I bought a box of frangible slugs for my .45.

They were designed to act like a hollow point while still loading smoothly into an automatic. Under the soft copper casing were four steel balls that split out at impact leaving a deep and wide ugly entry wound. Air marshals and city cops used them because they didn't over-penetrate, they hit like a fist but didn't come out the back to kill the innocent. I also bought a length of cannon fuse. From my trunk I took a red highway flare and jammed the fuse into its end. Acme couldn't have made a better fake stick of dynamite. Crawling back on the freeway I headed for Glendale.

I found the same ugly brown apartment building, pausing at the door I could hear the thump of rap music. I knocked and waited. After a moment the big Armenian opened the door, he didn't fight me this time, he stepped back and let me enter. The skinny boy in the cast was sitting on his sofa watching rap videos. "What the hell do you want now?" he squeaked. I dismissed him with a glance and focused on the big guy.

"You want some work?" I said, the big boy shrugged, noncommittal. "I need back up, pays a hundred. You interested?"

"Gregor does what I say," the skinny boy said.

"That true?" I said to the big boy, still not even looking at the punk on the sofa. Gregor shook his head. Grabbing his coat off the back of a chair he followed me out.

"You're a real chatterbox, aren't you?" I said, as we drove down Colorado. He shrugged looking out the window impassively. A layer of baby fat surrounded his face giving him a sweet look, his thick black hair was buzzed to a fine fur. The only thing really scary about him was his size and the dull look in his eyes that told you he just didn't care how things turned out.

"You packing?" I asked, he looked at me like that was the stupidest question he had heard in years. From under his shirt he pulled a matte black 9 mm with a squared trigger guard and a lanyard ring at the base of the grip. It looked more like a tool than the pimped out penis extensions most baby gangsters carry. "What's that, Russian?"

He shook his head like I was an idiot and handed me the piece. It was Czech, a CZ75. The kid knew his guns I'd give him that even if he wasn't a sparkling conversationalist. In Highland Park my street was quiet. The Lincoln was still parked down the block. Moving in the shadows I checked out their car, it was empty. Crawling along the hedge I slipped onto my porch. A dim light glowed behind the curtains. Slowly I slipped my key into the lock aware of every click. Striking a match I lit the fuse, it burst into sparks. Popping the door open I tossed the red flare into the room, and pulled the door closed. I waited for a second then burst in sweeping the room with my .45. On the living room floor two mob boys were diving for the flare. They looked up at me stunned. From the kitchen I heard the deep thud of a fist on flesh. The older well dressed thug tumbled into the room and went down. Gregor followed him in, leveling his CZ at the man's face. Moving between the other two I stepped on the fuse, crushing it out.

"Are you fucking nuts?" Jogging suit said.

"Yes, as a matter of fact I am. Guns on the floor

boys, before I have to make a mess I won't be able to explain to my maid."

"Do you have any idea who we are?" the sweater boy said, standing up into my face. A backhand sent him back down. "Oh, you're a dead man. I'm talking to a dead man."

"Shut up." The older well dressed man said, wiping a spot of blood off his lip onto a monogrammed handkerchief. The younger man closed his mouth, shooting me daggers with his eyes. "Now, let's see if there is a way we can all walk out of here with our heads held high. What do you say, Mr. McGuire?"

"That, or I kill you all and call it a day well spent."

"Obviously that remains a viable option, however, it will only lead to more destruction down the road. So let's say we put that option to the side for the moment, you can always pick it back up, but for the moment let's look down other avenues," he said as cool as a banker working out a loan.

"Do you like scotch?" I said.

"Single malt?"

"Of course." As an afterthought I bent to pull the sweater boy up, he smiled like I was finally showing him his due respect. Pistoning my arms I propelled him across the room backward. Stumbling over the coffee table he fell sideways onto the floor again. "Kill him first," I said to Gregor and left him covering the two young thugs, leading the suit man into the kitchen. "Ice?" I said, pulling down my McCallans.

"That would be a crime," he said. I poured us each a glass and sat down.

"You have a name?"

"Call me Leo."

"Is that your name?"

"It will do." He was around fifty with the body of a man who likes to keep in shape, his black suit hung beautifully, hand tailored I suspected. There was nothing off the rack about this man. "As I see it, you have accidentally stepped into a rather large bear trap. Now as for options, the cleanest would be for you to give us the girl. We part friends and all this becomes a sad but soon forgotten incident in your life." Looking at me he swirled the scotch around in the glass, then took a small sip. "This truly is fine scotch." I met his gaze, scratching my chin with the barrel of my .45.

"Twice, you and those two clowns have come after me, and twice I've handed you your ass. Now I'm supposed to wet myself 'cause you may or may not be connected. I'm not wearing a skirt, so don't treat me like your bitch."

"I meant no disrespect. And you could kill us, but it would solve nothing, and I think you know that." Again he sipped the scotch, closing his eyes he let it drift over his tongue.

"You want a deal? Tell me who your boss is and maybe I let you and Heckle and Jeckle walk. Or I let my boy go to work on them, see who talks first."

"My employer is not germane to this conversation. I think you'll be surprised by the effort we will go to protect his confidence."

"Do you care who I kill first?" I said, my blood starting to rise.

"Not really," he said, taking another sip. Rearing up, I toppled the table, sending the glasses smashing into the wall. Swinging the gun across his face he started to bleed but the calm never left his eyes.

"I'm through talking to errand boys. Collect your garbage and get out. Tell your boss, if he wants the girl he'll have to meet with me himself. And if he sends any more of you cheap suited bastards after me, I'll send them back in a box."

"A fair request, I don't think it will be met with much generosity, though."

"I don't give a rat's ass what you think. Tell him I'll be at The Barbary Coast in two days. I see any goons and the girl goes to the feds. Let them straighten this shit out."

"You seem destined to cut your life short. And all over a pretty face."

"Look around, you see anything here worth living for? Now get." Collecting their guns Gregor and I pushed them out the door. I watched out the window until the Lincoln was gone. Gregor smiled for the first time.

"That was fun," he said, just when I was starting to assume he was mute.

"Come on, I got one more cage to rattle before the

night is over." Tossing some spare clothes in a bag we headed across town.

It was ten thirty when I parked in the loading zone in front of Figueroa's. I left Gregor in the car and told him to keep his face in the shadows. Crunching four more whites I placed a roll of quarters into my fist and moved into the restaurant, I was rolling on pure instinct now playing it one move at time and seeing where it led. Eddie the Mechanic stepped up to block my advance. Before he could open his mouth I swung my weighted fist up into his jaw. His head snapped back, I crossed with a left that sent him spinning. He took a chair and small table down with him when he fell. I pulled a revolver from under his arm and slipped it into my belt.

"Eddie still alive?" Don Gallico's box squawked. He looked only mildly shocked when I sat at his table.

"I didn't check."

"Oh, Moses, you really have lost the will to live."

"Got that right, old man. The punks you set on me fucked up."

"Who are we talking about?"

"This is bullshit. Look out that window, see that man in my car? See him?" Gallico flicked his eyes past me to the widow then back to me. "He's a real sick person. I don't walk out of here, then he fades into the night. And one by one he takes your people off the count."

"You dumb Mic bastard. You dare threaten me?"

His face was dead still but I could see the veins in his neck popping, fighting for sounds his ravaged vocal cords could never produce. "You are a dead man."

"I keep hearing that. Just wish I gave a rat's ass. Look," I said, trying to be reasonable, "you let some boys try to kill me, they failed, I don't care, I know it's nothing personal. Damn it Sir, I've known you since I was a kid. I've never done you wrong. My ass is up against a wall. I don't want more blood spilled, don't think you do either. But we both know we'll do what it takes." He looked at me for a long moment then let out a sad sigh.

"Mickey Mouse Mafia, that's what they call us behind my back. LA gets no respect from New York and Chicago. They ask me to allow these punks into my city, I don't have any options but to say yes or go to mattresses in a war I can't win."

"Who's hunting me?"

"A San Francisco crew, big earners in stock scams… I don't know what you did to them but they want you and the girl dead."

"Who's the boss?"

"Jeffery Sabatini, a college man, he's got more degrees than a rectal thermometer." He chuckled at his own joke.

"Can I get a sit down with him?"

"Not in a million years. He wants you dead, he might agree to a sit down but it won't be one you walk away from. Not like the old days, when I was coming up we had honor. You went for a sit down, you went in light and came out alive. Sure they might clip you the next day, but the tradition of the sit down was respected. You hungry, you want a slice of pie?"

"I'm fine, sir, thanks."

"First time in thirty years."

"What is?"

"First time you ever refused a slice," he said, like it almost hurt him more than my threats.

"Times change. You got an address on this guy?"

"I know, you didn't hear any of this from me, ah fuck 'em, he lives on a big horse ranch up in Silicon Valley.
"

"Gino Torelli?"

"Never heard of him, truth. If he was one of the boys I'd know. You know if Eddie's still breathing, he'll need to square this with you, sooner or later."

"He knows where to find me. I'll see you around, Sir."

"Sure, kid." He shot me a sad smile and went back to his racing form. I dropped Gregor off in Glendale with a hundred dollars and a promise to call if I had any more fun gigs coming up. I jumped on the 5 and headed north, to the land of microchips and cyber porn kings. But it was about to become the land of blood and retribution or my unmarked grave.

CHAPTER 14

Mediocre scotch and bad speed tilted on the balance beam of my brain as I cruised up the hills, past Magic Mountain amusement park over the Cajon pass and down into the endless straight strip of the central valley. I tried not to think of Cass and was successful for about a hundred miles, but just past Button Willow I tasted her lips on mine. Was she playing me? When this was done if I was alive would she still want to be with me? Then again, what were the odds I'd live to see her again? All my life I'd been used and played by one person or another, that was the way the world worked. Isn't that what love is, two people with mutual need, two people playing each other and through some scam called romance they believe it's selfless?

At midnight, I passed a VW van full of college kids. A bumper sticker in their rear window read WAR IS NOT THE ANSWER. That all depends on the question. But I didn't have to tell them, they were young, with any luck the world wouldn't come along and smash their illusions.

At four AM I hit Palo Alto, I had crunched enough whites to know sleep was a distant dream. I parked on Hamilton and walked up to the Tudor. Moving down the driveway I noticed that the Volvo was gone. I let myself in the back door, the house was dark. At the top of the stairs I opened a door into a kid's room, all the toys were gone the beds had been stripped. In the beam of my Maglite the walls glowed with a bright field of sunflowers. Stars and a smiling moon were painted on the ceiling, it was every child's dream bedroom, but it was lacking any sign of children. Closing the door I tried not to think about the kids who had slept in that room. The master bedroom was large, in a carved oak bed the ponytail prick was sleeping, his face bruised and scabbed from our last meeting. I clamped my hand over his nose and mouth, cutting off his air.

He woke choking, his arms flailing. My grip was steel, his eyes bulged. He could feel the end coming near.

"Tell me about Jeffery Sabatini," I said, taking my hand off his face. He gasped for air, clutching his chest. "Whatever patience I had was lost a long way back down the road so start talking."

"I don't know what you want."

"Goodbye," I said and clamped my hand back over his airway. His eyes bugged wildly. "Jeffery Sabatini?" I said, letting him breath.

"I don't know him. Really, I don't."

"Good. Now where is Gino's cut for the last months?"

"No, he'll kill me," he said. My hand hovered over

222

his face. He lost all will to fight. "It's in a safe down in the den. But if you take it, you might as well kill me."

"I care as much about you, as you cared for those little girls, now move." I pulled him out of bed by his ponytail. He had on a pair of Ward Cleaver PJ bottoms that his wife probably bought him for Father's Day.

At the wall safe, he turned to me, for a moment he thought about trying to talk me out of it but one look into my eyes made him turn back to the dial. The steel door opened with a solid chunk. I pushed him out of the way and reached inside, pulling out stacks of banded hundreds.

"Half of that's mine," he said.

"And it's damn nice of you to donate it to a dead girl's sister," I said, and walked out. I knew if I stayed any longer, I might wind up killing the worthless piece of human flesh. I walked out the front door, then moved around the corner of the house and stood outside the den. Through the window the skinny punk slumped down into a leather club chair, he wiped sweat off his pale face. Moving to an ornate roll top desk he unlocked a small drawer and took out a piece of paper, he typed a number into the phone. I moved silently back into the house, hiding in the hall I could hear him. "...yes, it's late! Look, he was just here... yes in my house... No, I did not keep him here, he tried to kill me. I need traveling money and I need it fast...You promised... Screw you... You want me to go public is that what you want? No don't hang up, please I'm dying here... ok... two days, fine." I slipped back into the living room and hid in the shadows. I could hear the clink of a decanter against a glass then a long gulp. The skinny punk plodded upstairs with heavy footsteps. He was at the helm of a fast sinking ship, sharks were circling and I was sprinkling blood into the water. Slipping into the den I used a silver letter opener to jimmy open the small drawer, the phone number was missing but I did find a passbook to a savings account. It held a hundred and fifty grand plus change, it was in his name alone. Searching the desk I found a letter from his wife asking him not to contact her or the children. I was sure she would love to know about his hidden assets. I wrote her address on an envelope, slipped the passbook in, stole a stamp and put it in my pocket. The phone was very sleek and hi-tech, I hit redial and a number popped onto the L.E.D. readout. I scribbled down the number while it rang twice.

"Sanders here," a tired voice said. I could tell he was a cop, they always answered with their last name first.

"Your punk Jerry is dropping fast, I'd get out of the way if I was you."

"Who is this?"

"A concerned citizen."

"McGuire?" I placed his voice, he was the fed who had jammed me up at my place. "Didn't I warn you about walking away, wasn't I crystal clear about what would happen if you kept trampling around on my turf?" I hung up the phone, I was tired of people threatening me. I took the can of black spray paint from the trunk of the Crown Vic and scrawled in tall letters across the side of Jerry's BMW, "PORNOGRAPHER". It was childish but it made me feel a little better. On University Avenue I dropped the envelope into a mailbox, teach him the price of looking the other way while he collected a pay check.

I headed north on the Bayshore Freeway toward San Francisco. I pulled forty thousand dollars out of the safe, Cass and I could make a real border run on that kind of cash. Hole up in San Blas, eat fish fresh out of the sea, make love under the stars on a blanket down on the beach. So what if I had made a promise to Kelly, she hadn't told me one straight word. But I gave my word, all my life that was the only thing I ever had that was worth anything. My word. So I kept driving north. I got a room at the same dive across the street from the Barbary Coast. The junkie desk clerk looked up with dead eyes, if he recognized me it didn't show. I registered under the name Joe Strummer and asked for room two fourteen. I lay on top of the bed, my .45 clutched in my hand. The sky was turning gray when I finally drifted off.

I am running down the dusty Beirut streets. I am hunted from the alleys and windows all around me, I can hear the running of bare feet dashing across the roof tops. Circling, coming closer, on all sides. I keep pushing forward, I know salvation is ahead if I can only make it. I round a corner into an open plaza. On a carved sandstone platform a faceless man in a suit sits on a throne made of human bones, he looks at me laughing. Kelly is sitting at his feet. A chain around her neck leads up to his hand. I raise my M16, taking aim at him, he blinks and the gun turns to dust. He blinks again and the three thugs we killed in the desert rise up out of the dirt. They move slowly toward me...

My yell woke me. The muted afternoon sun was filling the room. Thankfully the fog kept the light soft, my head was splitting. I chased four aspirins with a deep drink of water from the tap then took a long shower. I changed the bandage on my leg, it looked good, no signs of infection.

Walking down to a Best Western I got a room in my name, taking several cards with the phone number. I couldn't remember the last time I ate so I found a small coffee shop and had steak and eggs and a bottomless mug of coffee. I was feeling almost human when I entered Java Enabler, the kid behind the counter's face lit up when he saw me. He looked around, clearly hoping Cass would trail in behind me.

"She's in school today." I answered the question he didn't ask.

"How'd that thing work out?" he said.

"I shut them down."

"Good for you, sir. I used to be proud to be on the cutting edge of geekdom, now I don't know, maybe I'll go back to school and learn to do something with my hands."

"Before you do all that, could you help a Neanderthal out with a problem?"

"Sure, what'd yah need?"

"I have an old war buddy I want to surprise, but he's unlisted." The kid gave me a long grin, I don't know if he knew I was lying or not.

"Hacking into the phone company is illegal," he

said.

"Yes son, it probably is."

"It's also easy. Their firewall is almost a welcome mat." I gave him Jeffery Sabatini's name and had him search the Bay Area, after a flurry of keystrokes he delivered an address on Skyline Boulevard in the mountains above Palo Alto. He smiled like a kid who had just won the spelling bee. I had given him a moment to shine, no need telling him that it would lead to some punk's bloody end. I thanked the kid and promised to send his greetings on to my niece and moved out into the thickening fog. It was time to start dropping some chum in the water and see what I could bring to the surface.

The Barbary Coast was in full gear when I entered. A short chunky black man in a derby with a tall blonde on his arm bumped into me, he looked up and let out a loud laugh. "Boy, you a mountain of a man! 'Scuse my rudeness, but my full attention is on this fine tail here."

"I completely understand," I said, flashing him a grin. At the bar, Jane was busy piling drinks onto a tray for a waiting waitress. I liked watching her, she had on low cut black jeans and a short tee-shirt with "Bitch" in rhinestones written across her chest. She caught me looking at her and her eyes twinkled. Working her way down the bar she joked with the drunks, serving drinks and flirts in equal portions, but from the corner of her eye she was watching me, getting closer and closer. It was a dance and I was her willing partner. Leaning over the bar so I could get an eye full down the cut in her tee-shirt, she looked deep into my eyes.

"For a man who isn't interested, you sure keep coming back.," she said in a quiet voice, meant just for me, I had to lean into her to hear.

"I didn't say I wasn't interested, just said it wasn't going to happen."

"Your eyes tell a very different tale. Now what is a girl to believe?" She ran her thumb down my jaw pausing to tug on my lower lip.

"Be a good girl and get me a drink," I said, fighting the urge to bite her thumb.

"Gimlet, right?"

"Absolutely." She poured the drink, set it down, gave me a wink, then moved back down the bar to service a cocktail waitress. I watched the money-mating dance gyrate around the room scanning for signs of mob boys. Rich men, poor men, old men, young men, hard men, soft men, but none had the look I was hunting for.

"I need you to do me a favor," I said, when Jane had returned from her round of the bar.

"Does it involve two sheets and a lot of sweat?"

"No."

"Then I'm not interested."

"How about as a favor to Benjamin Franklin?" I slid a bill onto the bar top.

"My old dear friend, what does he need?" she said,

scooping up the hundred.

"Some thugs may come looking for me, I need you to put the word out I'm staying at the Best Western down the street." I handed her one of the cards with the phone number on it.

"Is that where I can find you, say, two thirty when I get off?"

"Straight up, girl, nothing would be finer. But there are some very mean men bent on cutting my life short. Last thing I want to see is you getting caught in the crossfire. When the smoke clears, if I'm still standing maybe we'll go down to Chinatown have some dinner, see what happens. But until then, we better keep this bar between us." She took it all in, watching my eyes. I wasn't the first man she'd met who was in trouble, I doubted I'd be the last. Maybe that's what attracted her to me. She set a fresh drink in front of me and smiled.

"This one's on me big guy, and I prefer sushi, so when you get whatever it is you have to get done, done, we have a date. Right?"

"Right." I shot her a wink. She moved back down the bar, shaking her head once and dropping back into her bubbly barmaid character for the drunks. I watched her go and for the hundredth time in the past few days, I wondered why I didn't just let it all slip away, drift off into the night and forget I had ever heard of Kelly and Cass.

The fog had turned to an almost solid wall of white and grey in the streets outside. From the sidewalk I could see the glow of headlights but the cars were murky ghosts.

I moved slowly along, feeling my way to the curb. Out of the mist an arm reached up grabbing my shoulder, pulling me down. I stumbled falling into the fog, landing in the back seat of a car. Before I could react, I was roughly shoved inside and we were rolling. I was sandwiched between Agent Sanders and a large Black fed with a massive shaved head.

"We have a real problem, McGuire," Sanders said. I kept my eyes focused straight ahead fighting to steady my pulse, the illegal .38 in my boot holster weighed heavily on my mind. "We have a tap on some undesirables and it seems your name keeps coming up. In a very short time, you have stirred up quite a hornets' nest. What were their words exactly, Bob?"

"I want that big rat fuck dead, bring me his head on a platter," the bald fed said.

"Yes, that's it. So, I now have a couple of choices. A, let them kill you and hope to catch them in the act. B, cool you out in jail on some trumped up charge. Or C, you tell me everything you know to date and I see if I can keep you alive long enough to be an asset to us."

"How about I say fuck you and get out of the car," I said looking Sanders square in the eyes.

"Tell him what he gets, Bob," Sanders said, enjoying his power.

"You do not collect two hundred dollars, you go directly to jail," Bob said, flashing me a gold tooth. I could feel my blood starting to boil, I wanted to smash their faces in. They had me dangling and they knew it.

"You want to know what I know? I know that every time I turn around somebody is trying to jack me up. I'm just trying to make it home in one piece and it keeps getting harder every step I take. And now you want to take a shot at me? Well come on, let's dance. I've done jail time, it don't scare me. Now the next time I open my mouth it will be to my lawyer. We all clear on that?"

"Pull over," Sanders barked at the driver.

"What are you doing?" Bald Bob asked.

"I'm cutting him loose."

"No, he talks or he goes to jail."

"I'm the agent in charge of this case. I say he walks, then he walks, now pull over." As soon as we stopped he turned on me. "Get out."

He led me into the fog away from the car, out of earshot of the other cops. He leaned against an abandoned storefront plastered with torn posters. "Alright McGuire, look I've read your jacket. You did some dumb things when you were younger, but that was a long time ago. You were in the Root, right?"

"So?"

"I was there, army intel."

"Is that supposed to make us friends? You intel fucks killed more of my buddies than the enemy."

"You don't have to like me, I don't really care if you hate me. But believe this, I am your only hope."

"Then I'm fucked without a kiss."

"If you decide you want to live through this, give me a call." He faded away into the fog. I could hear the car door open and close and then move off down the street. It was a long slow walk back, stopping at street corners to search the mist for street names. At the Best Western I checked for messages from a way too cheerful young clerk. I took the elevator down to the parking lot, slipped out the side door and walked up the block to my little dive of a hotel. It was past midnight and the clerk was snoring away deep in some junkie dream.

From my room I called a number in Glendale, a groggy high-pitched voice answered. "Put Gregor on," I demanded.

"Who the fuck is this?" he squeaked.

"Gregor, now." After a few long moments Gregor picked up.

"Moses?"

"Want to make five large?"

"I'm there."

"May get ugly."

"So?"

CHAPTER 15

I woke at nine, rolled over and started to search for my white wake up pills, only to realize I had left them in the Crown Vic. Maybe it was a sign. My head hurt and my body felt like it had been run through a meat grinder. Between the feds and the mob I was dancing blindfolded in a minefield. Whatever brain cells I had left would need to be in fine tune if I had any hope of seeing my way clear to the DMZ.

I called the Best Western but there were no messages. Slipping my .38 into my pocket I had no desire to put it against my head. There were too many bastards out there who needed the bullet more than I did.

At a convenience store I bought a six-pack of Red Bull and a fistful of ready-pac vitamins. In Golden Gate Park I switched my boots for high-tops, wrapped an ace bandage tight around the gauze to keep my stitches from popping and started to run. After only a mile, I doubled over and threw up in the bushes. I never will understand why tossing your cookies makes you feel so much better.

After another three miles I started to sweat and feel like I might survive the run back to the car.

Showered and dressed I drank another Red Bull and joined the world moving by on the street, firm in the belief that I was on the path to a healthier life. No more speed, no more booze, all I had left to worry about was dying of lead poisoning.

Billy Joe's Pleasure Hole was a supermarket of porno just off O'Farrell street. In the back room men sat in private booths watching small screens and doing who knows what. You'd think the advent of the VCR would have done them in, but they were doing landmark business. The walls were lined with every kind of device imaginable, whatever your kink Billy Joe had you covered. A happy yuppie couple was looking at a huge studded black dildo with glee. Along the back wall I found what I was looking for, a life size love doll. She had realistic features made from latex; her glass eyes stared out at the room vacantly. The price tag touted three entries and fully articulated limbs all for only $1,500.00. Not a bad price considering what my last wife had cost me. I paid the sweaty old man behind the counter and carried my new friend out into the street. She was 5'2" with long curly dark hair and dressed in a baby doll nightgown. We got more than one glare from passers by until I got her into the Crown Vic's trunk.

At a small wig shop on Market I bypassed the rainbow afro and chose a short platinum blonde job. I also picked up a pair of lightly tinted pink glasses and a floral print sun dress.

Gregor was standing outside the airport in a black wool trench coat, a black fedora and sunglasses looking very much the Eastern European thug that he was. He slid in and we rolled off. He didn't ask me what the job was, he didn't ask for his cash, he just watched the road go by. I passed him an envelope, he didn't open it. It disappeared into his coat. "I put two bills in to cover the plane."

"Cool," he said.

"Let's go shopping." I slid along in the now constant Bay-shore freeway traffic. There was a time when the run to the south bay would have taken twenty minutes. But that was long before the microchip mavens turned this whole end of the state into their own personal Mecca. Now Beemers and Saabs lined up to crawl up and down the bay.

Benny King worked out of a pawn shop on Broadway, just down the street from The California Hotel in the heart of Oakland. Stepping around the hookers trolling the sidewalk we moved under the three giant brass balls. The shop was crammed to the rafters with everything from tubas to baby strollers. A cage in the back held the real valuables. Guns and gold, the universal coin of the realm. A half foot of glass kept the clerk protected from his customers.

"Benny around?" I asked the middle-aged egg shaped man in a Grateful Dead tee shirt.

"That depends, dude," the clerk said, picking a loose piece of tobacco from his lip. His fingers were stained yellow from the nicotine.

"Tell him Moses McGuire is here." I dropped seven

hundred dollar bills into the cash troth below the bulletproof glass.

"Sweet, I'll check it out." The clerk scooped up the greenbacks and disappeared past a steel door.

"You have some interesting friends," Gregor said, looking around at the odd collection of junk piled high around us.

"Live long enough, and you accumulate all sorts of connections. Benny's alright, as long as you don't take his word on anything."

After about ten minutes the clerk came and led us through the three locked doors into the back of the shop. The clutter was out front, all for show. The back room was clean and orderly with rifle racks lining the walls and glass cases filled with every imaginable handgun laid out on black velvet.

"Moses mother fucking McGuire, man, I thought you were dead." Benny was a half Black, half Hawaiian, all huge man. The only sign of his aging was the white starting to show in his tight afro and scraggly beard. He had a FFL that allowed him to legally sell firearms. He also did business in straw purchases out of Texas, and took in hot guns off the street. He was connected to Chinese smugglers, Russian mobsters and crack dealers. He never took sides, and always made a profit. "Who's the mug?" He nodded his head towards Gregor.

"Terror of the Eastern Block. Gregor, shake hands with a living legend."

"Too young to be a partner," Benny said, taking

Gregor's hand, searching his face. "You taking in trainees Moses?"

"No, he carries his own weight."

"Bet he does." Benny finally let go of Gregor's hand and turned back to me. "Now what can I do you for, got a new shipment from Norinco, clean AK's."

"CZ75," Gregor said.

"Washed if you got it," I said.

"Sure, no problemo, got one out of Alabama just burned the numbers off. But CZ ain't cheap. Sure you don't want a Desert Eagle. Same gun, but knocked off in Israel."

"CZ," Gregor grunted.

"$450, ok with you Moses?"

"It catalogs for what? $370 and change, new."

"How about I toss in four fifteen round pre-ban mags, round it up to five bills and call it a day." Benny was grinning. He truly loved the haggle. Gregor had turned away and was inspecting a cut-down double-barreled 12 gauge. The wood stock had been filed into a pistol grip and the barrels were several inches shorter than the legal eighteen.

"Now that baby's a real classic." Benny pointed at the shotgun with pride. "Takes a man to keep that bitch from roaring out of your hands, but it will clean a street."

"It'll do the job." Gregor looked from the gun up to

me.

"The $700 I dropped on your boy. Both guns and you toss in two boxes of factory for both and two for my .45."

"If you wanted to rob me why didn't you wear a mask?"

"Rob you? Shit if I wanted to rob you you'd be on the floor face down and begging for your momma."

"$750, and I toss in a shoulder strap for the sweeper." I dropped a fifty on the counter before he could sweeten the deal and cost me another hundred. "Fine, as always, doing business with you Moses." He dropped our purchases into a cheap canvas bag. "Come back any time." He reached out shaking Gregor's hand again.

"Better count your fingers." I told Gregor. Grabbing the guns and ammo we hit the street. At a corner market I bought four Red Bulls and a potato. Gregor's eye brow shot up, but as was his way he said nothing.

"Potato, vegetable with a million uses. Eat 'em, make vodka and drink 'em, shoved on the barrel of a .38 they make a passable silencer." I told him, tossing the potato into my pocket.

From the window of my room in the dive we took turns watching the Coast and the Best Western through my field glasses. Around six thirty I brought in some Chinese and black coffee. What I wanted was a tall scotch, a fist full of whites and the love of a lying woman but my old ways were likely to get me killed right now. Evolve or die, those are the choices we are given, evolve or die.

Helen sounded worried when I called her. "Cass said she was just going for a walk, get some air, that was four hours ago. She still isn't back Moses."

"I'm sure it's nothing, she's a tough girl."

"Bingo!" Gregor said.

"Look Helen, I have to go. Call me when she comes back." I gave her the number at the Best Western and hung up. Out the window I could see a Cadillac double parked in front of the Barbary Coast.

"They went inside," Gregor said. Fifteen minutes later the sweater boy, now in a tweed suit and the beef in sweats came out of the club. They got in the Cadillac, pulled a U-turn and parked in front of the Best Western. I could see the sweater boy go into the hotel and after a few minutes come out. They sat in the car, waiting.

"Let's roll," I said to Gregor. The nasty little cut-down shotgun hung on a leather strap under his trench coat. He dropped the CZ75 into his huge outside pocket. If this thing went sideways they were going to pay hard.

The fog was a light mist as I crossed the street moving up to the back of the Cadillac. Taking the potato, I crammed it into their tail pipe, pushing until it sealed it closed. I crept along below the window line then popped up into the driver's window. The sweater boy's eyes went wild, he started to reach into his jacket. Gregor tapped on the passenger window with the two barrels of his shotgun. The men in the car didn't know who to look at. I burned holes into the sweater boy's eyes, as his hand hovered in his jacket.

"Do you really want to do this here? Really? I'm here to make a deal. I'm tired of running and I just want to get the hell out of this thing. So if you and monkey boy over there want to calm down, take your hands off your piece and listen. I think we can all go home happy campers. But you want to play who's got the bigger balls, well then someone's going down. Odds are it ain't me."

"Do what the gentleman says," a voice from the back said.

"You ain't my boss Leo. I ain't backing down 'til his goon lowers that cannon."

"I think you should kill him." Leo sat in the back, his suit was perfect, he was dead calm.

"So do I, but I doubt it will solve my problem with your boss. Ok boys keep your hands wherever you want them, grab your dicks if it makes you feel better. I have a one-time offer. No negotiations, you want the girl, I want out. You be at the Cow Palace parking lot at midnight tonight with forty grand and a guarantee from your boss that I walk away. You do that and she's all yours. You fuck me and I drop her off at the feds."

"Fuck you dead man, you don't give us terms, we tell you how it goes, who the fuck do you think you are?" sweater boy spat at me.

"One more thing, just you two show up for the drop. I see Leo or anyone else there, I roll." Over the roof of the car I nodded at Gregor and he took off down the sidewalk. I spun running into the slow moving traffic. Behind me I heard the Cadillac fighting to turn over, the starter motor grinding, but with no place for the exhaust to escape it was futile. As I rounded the corner I heard the loud blast of the seals blowing on the exhaust pipes, the Cadillac rambled down the street but I was safely down an alley.

From the room, I checked the messages over at Best Western, Helen hadn't called. If the mob boys had Cass, then I was about to walk into a death trap. I called Sanders. "I'm ready to deal."

"Alright, bring in the girl and we'll see if we can keep you alive," he said.

"Couldn't do it if I wanted to, dropped her at the airport and told her to get lost."

"What?"

"You heard me, she's in the wind."

"Then why am I talking to you?"

"Same reason you let me walk last night. Do you know how they hunt wolves? They stake out a lamb, then hide in the brush and wait. Baaa. See I don't mind being your lamb, but we're going to play it my way. Who is Gino Torelli?"

"That's classified."

"So that's how we're going to play it, fine. Have a nice life, officer." I started to hang up.

"Wait, McGuire, did you have an offer in mind or

did you just call for a pissing contest?"

"You're going after Sabatini, right? He's the brass ring you suits are all fighting to catch. I can deliver two of his soldiers. Solid busts and you take the credit."

"And in return you want what?"

"The truth, everything you know about Torelli, Cass, the whole enchilada." There was a long pause while he mulled over his options. "Look, Sanders, I have you by the short hairs and I'm tugging. This deal goes down at midnight. You in or out?"

"Ok," he finally said.

"Be at the Cow Palace parking lot at midnight. They'll be packing and if you search their car I'll make sure you find enough to hold them."

"We'll need just cause to search them, I can't get a warrant on some ex-con's word."

"If you and your crew happened to be rolling by and heard gunfire, you would have to respond, right?"

"Yes."

"Then that will be your signal."

"Be careful." He said without meaning it.

"What the hell, if they kill me, you'll really have something to take them down for." I said and clicked off. What I didn't tell him was I had taped our conversation with the small digital recorder that I had picked up that morning. Trust no one and you can't get burned. Out of the closet I took a dress I bought for my latex girlfriend. Gregor gave me an odd look.

"I'm not wearing that."

"No Gregor, you are not. Now let's roll." In a back alley I popped the trunk, Gregor gave me one of his rare smiles when he saw the sex doll. The detail work on her body was frighteningly real. From her perfect pink nipples down to her heart shaped pubic hair she was a necrophiliac's dream date. It took both of us to dress her, she wasn't light. Bending her knees we sat her in the front seat and belted her in. It was scary how lifelike she looked at a quick glance. Placing the wig and glasses on her head I started to feel a little queasy. I had turned a fuck doll into a faux Cass, who was, at least for me a faux Kelly. It was truly three degrees of screwed up.

Gregor shook his head sadly when I rolled into the bad section of the Mission District and bought $20 worth of crack from a pre-teen working the corner. But he had the good grace not to ask any questions. That was one of his better qualities, he took it as it came and trusted himself to be strong enough to dig out of any hole I dug for him.

A three-quarter moon hung over the bay as we drove down toward the Cow Palace. It was a huge tin structure used for concerts, county fairs and now deadly trades. We arrived with thirty minutes to spare. I snapped the lock on the parking lot gate with a pair of bolt cutters. Pulling to the far end of the lot I parked under a light. I left Gregor in the Crown Vic and walked out about a hundred yards and stood waiting. My nerves were jangling, I had picked the wrong night to quit drinking. Patting my pocket I felt the reassuring weight of my .45, cocked, locked and ready. Someone was going down tonight. With any luck it wouldn't be me.

Two beams moved slowly through the gate shooting shafts into the dust. A black Lincoln appeared behind the headlights, it rolled to a stop, blinding me. I heard a door open and sweater boy moved in front of the lights, in his outline a pistol was clearly held in his hand. "Where's the bitch?" he said pointing the pistol at me. I raised my left hand, keeping the right close to my pocket. Inside the Crown Vic Gregor flashed a light on the girl.

"Now turn off the lights before we attract attention, and let's get down to business." I said.

"You don't give the orders anymore got it?"

"Got it. You, my friend, are the big swinging dick here. So what do you want to do?" I said with a disarming smile.

"That's right, damn it. Larry, kill the fucking lights, you want the cops coming or what?" The driver killed the lights and I could see he was alone in the car. "Ok tough guy, now you bring me the girl."

"I will, because you asked me to. But um, first, just to keep things straight, I should see the cash. Not that I don't trust you. You are in charge here."

"See that's nice, you're respectful, if you were like that from the start this whole thing would have gone a lot easier."

"Trust me I see the error of my ways."

"Good. Larry, you lazy fuck, get the bag." The driver got out and moved to the trunk.

"Not for nothing, but, did you guys do the girl in LA?" I tossed it off like I was asking if he thought it might rain.

"That bitch was fine. A real screamer." The blood in my veins started to boil. My head pounded. Every cell in my body screamed. This smarmy mother fucker had to die. My hand snaked towards my pocket.

"Whoa! Dumb fucking move ace!" Sweater boy snapped the hammer back on his pistol. From ten feet he couldn't miss my head. My hand moved into my pocket. "Pull out your hand, slow!" he yelled.

The beef in a running suit dropped the black gym bag he was holding and reached for his shoulder holster.

My .45 was almost clear of my pocket when I heard the report of a high-powered rifle. The passenger window of the Crown Vic popped and the sex doll's head exploded. Dropping to the ground the sniper's second shot whizzed over me. Sweater Boy swung his barrel down. The .45 rocked in my hand, flame flashed and his ankle shattered into a bloody mess. He went down howling, his pistol slid across the gravel. I rolled to the left as a third rifle bullet puffed the ground beside me.

The son of a bitch had a night scope.

Gregor fired up the Crown Vic and had her rolling

towards me. He fired wild shots out the window. Skidding to a stop he blocked the snipers view of me. The metal pinged as a slug tore through the car door.

Sirens wailed and two unmarked cars burst through the gate, their cherry tops spinning red into the night. The beefy goon had his arm under Sweater Boy and was trying to get him into the Lincoln. Kneeling against the Vic's front fender I took aim. My first hardball ripped a hole in the back of his cardigan and ruined his spine. Beef dropped his pal and leapt for the car. I popped him in the knee and watched him go down. Running towards them I hoped the cops had scared off the sniper.

I kicked the piece out of Beef's hand and tossed the crack vials into their car. A gurgled breath came from the crumpled Sweater Boy. He looked up at me, his eyes pleading, his mouth unable to form words. I stomped my boot down on his head. I could feel his skull crack.

"Boss!" Gregor yelled. The cops were almost on us.

The second stomp ended the punk's breathing. It wasn't enough. Nothing would have been.

Grabbing the gym bag, I was barely into the Vic when Gregor hit it hard and we spun out the opposite direction from the cops. We were doing seventy-five when we hit the chain link fence. Bouncing over a planter the Vic skidded onto the city streets and didn't slow down until we saw the glittering city by the bay rising up out of the mist.

CHAPTER 16

In a filling station, Gregor held up the flap on his coat. A sniper bullet meant for me had passed through the car, through his coat and punched a hole in the door. "Bastards. Somebody's buying me a new coat," Gregor said.

"You want a new coat? I'll buy you a new coat."

"You didn't put the hole in it."

"No, I didn't."

"Then you don't have to buy me one, but somebody does."

"Yeah, I see your point." I left him in the car to worry about his wardrobe while I went to the phone booth. First I dialed the number my hacker buddy had gotten for Sabatini. It rang three times before a thick headed bruiser answered, I asked him to put Leo on.

"Pal, you got the wrong number, no Leo's here."

"Tell him it's McGuire. Tell him I ain't dead."

Twenty seconds later I heard Leo pick up.

"Mr. McGuire, I'm glad to hear your voice."

"But not surprised, are you?"

"No, I was told you had been lucky."

"I whacked your skinny friend. Cops have the fat one."

"I heard that as well. But you didn't call me to recount old times, did you?"

"No, the girl's dead, I got my cash. I just need to know no one is coming after me for the punk."

"No one will be coming after you."

"No offense, but that's not just coming from you is it? You're with Sabatini?"

"Yes, he's here and we both agree you have earned a walkway."

"Good." I hung up and dialed Agent Sanders' cell.

"I'm a little busy right now McGuire, some perp blew holes in a couple of mobsters and ran off." Sanders said when I reached him.

"What a shame."

"You've got some real issues with anger, that boy's head looked like so many pounds of ground chuck."

"Fuck him, how's the fat one?"

"He'll probably lose a leg, but he'll live to see trial. "

"Then you should be happy. Now you owe me a cup of coffee."

"I should put an APB out on you."

"But you won't, not until you know what I'm holding. And trust me you don't want to find out in a room full of your brother cops." He tried to play it tough, keep control but I knew he'd meet me. After a bit of arguing we settled on a coffee shop down in the Mission district. He said he could be there in twenty minutes. So we headed over.

Ten years ago, Mission had been home to heroin, jazz, street kids, pimps and whores. Dot com money had driven most of them out of one end, moved the poor and beat down onto a reservation of two city blocks while they gentrified the rest. Eddie's Café was a lone hold out, it still had the original grease on the walls. I took a booth that was upholstered more in duct tape than vinyl and told Gregor to sit at the counter. I had the recorder in my pocket ready and waiting.   Gregor was well into his second stack of pancakes when Sanders walked in.

"What is keeping me from arresting you for murder?" he said as a greeting.

I set the digital recorder on the table and pushed play. Sanders went a lighter shade of pale when he heard his voice agreeing to the setup. "You know I have copies of this, so why don't you stop hyperventilating and tell me about Torelli."

"You son of a bitch."

"Yes I am, but let's leave her out of this. Torelli?"

"Alfred 'the Animal' Stolloti," he said in a defeated drone. "Two years ago he turned state's evidence against the Chicago mob. Since then he's been living in witness protection. Three months ago he fell off the map."

"He was Gino?"

"Yes."

"And you think Sabatini had him clipped."

"That's the working theory."

"And you figured Kelly saw it go down?"

"No, Bette, her sister."

"Bette?"

"You know her as Cass."

"You got it wrong, Kelly was dating Gino, she's your witness and she's dead. If the punk I gave you doesn't roll over you're just going to have to make your case another way."

"That's not the way we see it. No, it was Bette and we'll find her sooner or later. If the mob doesn't find her first." His courage was coming back as he saw a way to spin it on me. "What do you think their response might be if it slipped that you set up their men? If I was you, I'd go home, pull the blankets over my head and say my prayers. Bring me the girl, or tomorrow I call them. "

"I don't know where she is."

"So you said. I'll see you around McGuire." As he walked out he stopped at the counter, leaned over and said something to Gregor, then left without looking back.

"What'd he say to you?" I asked Gregor as we were driving back to the hotel.

"Said I should leave town before we both wound up in a box."

"So what do you think?"

"About what?"

"Leaving town."

"And miss all this fun?" The corners of his mouth almost curled into a smile.

"Tonight's going to get ugly, a lot of bad craziness is going to have to go down before it's over. Are you sure you're up for the ride? You've been paid, there's no honor lost if you want to walk." He looked at me and then out the window. We climbed a steep hill lined with gingerbread Victorians, it was hard to believe anything bad could happen in this city.

"Yeah, I'm in," he said. "Will you drop me off at that church?" He pointed to the spires of a Catholic Church looming ahead of us.

"What?"

"The church. I'll meet you at the hotel in an hour." I pulled to the curb without asking any more questions. He slipped his 9 mm under the seat and walked up the stone steps, his great coat flapping behind him like huge black wings.

Parking the Crown Vic at the Best Western I checked for messages. Nothing. I took the elevator to the parking lot and slipped out the side door. I headed towards my hotel, the flashing neon of the Barbary Coast called to me, beckoning with its cool gin and willing girls. One drink wouldn't kill me. I was standing at the mouth of an alley next to my hotel, about to cross the street when I felt a hand on my shoulder. I spun around swinging out a left haymaker that would have taken Cass' head off if she had been six inches taller, instead the blow sailed over her head grazing her hair.

"I'm glad to see you too, Moses." She smiled up at me.

"What the hell are you doing here?" I didn't know if I wanted to hit Cass or lift her into my arms.

"I was losing my mind waiting, wondering if you were dead. I'm your girl." She moved in close placing those soft full lips on mine. One kiss and I was lost. Linking her arm in mine we went up to the room.

"I'm taking down Sabatini tonight," I told her as we sat on the bed holding hands.

"Then I'm going with you."

"No, you are not. Look, I don't care about much in this life. I don't think I could stand to see you die."

"Then you know how I feel. Mo, these scum bags killed my only sister, I am going to be there when they go down." I looked at her set jaw and knew she spoke the truth. Pulling her hand up to my mouth, I nodded and kissed her. Our bargain was struck, there was no turning back

252

now. Pulling her face to mine, I kissed her, her lips parted letting my tongue dart in. There was a hungry look in her eyes, we kissed and ripped at each other's clothes with no regard for buttons or zippers. She hiked up her skirt and I made love to her standing up with my pants down around my ankles. I could taste blood on my lip from where she bit me but I didn't care. We were tossed in a passion driven storm. The dresser I pushed her against fell with a crash but we kept our rhythm, moving to the closet door I slammed her against the mirror. Grabbing her ass in my big hand I looked into the mirror. There on her ass cheek was a fairy sprinkling pixie dust. The room spun out of focus for a moment, but my lust was boiling so I pushed away the meaning of her tattoo. She was screaming wild war cries as we collapsed onto the floor.

In a post-coital lump we lay tangled on the floor. I gently traced the fairy tattooed on her backside. It was the same mark as the girl in the porn video. I never had the pleasure of seeing Kelly's ass but I now doubted she was tattooed.

"Did Kell have any tattoos?" I said as casually as I could.

"Why do you want to talk about Kelly? Do you wish you had just fucked her?"

"No, I was..."

"I'm not Kelly, hell, Kelly wasn't even Kelly. I'm here, I'm alive and I'm the best you're ever going to get." To prove it she started kissing my neck and moved slowly down my belly. My desire to question her dissolved when she took me into her mouth.

We woke to the sound of a knock at the door. I pulled my pants up and righted the dresser. Cass gave me a wink and slid into the bathroom. Gregor came in, looked around the room but asked no questions. Cass came out of the bathroom looking fresh as a new picked flower. "She'll be riding with us tonight," I told Gregor.

"It's your party boss."

"Then let's roll."

CHAPTER 17

As a kid, my grandmother Therkleson told me about the Valkyrie, beautiful bare-chested winged warriors who dropped down onto the Viking battlefields and picked the bravest of the fallen dead to take to live in the halls of Valhalla, where they could drink and fight and fuck until the end of time. In a hard world a good death was sometimes the best a man could hope for. That, and a big breasted chick with wings to swoop out of the sky.

Soaring down 280, I watched San Francisco disappear into the rear view like a glittering dream calling me back to bed. The highway was smooth and nicely banked, built for speed, I fought the urge to pin the needle and kept at a safe eighty miles an hour. The CHP might frown on rolling arsenals crowding up their highways.

I dropped in Give 'em Enough Rope, by far the Clash's best album. London Calling was for posers and Johnny come late to the party wanna' be punk college kids. Melancholic Island influenced punk, with enough melody not to drive my traveling comrades screaming from the car and enough overdriven guitars to keep me from blowing my brains out. Mick Jones, that pussy, was telling me to step lightly and stay free when we hit Palo Alto. Taking the Sand Hill exit we headed up into the mountains. The streetlights disappeared and there were damn few homes as we snaked our way into the country. A warm blanket of black fell around us, pierced by our headlight beams. The stars filled the sky above, silhouetting old oak trees on the rolling hills.

"When this is over, I was thinking about going down to Mexico," I said to Cass, she was resting her head on my shoulder. "I was thinking you might want to go with me."

"What's in Mexico?"

"Warm beaches, good food."

"Ok." We slipped back into silence. Gregor sat in the back with his fedora down over his eyes. Old La Honda Road twisted its way up the dark mountain, redwoods speared up into a forest above the road, cliffs dropped off to the right, so that one wrong turn would take you into the next life in a wailing plunge. A flash of white spread out in the headlights as a barn owl crossed our path. Tommy Cavasos told me that if you saw an owl in flight you should look away because it was a brujo, who could make you sick or cast a dark spell on you. Tommy swore by that border magic. I watched the owl fly up and disappear into the dark forest. What was it going to do to me I hadn't already done to myself? Luck was for suckers, and magic was what that freak in the top hat did down on Hollywood Boulevard for turista quarters. I was done gambling in games where others set the rules, and all odds went to the house. From here on out I only wanted to play when I chose the deck and dealt the cards.

Twenty minutes later we hit Skylonda, a small mountain town consisting of a general store, two restaurants and a two pump gas station, they all were dark and silent at this early hour. I pulled in and used a payphone to call Sanders.

"You want Sabatini, get your ass up to his ranch."

"What are you talking about, McGuire?" he mumbled into the phone.

"I'm dropping Sabatini in a package for you, but me and mine walk. No witness protection, no DA, no bullshit."

"Who exactly do you think you are?" he said, waking quickly.

"The man who's about to make you a hero," I said and hung up.

Pulling out onto Skyline Boulevard, a two lane black top stretched out along the ridge of the mountains all the way to Santa Cruz, I switched The Clash out for Iggy and the Stooges. I nodded along to Search and Destroy, anger driven three chords of pure rage. Cass and Gregor were flicking glances that said the old man has lost his noodle and what was that god awful music? No sense of history, fuck 'em. I needed the raw power jangle and Iggy knew how to deliver.

Breaking through the tree line we could see down rolling hills to the ocean on one side and all the way to Palo Alto and the bay beyond on the other. Twenty minutes later I spotted the address I was searching for. A tall iron gate blocked the entry, just inside it was a stone guard house. I checked my watch, I knew it would take Sanders at least an hour to assemble his troops and make the drive. I didn't have much fear that he would call in the locals and give them a shot at his glory.

I parked around a bend in the road from the gate's entrance. Looking over my two comrades, I thought about how good a drink would feel right about then.

"What's the plan baby?" Cass had grown nervous as the reality of what we were about to undertake sank in.

"We go in, find Sabatini and try not to get too dead in the process."

"What's he look like?" Gregor said.

"Like the chief Greaseball, I figure we'll know him when we see him. He'll be the one giving orders."

"I don't mean any disrespect Moses, but the plan sucks," Gregor said, not worried, just stating a fact.

"I know what he looks like," Cass whispered. I looked at her stunned.

"How the hell do you know him?"

"It doesn't matter." She looked away, out the window.

"Only a little."

"Why?" She looked back at me, innocent.

"Because it does. If I don't get all the facts, I'm spinning this car around and going home," I yelled.

"No you're not." She called my bluff. "They know your name." Her voice was calm and her eyes had gone cold. "They won't stop hunting you until you stop them."

"She's right boss," Gregor spoke from the back seat.

"I know she is damn it. I just don't know who she is!"

"I'm your girl and you are my man." She softened, clasping her little hand around my three middle fingers, "I would never do anything to hurt you." She caressed my hand focusing her attention down so she wouldn't have to see my eyes if I rebuffed her. Who was I kidding, this wasn't about her, or me, it was about Kelly and me setting my conscience to rest. I had killed the punk who killed her but the mouth breather who ordered it was still walking free.

"Ok, fuck it, let's go bowling," I said and fired up the Crown Vic. Fishtailing onto Skyline I let the V8 roar. Pushing hard, I was going ninety-five when I slammed into the gate. The iron snapped and bent around the hood, ripping from its post. I hit the brakes slamming it in reverse, smoking the tires. On the second hit the gate toppled off its hinges and fell to the side. A tall ape of a man in a tee-shirt jumped out of the guardhouse, aiming a pump shotgun at me. I locked up the brakes, pressing my .45 against the inside of my door, I tapped off three quick shots. They punched through the sheet metal of my door and into his gut. He fell, stumbling back into the guardhouse. I stomped on the gas and we flew down the twisting driveway. Around two bends and past a small pond lay a large two-story wood home. Six cars were parked on the circular drive. Half dressed men ran from the front door as we approached. The rhythmic rattle of automatic fire blasted as bullet holes punched into the Crown Vic's body. I wrenched the wheel to the left sliding it sideways, blocking the exit. Bullets tore through the cab, ripping shredded holes into upholstery and sparking in the darkness.

Gregor dove out of the back seat, he rolled and came up firing. Emptying his clip he scattered the men coming from the house. On the run, he used the parked cars for cover while he reloaded. Cass and I crawled out my door and down a small embankment that led to the pond. Moving quickly over the wet ground we headed toward the house. I pushed my way up through tall cattails. A pair of legs in wool slacks moved in front of me. I pulled the trigger on the Mossberg, the buck shot cut a wide path through the water grasses and the man went down screaming.

Springing to my feet I ran for the house. A shirtless punk spun from the porch and fired three wild shots before I blew him back through a picture window, glass and man both tumbled into the house. A huge form rose up beside me, I heard Cass' gun go off, the man tumbled over grabbing his fountaining throat. From the porch I leapt into the ruined window. Cass was in mid-air following me when something hit her, she twisted and blood bloomed from her upper body. She fell sliding across the floor. On a wide staircase I sensed movement and fired without thought. A fat man with a bad rug slid down the stairs leaving a red stain behind him. Dragging Cass behind an obese sofa I checked her wound.

"Goddamn it Mo, they shot me."

"Sure did baby girl." Bullets struck the sofa, bursting the upholstery and filling the air with floating tufts of down.

"Kill Sabatini, do that for me," she said. No organs had been hit, but she was bleeding profusely. "Leave me and go get him. Damn it, Mo."

"Forget it kiddo, I'm not leaving you."

Shots thudded into the sofa and floor around us. Popping my head up multiple muzzles flashed from the stairs. We were trapped between the men outside who were firing at Gregor and the men on the stairs. A bullet took out two inches of masonry next to my head.

Gregor spun across the hood of a Mercedes, blood bursting from his hip. He crawled for cover behind the car but bullets were raining down on him from the second story.

The time for choosing was over. Tearing a strip from my shirt so Cass could stanch the bleeding I said, "Don't go nowhere baby girl." Jumping up I let out a wild war cry and charged the stairway. Firing on the run I vaulted the steps, a young man with long jet black hair fell gripping his bleeding gut. I leapt over him and kept moving. The second story hall split off in two directions. To the left I could hear the automatic fire that was being dumped down on Gregor. I ran to the door and pumped four loads of double aught through it. Their rifles went silent. Through the grapefruit sized holes I saw a man hanging limply out the window. Racking a fresh shell into the Mossberg I stormed down the hall kicking doors open. Moving into a bedroom that was bigger than my house I found three party girls in Frederick's best huddled in the corner. Their eyes went wide when they saw me. I tried to give them a calming smile, but in my battle blood mood it must have looked like a deadly grimace, they sank farther back into the wall. A way too skinny redhead with fake tits flicked her eyes involuntarily at the bed. I rolled to my right just as flame exploded from under the bed and bullets ripped up the wall where I had been standing. From the floor I emptied the clip of my .45. I could hear the meaty thud of bullets striking the flesh I couldn't see. Rich red ran from under the bed, mixing the smell of iron with cordite. Dropping the clip on my .45 I slapped in a fresh one and slipped it into my belt. Leaving the trembling girls, I sprinted back down the hall. In a large bathroom I heard a sound behind the shower curtain, snapping it back I found a man crumpled up in the fetal position sobbing.

"I'm just an accountant... don't kill me..." I did a quick pat search and came up with his wallet while he blathered on, "I have a wife and kids... I'm not one of them really..." I left him in the tub sobbing. He wasn't Sabatini, he wasn't even Italian. Clearing the second floor I moved back down the stairs. Outside the shooting had mostly subsided. Running to the sofa I discovered Cass was no longer there. Dread swept over me. Turning back to the room I found three bloody men aiming pistols up at me. Fuck it at least I wasn't going out alone. Gripping my pistol in one hand and the shotgun in other I got ready for one last charge. Leo stepped out of a doorway and stood between me and the three killers. His hands were empty, palms up.

"You are one incredible pain in the ass, you know that Mr. McGuire?" Looking natty as ever, he smiled.

"What now Leo, do I start pulling the trigger and see how many die before your boys can drop me?"

"As much fun as that sounds, Mr. Sabatini and your lady friend would love to have a chat with you. So why don't we delay the whole macho blaze of glory act at least for the moment, ok?"

I moved past the stairs and the goons with their guns aimed at me. They hated not to blow me away, their blood was as high as mine I'm sure.

I set the shotgun down in the oak paneled hallway, but kept the .45 firmly in my hand. Leo watched me without much interest. He opened the door into a large den that would have done Hemingway proud. A lion's head stared at me from over a fireplace. A myriad collection of other dead beasts lined the walls. Cass was sitting on a leather sofa next to a fit looking dark haired man of maybe forty. He had a sharp Roman nose and intelligent eyes that made me feel like whatever I was thinking he was two steps ahead of me. He was holding a small automatic against Cass' temple. Leo stepped out of the room, closing the door behind himself.

"Check and mate. I have your queen, now why don't you put your gun down and we can see if there is any way to salvage your life," he said in a soft, almost melodic voice.

"I don't think so, no, I think I'd rather blow a hole in your ugly mug."

"Then what? There's a room full of guns out there waiting for you."

"Yup."

"Are you suicidal?"

"Yup," I said with a slight smile, screw him if he didn't get it.

"But you do care about her? This little skirt. This twist that has caused so much trouble. You care about her." He pushed the barrel harder into her head.

"Kill him," she whispered, she was pale from loss of blood and her eyes were starting to glaze with shock.

"Don't get me wrong," he said, "I understand your attraction, our little minx is one of the best pieces of ass I've ever had. But she has a real problem with loyalty."

"Shoot him Moses!" Cass pleaded.

"See what I mean?" Sabatini tapped her skull with the pistol, causing her to wince. "After all she and I have shared, now she wants you to kill me."

"He's lying, Moses, kill him."

"Truth? Shall we talk about the truth?" Sabatini said, "She came to me, offered where I could find an associate who had strayed from the pack."

"I didn't." Cass was losing gas.

"I paid her ten large to rat out Stolloti."

"It was my sister." Cass' voice was becoming a hissed whisper. Sabatini slapped the pistol up under her chin, she let out a high gasp.

"Hurt her again, and it's over," I said, starting to tighten on the trigger.

"Even if it means my men kill you, which you have said you don't care about, interesting problem we have here." He turned it over in his mind looking for the angle.

"I just figured it out, I've been looking at it backwards all this time," I said smiling at him.

"That's a bit cryptic."

"I was wondering why go to all this trouble to take out one girl. So what if she saw Gino get whacked. Get rid of the hitter, cover your tracks, then who cares who she tells. You kill all of these yourself? Huh, killer?" I motioned to the trophies hung on the walls .

"Yes. Hunting is where a man discovers his true nature."

"And what did you discover when you killed Gino?"

"Always wear a raincoat when you use a shotgun at close range."

"That's funny, wear a raincoat huh? I'll have to remember that."

"I don't think you will be around long enough to have to worry about remembering anything," he said, his smile fading.

"Really, I wasn't planning on going anywhere. You getting hungry, want to order a pizza?" I said, flashing him a shit eating grin. Cass' eyes fluttered slowly closed. Blood had soaked through her makeshift bandage and was staining the sofa in an ever widening red blotch.

"I don't know what game you think you are playing," he said, "but I can assure you, you will not win. Your kind never do, so perhaps you would like to discuss a fallback plan? One where you don't necessarily die, maybe even keep the girl if I get certain assurances." He was treading water, looking for my chink.

"Here's what I think, pal, I think you're a dago pussy who kills defenseless animals and people your goons hold down." His face went red, veins popping in his forehead. I let the .45 drop and hang at my side as I taunted him, "I think you're a weak freak, a ball-less bastard who should have been stepped on at birth. You're a spineless little..." Before I could finish he whipped the pistol off of Cass' head swinging it toward my face. Arcing the .45 up we fired at the same moment. I could see flame spitting out of the barrel of his pistol, flying at me, then I felt a hot burn on my head that spun me backward.

"Moses," Cass was whimpering as I pulled myself up, crawling to the sofa. My left eye was covered in a stream of free flowing blood. Sabatini was flopped back moaning. The slug had taken a chunk the size of a small apple out of his right shoulder and smeared his chest and face in blood and meat chunks. I ran my hand up my scalp looking for the hole, half expecting to find gray matter leaking out. What I had was a three inch gash, a lot of blood and a headache, but nothing that was going to kill me today. Fastening my trusty bandana around my head to staunch the flow, pirate Moses took a seat on the sofa next to Sabatini. I grabbed his chin forcing his face to look at me.

"Pay real close attention, you are hanging by a

fucking thread here, and I'm the fucking thread. Got that you arrogant fuck?" I said, when he didn't answer quick enough I slapped his face hard enough to knock out a loose filling. Slowly he nodded. "Who did her sister? And don't even think about lying or I'll make this slow." His eyes focused on me.

"Johny B…" he gasped.

"The prep school boy I killed?"

"Yes…" he said.

"Leo? Was he in on it?"

"No, they sent him later."

"Did you tell them to do her rough, maybe even have them take snaps to prove it?" He just looked at me, fear filling his rabbit eyes, he knew it was over. Slowly a new strength came into his face, as if he had known this day would come and now that it was here maybe it wasn't that bad. Maybe fear of death is worse than death itself.

"Get it over with," he said, closing his eyes, settling back into the sofa cushions.

"You think it's over asshole? It's just begun. Some hillbilly named Bubba's gonna make you his wife, bitch," I said. In the distance I could hear the wail of sirens. "Game's over pal. I'm taking my pieces and going home." I picked Cass up into my arms, she was weak and drifting, she nuzzled her face into my neck. I pushed the door open with my foot. Leo was standing guard. He looked into the room at Sabatini's sunken form, shook his head like it was the outcome he expected. He stepped out of our way giving me a nod that told me he was no threat. From outside tires skidded to a stop and sirens screamed. There was a brief burst of gunfire then none at all.

"Let him walk," Leo said to the panicked mobsters in the shattered living room. From the porch I could see a Lexus was on fire. The sky was pale blue as dawn broke soft and gentle over the violent scene. Three black Suburbans full of Feds in SWAT gear swarmed over the lawns and into the house. A baby faced officer pointed an assault rifle in my face demanding I get face down. I just kept walking, luckily Sanders arrived before I was shot.

"Jeffery Sabatini just admitted to the murder of Gino," I said and handed him the digital recorder from my pocket.

He took the recorder and looked at Cass. "Will she make it?"

"She better."

"Medivac is five minutes out. Your big guy was hit bad." I turned away, holding Cass to me, her breathing was shallow against my neck. I looked down over the pond, its water mirror still. I didn't feel flushed with victory, I felt small and helpless against a world that let its most amazing flowers get trampled. A world that ate the young and spit out the bones and left the children of the battle zone to stumble blindly on searching for answers. Answers that never came, or came too late.

Over the hills I could hear the familiar thump thump of a chopper. They set down flattening the grass around them. I ran with Cass to them, lifting her into the waiting arms of the paramedics. She didn't want to let go of my neck, I had to pull her arms free. I wanted to kiss her goodbye but was pushed aside by a woman bent on saving her life. Two paramedics ran up with Gregor on a stretcher, his chest and left leg were tore up and bled wildly. He looked up as he passed and grinned. "Hell of a party boss, hell of a party," he said and then closed his eyes. I stood, staring until the chopper was over the hill.

"You were the one who turned Cass onto Sabatini," I said. Sanders looked past me and didn't deny it. "Your computer pimp told you about her and you saw an opening."

"I may have opened the door, but she walked through it willingly." He still wasn't meeting my eyes. "And an innocent girl died so you could make a collar. You sleeping well at night?"

"Like a baby. There are no innocents in this game, only differing degrees of guilty."

"Bullshit, and you know it. So what now, are you going to keep your word and let us fade?"

"Your tape may be enough to get Sabatini to plea out, but if it goes to trail the D.A. will want you and Bette to testify." His face was still and emotionless, just giving me the facts.

"That wasn't the deal."

"So sue me."

"I don't think so. Here's how it's going down, if any of my people hear from you again, the LA Times gets a package, the recording of you allowing a known felon to plant drugs and kill gangsters. I'll give them the porno boy you let operate and tell them how you sold out a government witness you were sworn to protect." I was guessing he had tipped Cass to Gino's identity, hoping she would witness Gino's death. Then to keep from being killed herself she would have to turn Sabatini in. Only she had outsmarted them all and run. The twitch developing in the corner of Sanders' eye told me I had hit the mark. "The marshals aren't going to be too happy that you screwed up the witness protection plan."

"You'll never make it stick." He wasn't sounding too sure.

"I don't have to, the suspicion will be enough to derail any career plans you have." I had his balls in the ringer. He could either kill me or let us walk clean. He shook his head slowly and walked past me, I followed him down to the house.

The party was over. Sabatini was being loaded into the back of an ambulance, his face covered by an oxygen mask and his hands cuffed. His eyes locked on me for a moment and seemed to say I'll get you yet. I just shot him the smile of a man who just didn't give a rat's ass. The goons not being treated were sitting down in handcuffs.

Bob brought Leo over to Sanders, shoving him forward with a pistol in between his shoulder blades. Leo took it calmly as if it was only a speeding ticket he was facing.

"Says he needs to speak to you," Bob said.

"He's one of mine," I told Sanders, "My inside man." Sanders looked Leo over with undisguised disgust.

"Fine, take the cuffs off him Bob."

"If you say so."

"I do." Bob told Sanders about the accountant they found in the bathtub who was pleading to sing his heart out. That put the first smile I had seen on Sanders' face.

"This is turning out to be a banner day," he said as he and Bob went off to talk to the accountant.

Pulling out onto Skyline the Crown Vic rattled like a mother and the wind whistled through the broken windows, but it ran. God bless Detroit iron.

"Where can I drop you?" I asked Leo as we rumbled along.

"The airport, I think I would like to go home and take a very long bath."

"You weren't part of that crew, so what's the deal."

"No, I wasn't part of that mess. My employers sent me out to sweep up, after those idiots bungled a very simple job."

"When you get home, tell your bosses I'm through. If they want to come after me or mine, then buckle your seat belts, I will not go down lightly."

"No, that is clear as crystal. From my perspective the less mentioned about you the better. I plan to forget your name the minute I leave this car. As for Mr. Sabatini, after this and what he lost in tech stocks, I suspect he is due for an unfortunate accident while in custody."

I dropped him at the airport and drove down to Palo Alto. Cass and Gregor were taken to Stanford Emergency. I was told the Justice Department was picking up the tab for the hospital, so maybe Sanders wasn't a total waste of DNA. Around eleven a young doctor came into the waiting room and told me Cass had lost a lot of blood, the bullet entered above her right breast, but missed the lung. She might lose some strength in her arm but she was going to pull through. Gregor was still in surgery when I finally passed out.

CHAPTER 18

The sun shot golden rays out across the bay, white caps danced on waves below as we stood on the Golden Gate Bridge. Cass was in the hospital for eight days, I stayed with her, sleeping on a cot at her side. She woke crying at night and I would hush her back to sleep. Gregor did three days in the I.C.U. and was still laid up with tubes running in and out of him, but he was recovering quicker than any of his doctors expected.

Cass lifted the Marilyn Monroe cookie jar onto the railing, tears filling her eyes. "She always loved this city," she said.

"It was you Cass, the whole time, Kelly didn't do any of those things," I said in a soft voice.

"I don't know what you're talking about baby, Kelly…" she drifted off looking out to sea.

"Hell Cass, Kell didn't even like stripping. You talked her into it. You slept with Gino and then Sabatini.

You saw the murder go down. You, not Kelly. She was the soft one, in LA she chose to be a waitress instead of stripping. You chose hooking. She wasn't hard like you. The girl in the porn, the girl with the fairy tattoo, that wasn't Kelly, was it?"

"Fuck you Moses. How dare you, here, now? You choose now to pull this?"

"Has to be now, Kelly deserves the truth." She slapped my face hard, but it didn't hurt, nothing hurt anymore. I had been through hell and I had finally found Kelly. I couldn't bring her back, but I had found her. She was the girl I had known, our friendship wasn't an act or a manipulation. She hadn't played me, but I had been played. "You ready for the funny part Cass? Your big dark secret is out, and I don't care."

"But it's not true, Mo," she pleaded.

"You didn't have to play me... I'd have laid down my life for you, all you had to do was ask." I pulled her to me kissing her forehead. I let her cry against my chest. When she was done we opened the cookie jar and let the ashes drift out over the bay. The sun was dropping down and city lights were winking on giving the skyline that magic wonderland Oz feeling.

Gregor spent three weeks in the hospital, they would have kept him longer but as soon as he could walk he disappeared from the ward. I left a new black great coat with $5,000 in the pocket for battle pay, on his apartment stoop. Ringing the bell, I walked away. I was proud to have gone to war with him and hoped I never had to do it again.

I combined what was left of the porno boy's money with that from the Cow Palace parking lot and split it with Cass. Paid off my heartless ex-wife and my debt to the Pope, who on the word of a Chicago lieutenant decided to forgive and forget my fronting him. It might not ever be easy with him again but at least I didn't have to worry about him clipping me. Eddy The Mechanic still had a place on his dance card reserved for me. Maybe old age would take him before he got to me. Stranger things have happened.

Cass and I loaded up Angel and went down to San Blas for a vacation. We lay on the beach and made love in the moonlight and we never talked about the lies she had told me. For the time it lasted she made me feel young and powerful and good. And on the rainy December night when she left, my little house felt empty and sad. You don't really know what you're missing until you've had it, like kisses and waking up next to a pretty girl who tells you you're her man.

I've stopped putting guns in my mouth and whiskey in my gut. Somewhere on the road, I had traveled from suicidal to homicidal, not much, but it's growth. All in all, I have a good life, a dog who adores me, a friend to drink coffee with and another day above ground. For children of the battle zone that's called winning.

COMING SOON

OUT THERE BAD – A Moses McGuire Novel.

Armenian mobsters, Russian strippers, human traffickers, Mexican assassins, they all want Moses dead. Hell most days, even Moses wants Moses dead, but he'll have to put his dark thoughts on hold. Somewhere between Moscow and LA a young girl has disappeared. The hunt for her will take Moses deep into the heart of Mexico. He will be taught once again that that which does not kill you, leaves you scared for life.